COURTING TROUBLE

"Is my company truly so unpleasant that you can't spend a few minutes alone with me?" Lucas asked Delaney.

She didn't want to admit that she found the lawyer's company immensely pleasant. That when she was alone with him she found herself remembering how the contours of his hard body felt beneath her hands. That she inhaled deeply, as if her breaths were numbered, so she could recall his scent when he departed. That if she spent another five minutes with him being so considerate and honorable she was going to find herself being very inconsiderate and dishonorable by throwing him into the bushes and ravishing him.

"You're not all that unpleasant," she admitted. "I just think it probably isn't appropriate for us to be out here. Alone. Considering who you are and who I am and what we've already done and what we can't do again because of who we are."

He shifted, shuffling his feet against the cobbled terrace floor.

"Not that you even want to…," she continued. "Do it again, I mean."

"Do *you* want to?"

Just the thought of doing it again made her flush. She raked her teeth across her bottom lip and looked at him from beneath her lashes. Even without that seductive glance, her silence was answer enough.

He cleared his throat and rocked back on his heels. "Me too."

REMEMBER THE ALIMONY

BETHANY TRUE

LEISURE BOOKS NEW YORK CITY

To my family, one and all.
Without your love, support, and constant
reassurance, this would not be possible.

A LEISURE BOOK®

February 2007

Published by

Dorchester Publishing Co., Inc.
200 Madison Avenue
New York, NY 10016

ISBN 0-8439-5788-3

The name "Leisure Books" and the stylized "L" with design are
trademarks of Dorchester Publishing Co., Inc.

Printed in the United States of America.

Visit us on the web at www.dorchesterpub.com.

ACKNOWLEDGMENTS

Special thanks to my agent, Cheryl Ferguson, for falling in love with this manuscript; Leah Hultenschmidt, my editor, for helping to make it worth loving; and everyone at Dorchester for making this dream a reality.

Kisses to Jon, Mom, Father, Lynn, Davona, Debbe, James, Felicia, Joshua, Hannah, Jared and last but certainly not least, all things Disney for loving, nurturing or otherwise helping to keep a certain toddler busy for countless hours while his mommy pecked away at her desktop.

Hugs to Nicole McAleb, who saved millions of lives by convincing me to write instead of going into medicine (and extra hugs for my beautiful jacket photo) and to Cheryl Behr, whose advice and input gave me the encouragement to finish this manuscript. I can't thank either one of you enough.

Air kisses and waves to teachers and friends: David, Shonna, Rosalyn, Terry, New Girl, Nikki, Amie, Lasha, Angelita, Allyson, Miss Debbie, Ella, and Mike. I beg forgiveness for any names I might have overlooked in my excitement. In ways small and great you all are a part of this book.

Mwah!

Remember
the
Alimony

Prologue

"I suppose it feels a bit like being a priceless doll in a glass case. Sure, she's beautiful, but she's not serving her designed purpose. She might be coveted but she's really not appreciated. It feels like a million people look at you every day but nobody really sees you," was what Delaney Davis **really** wanted to say in response to the question: *"How does it feel like to be Miss Texas, the most beautiful woman in the state?"*

In Delaney's opinion, her mind-dulling mediocrity was precisely the reason she wasn't *chosen* to be Miss Texas ten years ago—she was chosen to be first runner-up, even though all the contestants assured her she was by far the prettiest, and it was just too bad about that note she missed right at the end of her song. So there Delaney was, blinded by flashing bulbs as she accepted the crown, by default—for the *real* Miss Texas had found herself pregnant, engaged and eloped (in that order) just weeks after winning—

standing at a podium answering idiotic questions like "How does it feel to be Miss Texas, the most beautiful woman in the state?"

To which she politely replied, "Wonderful."

Chapter One

Break in new shoes! You want to look completely comfortable and natural walking around in a bathing suit and four-inch stilettos.
—Everything I Never Needed to Know I
  Learned from a Beauty Pageant *by Delaney*
  Davis-Daniels
  (unpublished, of course)

"You need to get laid."

"What?" Delaney asked. She adjusted the earpiece of her hands-free cell phone. "Say that again. I have my top down."

"I guess you beat us to the punch then." Macy laughed.

"On my car, moron. I have the top down on my car. I'm sure I didn't hear you correctly."

"Of course you did. I said you need to get laid. Your sister and I have discussed it at length and we've determined it's been too long. So we're going out tonight with one mission in mind: finding you a man."

"It comforts me so to know that you and Phoebe are discussing my sex life."

"Your sex life doesn't exist."

Not for two years, Delaney lamented.

"And we're just worried about you because it just isn't natural. I've read about things like this in *Cosmo* . . ." *Cosmo* was Macy's holy scripture. "Women who go too long without having sex, all sorts of terrible things happen to them. There was one case where this lady blew up right in the middle of nowhere and when they investigated her death, they discovered she hadn't had sex in over a year. She was so horny she blew up!"

Delaney laughed. "Mace, that's a suburban legend. Stories soccer moms pass back and forth across the open windows of their SUVs. I read a similar story. Only *Ladies' Home Journal* attributed the not-so-spontaneous combustion to the woman talking on her cell while pumping her gas."

"Whatever. I'm just saying, it's not healthy. Look at you, you're twenty-seven years old and you're reading *Ladies' Home Journal*? I didn't think they even sold that without a box of estrogen patches and an accordion fan."

"I appreciate your concern, but I assure you there is nothing to worry about. I am perfectly comfortable with my life just the way it is," she lied.

She hadn't been comfortable in quite some time. Truth be told, her frustration had reached an all-new peak. Lately, she couldn't even reach orgasm with her vibrator.

She sighed deeply into the phone. "Besides, *Ladies' Home Journal* has lots of good recipes."

"None of which are doing you any good unless you have somebody to cook for. Which you don't," Macy was quick to point out. "So unless they have a recipe for getting laid, I don't know why you bother reading it."

"How'd you two get on the topic of my sex life anyway?"

"I just had the most amazing, mind-blowing sex of my entire life with the copy boy."

When Macy said "just had," Delaney knew it wasn't last-night-after-work-we-went-out-for-drinks just had. It was we-flirted-all-morning-then-locked-the-door-to-the-copy-room-bit-my-knuckles-to-stifle-my-screams just had. That was Macy. A raging ball of sex energy that burned hotter than her hair was red.

Delaney smiled. She was a little envious of Macy. Macy was completely comfortable in her skin. For Macy, there was sex and there was love and if the two hooked up in the middle, you were damn lucky. Delaney, of course, would never dream of doing anything so spontaneous. She hadn't been on the dating scene in five years. Just before she got married she had dated a short string of guys who couldn't believe they were out on dates with Miss Texas. Other than getting in bed with her, they had no desire to get to know her any better. After she made it abundantly clear that she wasn't sleeping with them, they never called her back. Macy and Phoebe were right. Her sex life was nonexistent.

"And Phebes was telling about her make-up sex with Matt."

If Phoebe and Matt were having make-up sex, they were fighting. Again. The two had been dating since tenth grade. On again, off again, on again. They spent all their time arguing over who forgot to pay the cable bill, who left the empty toilet paper tube on the holder, who erased whose messages on the voice mail. All their fights ended the same way: the two of them tumbling into bed for a night of marathon sex. They might as well just make it official and get married.

"And we realized the only one of the three of us who doesn't have any incredible sex stories to share is . . . you."

Whenever Delaney talked about sex she got flushed or fanned herself or had to stop halfway through for a sip of ice water. She didn't have all that much experience with guys before she got married—three lovers (the guy in high school, the guy in college and the guy she married). Orgasms (and she used that term loosely) with any one of them were a distant second to the nervous giddiness she felt when she plunked down $395 for her first pair of Jimmy Choos.

"The problem is you spend three days a week at the boutique and any free time you get at Through the Looking Glass. You are surrounded by women twenty-four seven. You're never going to find a man that way."

Delaney bit her lip and inhaled generously. With Macy it was always men! "Who says I need a man? The whole reason I started Through the Looking Glass is to teach the girls I work with that they can't define themselves through their romantic or physical relationships. I want them to be strong and independent. What kind of simpering, whimpering hypocrite would I be if I went home every night and fell right into bed with some random guy?"

"It doesn't make you a hypocrite to enjoy being with a man, Laney. You'd be relaxed. You'd be satisfied. You'd be happy."

"Contrary to popular belief, Macy, sex is not the end all be all."

"Then you've been sleeping with the wrong men, honey."

Delaney sighed. This was not a battle she was going to win.

Best friend conquered, Macy turned to attire.

"Dress to kill. Wear the strappy Jimmy Choo stilettos. *Cosmo* says no guy can resist a stiletto. We'll pick you up at eight."

Delaney disconnected the call as she pulled in front of the posh boutique. She finger combed her wind-tossed hair and applied a sheer pink gloss to her lips. She rubbed her lips together, then kiss-blotted on her wrist. She checked her reflection in the rearview mirror.

"Another day, another dollar," she told her reflection. She just wished a dollar were all she needed.

Chapter Two

Every beauty pageant is like Little League sports. At the end of the game, somebody's going home with the trophy and somebody's going home with tears.

"I don't see him. We've been here an hour. We should go already," Macy said.

"Matt's here!" Phoebe squinted through tendrils of smoke curling in the air. "I just know he's here. If he's not here, trust me, he's coming. I snooped through three months of bank statements and he's been at this strip club every Thursday night. He's more regular than my period." Phoebe none too casually twisted in her seat to get a better view of the endless sea of heads bobbing and cresting to the tune of top forty pop music.

"'I'm just going to the library to do some research,'" she said, mocking her boyfriend's pretentious tone. "Lying sack of shit."

"Delaney, tell her it's time to go. Tell her you don't want to be here," Macy pleaded.

Delaney shrugged. The longer they hung out at Foxy's, the longer they could avoid the real reason for their evening out. If they stayed here long enough, eventually she could claim a headache, force them to take her home, and then crawl in bed with a steamy mug of chai and a dog-eared book by Jane Austen.

"Come on, Mace. Her life is hanging in the balance here. This could mean the difference between 'I do' and 'I don't think so.' Well, this week anyway. Besides, we owe it to Phebes to stick it out another hour or so. She's my baby sis. I don't want her in my shoes in five years."

Macy glanced down at Delaney's grossly expensive Manolo sandals. Pink, of course, sexy, strappy and encrusted with genuine Swarovski crystals.

"Six-hundred-dollar shoes. Yeah, that would *really* suck," she said, her voice dripping with cordial sarcasm.

Delaney sighed. "I meant the divorce."

Her marriage had been short and not so sweet. For five years she had either played the role of J.D. Daniels' dutiful trophy wife or sat at home, alone, wondering whether he was having sex with a younger, more eager facsimile of herself.

She loathed to admit that he had been unfaithful during the bulk of their marriage—and that she tolerated it. It took his current mistress—Misty, quite ironically—to clear things up. Misty was a social climber and when J.D. hooked up with her, she immediately demanded all kinds of outrageous displays of his affections—progressively more outrageous the longer he stayed in artificial marital accord with Delaney. Even though Delaney had given up on their marriage long before she found him screwing Misty in their Galveston beach house, walking in on that scenario did little to ease the smarting of her wounded pride.

And now she was on the eve of meeting with her soon-to-be-ex husband's newest attorney—his third so far this divorce—without a dime to pay her own counsel (fortunately she hadn't lost her charm and wit and she ably convinced him to wait a few weeks on a good and proper retainer), looking for her sister's soon-to-be-ex fiancé at the most elite strip joint in Austin.

Way to go, Miss Teen Texas.

"Aren't you having even a little fun?" Phoebe asked as she bounced and twisted to the music.

Macy shrugged and rolled her eyes and motioned for the waitress to come over. "I thought we were going out to find Laney a piece of ass."

"Laney thinks we should stay, right Laney?"

Delaney nodded and sipped her pink drink. She didn't want to talk about it, much less think about it . . . except she couldn't stop thinking about it. So she would just have a drink or two to take the edge off.

"The only reason Laney is siding with you is because she is trying to avoid our original mission—to find her a man. Admit it, Laney," Macy yelled over the loud music.

Delaney shrugged and took a long sip of her pink drink.

"Look around, Mace," Phoebe argued. "Seriously, what better place to find her a man? This place is packed with men. Every eligible man in Austin is probably sitting in this very club."

Eligible man-hunting in a strip club. That made Delaney giggle. She looked around. Lots and lots and lots of men. If the number of wrists bearing Swiss chronographs was an indicator, lots and lots and lots of money too. Money, however, was not indicative of eligibility. She had already learned that the hard way. She caught the eye of a dark-haired, azure-eyed Adonis a few tables over. He winked. She blushed, smiled and took a *very* long sip of her pink drink.

"What kind of creep would she find here? Right, Laney?"

Delaney inclined her head in agreement, not a full nod as she noisily sucked air through her straw. Her drink was gone already? Funny, she didn't even feel it yet. She placed her empty glass on the table and started on Macy's abandoned drink. It wasn't pink, but it would do.

She looked back over her shoulder to see if he was still looking. Yep. Still looking, no, unapologetically staring.

"They look normal." Phoebe pointed at Adonis's table.

She guessed it was a bachelor party since one of the guys was wearing a construction paper chain attached to a big foam ball painted black. Most of the other guys were dispensing twenties like ATMs to get girls over to give the guy a lap dance.

Her Adonis didn't seem all that into the celebration. He was relaxed in his chair, nursing his beer and laughing obligingly whenever one of the other suits elbowed him.

When he caught Delaney looking at him again—now *she* was staring—he smiled a crooked Harrison Ford smile and raised his beer stein to her. She was thankful for the low lighting because now her cheeks were competing with the pink of her drink. She snapped her gaze back to the stage where the dancer had just bared all, and Delaney's face went from a pretty blush to that awful shade of fuchsia that looks good on exactly .001% of the population. She tilted her head to glance out of the corner of her eye to see if he was laughing at her. He was. Her body tingled from head to toe and back up again, pooling in her center and, suddenly, she was hot. She picked up a napkin and fanned herself.

"I don't need a piece of ass. I do, however, need another drink," Delaney declared. She motioned for the waitress by holding up her empty glass. "Remember where my last adventure in sexual spontaneity got me?"

"Yeah, to the altar. Marrying James David Daniels, one of the richest men in Texas."

"And now divorcing him, thank you very much, but we're not divorced yet."

"Semantics," Phoebe said. "He kicked you out of the house over a year ago. You're just waiting for the judge to grant it. Not to mention, he'd moved the new honey into your house before the dust settled after you left. . . ." Delaney hated when people said "not to mention" if they were just going to mention it anyway.

"I moved out of my own free volition." She had wanted out as much as J.D. wanted to get her out.

"You two are so over, it's just not official yet. Once you meet with your lawyers tomorrow it's all downhill. Where is that prick?" Phoebe returned to scanning the crowd in hopes of sighting Matt.

"Don't remind me." Delaney dreaded the meeting. Her attorney, Lawrence, promised Delaney that J.D.'s technique of hiring and firing legal counsel, drawing out the battle, was his way of trying to make her weary, to give up any alimony claims and walk away empty-handed. Lawrence promised it would not make him weary and they would not leave the table with anything less than she deserved.

A waitress finally sashayed toward their table, making a pit stop by the bachelor party table. She swatted at a couple of hands making a grab for her bushy tail.

"There are a lot of women here," Delaney noted, looking around.

"Ha-llo! Titty bar," Macy reminded her.

"No, I mean in the audience. As a matter of fact there are almost as many women here as men. I'll take another . . . ummm. . . . ummm . . ." She held up her empty glass. She couldn't remember what she was drinking and thought for a moment it might be because she had one too many already. She normally had a two-drink limit, but what the hell, she was divorcing one of the richest men in Texas. She was allowed a little celebration libation, wasn't she? "I dunno what it was. It was a glossy martini. Not a cosmopolitan but pink." Her signature color.

"Bikini martini," the waitress in the fox costume told them. At least it was supposed to be a fox costume. What there was of it. It basically boiled down to a bronze teeny bikini and a headband adorned with furry little pointy ears. There was a bushy tail attached to the impossibly small satin triangle of her thong and she wore fishnets—just to sex it all up.

Delaney fished a ten out of her handbag and handed it toward the waitress.

She shook her head. "You're covered."

"Covered?"

"The hottie in the suit." The fox pointed to Mr. Adonis. "He said all the drinks for this table should go on his tab."

"He's a regular?" Delaney asked, wrinkling her nose.

"Never seen him before. But he's wearing a twenty-five-hundred-dollar Armani and he left his platinum card with the bar to cover all the drinks at his table, so I'm guessing he can cover a couple of yours."

Macy tilted her head to get a better look. "He's hot."

"Off the charts," Phoebe agreed.

"You'll thank him for us?" Delaney asked the waitress.

"Honey, I'm guessing before this night is over, you'll get to thank him yourself."

"So how come there's so many women here?" Macy asked when the waitress had finished taking the rest of the order.

"Amateur night," the waitress said.

"Amateur night?" Macy raised a questioning eyebrow.

"Everybody wants to work for Foxy's, right? So many that Mick, the manager, doesn't have time to do all the auditions anymore. So he has amateur night. All ladies get in for half cover and those brave enough to get up on stage and shake their asses can semi-audition."

"What do they win?"

"A chance at a real audition. Mick figures if she drives the crowd wild, he might as well give her a chance to dance . . . and a thousand bucks." She added the last part casually as if it were the least important piece of information.

Delaney's interest piqued. Not that she would actually do it. She would never in a million years do anything like that, but . . .

A thousand dollars!

It was like the lotto. Only millions of dollars less.

Three or fours years ago she would have dropped a thousand dollars on a small leather accessory—a Prada handbag, a Coco belt. Now she needed to horde every penny just to survive. Funny how life turns out.

"A thousand bucks." Macy poked Delaney with her elbow.

"Winner takes a thousand dollars home and even if she isn't interested in auditioning for a job, she's invited back for the Annual Fox Hunt. Fox of the Year takes home five thousand dollars plus a lot of freebies—spa visits, luxury rental car for a week, trip to Cancun. Stuff like that."

"Do you have to get naked?" Phoebe asked.

"Helps, but no. All you gotta do is dance. The dancer who impresses the audience the most wins. Old-fashioned popularity contest. Just like being back in tenth grade. If any of y'all are interested in signing up, you'd better hurry, the best costumes go quick. I'll be right back with your drinks."

Phoebe nudged Delaney this time. "Did you hear her? A thousand dollars."

"So?" Delaney said, wishing the waitress would hurry back with her third? fourth? round.

"So you said you needed cash for the lawyer. You're robbing Peter to pay Paul on all your plastic. Here's a thousand dollars right on the table."

Delaney laughed. Guffawed, actually, drawing a few curious stares from the tables of leering potbellies in their immediate vicinity. "I am not going to dance bare butt in front of hundreds of strangers."

"You heard the waitress; you don't have to get naked. Just dance. You're an incredible dancer."

"It doesn't even matter. With looks like yours, you'd win even if you danced in knee-highs and a house dress."

"Momma and Daddy would kill me."

"Who's gonna tell them? Me? They still don't know I'm shacking up with Matt. Besides, anybody who knows them wouldn't admit they were here. And they'd have to tell them they were here to tell them they had seen you dancing," Phoebe reasoned.

"It's absolutely no different from prancing around in your swimsuit in all those pageants your mother dragged you through," Macy added. "And you know you need the money. If I give you another dime, I won't be able to make rent this month."

"I'm gonna pay you back. Every last cent." Delaney hated that her parents, her sister and her best friend were giving her money. Last year when J.D. first moved her out, things weren't as tough. He set her up in a decent suburb and was paying the mortgage, the utilities, even giving her a little allowance. But then, very suddenly, he shut her off. He told her that Daniels Enterprises was having a bad year. Odd, considering his company made billions. Her mortgage couldn't have been more than a drop in the bucket to him. She was certain he had told her that to force her into filing for divorce when she had first suggested counseling. Then, after she filed, he turned down every offer her lawyer presented. She knew she was being more than reasonable. No matter what she asked for, the answer was a resolute no.

Even though Delaney had found a job as a personal jobber and image advisor at some hoity-toity boutique, she barely earned enough to cover her mortgage and utilities. Anything extra like say, food, she relied on the grace of her friends and family. Lawrence assured her there was no way she wasn't walking away without a decent settlement, but she wasn't seeing any of that at the moment. But even Lawrence was beginning to drop hints about when she would pay the rest of his retainer. He'd already cut his usual price in half out of pity.

"I know, I know. And I would give you the last penny I had. I'm just saying, I don't have that much extra. You could use the money. You're a great dancer and you were friggin' Miss Teen Texas ten years ago, Miss Rio Grande the year after that and first runner-up to Miss Texas. You would win this gig hands down."

"One. Thousand. Dollars," Phoebe sang.

Delaney thought it over. Why shouldn't she do it? She'd spent her entire life doing what others expected of her and where had it landed her? Divorced and washed up at the ripe old age of twenty-seven. When she was a kid, she had been her mother's helper. Not that she resented it, she didn't. But when the younger girls were exploring and playing, she was inside washing and folding diapers and helping with supper. When she was full swing into the pageant circuit, every movement was measured and calculated—everything a question as to whether it would cost her a crown. After she got married she was expected to be the dutiful trophy wife. She could wear designer originals, but she was never expected to be original. She'd never done anything wild or off the cuff like Macy and Phoebe. She was always the one on the sidelines listening to the tales they told of their escapades. It was right at that moment she came to a realization: Delaney Daniels was sick and tired of being Delaney Daniels.

The waitress came back and set their drinks in front of them. Delaney took a long swallow, then caught the fox by her tail before she rounded the table.

"Where's the costume room?"

Chapter Three

It's not about what you give them; it's about what you don't give them. . . . Always leave the judges wanting more, and you'll always be invited back to the next round.

His name was Lucas Church. But there was nothing holy about that man. Not his sinful good looks, not his devil-may-care attitude, and certainly not one of the thoughts going through his head about the girl dancing on stage at the present moment. Just as he was about to declare this the worst bachelor party he'd ever attended and make his exit, some guy in hunting digs (yes, red coat and jodhpurs) announced the onset of the weekly amateur night contest.

Lucas thought, *What the hell?* Stay-at-home moms and sorority bowheads hungry for fifteen minutes of attention? It was worth a good laugh.

The first few girls had been intolerably young and uncoordinated, gyrating with moves copied from the newest MTV pop tart. They probably thought they came across as sexy, but to him it looked as though they had eaten bad shrimp or something. Lucas was uncomfortable even watching them. A couple of others had been a little older, maybe mid-twenties. They were decent dancers, but within seconds they'd bared it all, leaving nothing to the imagination.

Then *she* came on stage. She was all sex and style. The doe-eyed beauty he'd noticed earlier in the evening. She'd looked misplaced with her hair in a tightly wound chignon, a designer suit and impossibly high heels. Her friends were comfortably dressed in tanks and jeans. It wasn't difficult to tell that— aside from savoring every last drop of her frilly pink drink—she was miserable in the surroundings. Even when she smiled, it only turned the corners of her perfect pink pout but missed sending light to her dark chocolate brown eyes.

So he was surprised when, just as he was settling the tab, he turned from the bar and saw her on stage. Something in her had changed. She had gone from ultra conservative to all pomp and circumstance. This one came out in her hot pink bikini and tiara. The white sash diagonally bisecting her read "Miss Behavin'," which made him smirk. And wonder, *What the hell she has left to take off?* She was older than the other girls, not that she looked it so much, but she had a poise and confidence that the previous girls lacked. This time when she smiled, sexy and seductive, she was smiling for the audience. Drawing them in.

Siren.

She was long and blond with great boobs and a tight round J. Lo ass. She was exactly the type he would take home and, in that moment, he decided he would. Take her home.

She could dance. Not the jerky gyrations of some twenty-come-lately who watched way too many music videos. No, Lucas could tell she had studied the classics—ballet, jazz, tap. And her choice of music made him hesitate. The other girls had danced to the annoying tunes of whatever pop princess they thought they looked the most like, but she had chosen the title song to the Broadway blues revue "Ain't Misbehavin' "—only slower and sexier than he had remembered. She not only danced to it but she sang it. Low and breathy. Arousing as hell. Just barely loud enough to be heard over the waves of hoots and whistles. His instant hard-on surprised him. He had had his fair share of women and he did not react to them like a schoolboy with raging hormones.

There was something different about this one. She was beautiful, to be sure, but something more. She was not just sexy; she was alluring. Her routine was slow and methodical. Like something out of the fifties—teasing, taunting. She strutted. She swayed. She sashayed. She dipped her chin and looked at the audience. Lucas would have sworn (along with half the men there) that she looked *directly at him* from beneath her heavy fringe of lashes, puckered her Angelina Jolie lips and kissed the air. Just a peck. That sent him reeling, his penis surging. Twice she leisurely slid her finger down her tongue, down her neck, her collarbone, the swell of her breast almost to her nipple, hardened and erect by the blast of cold air directed at the stage. He motioned for a glass of water from the fox behind the bar, gulping the entire tumbler in two swallows.

She was almost through with the song before Lucas realized she hadn't taken off a stitch. Well, that wasn't exactly true. At some point she had taken off the tiara and shaken out her hair, longer than what was probably considered fashionable with the popularity of cropped pixie cuts and blunted bobs, but on her, bombshell sexy. She had discarded the sash at some point, too. That must have been the moment she knelt and wrapped it around the chin of the bald man front and center, but Lucas couldn't remember the action, just that he wished he could turn back the hands of time and unrelinquish that very seat he had abandoned when he came to settle his tab.

At the last chords of the song, she turned her back on the audience and very slowly dropped the top of her bikini. His breath caught in his throat, and in that moment, Lucas wanted her to turn around more than he had ever wanted anything. But she didn't. She looked back over her shoulder, cast her heavily lidded lashes downward, wiggled her butt, smiled, winked (at him, he was certain) and let the curtain drop.

The entire club was quiet, and Lucas realized he wasn't the only one in the room with a boner hard enough to cut diamonds. He painfully suffered through two or three more routines before the hunter-clad M.C. brought all nine girls out on the stage again. One of the foxy waitresses pointed to each girl in the fashion of Barker's Beauties and held up some fake "applause-o-meter." When she stood in front of the "beauty queen," the crowd went wild. In the front, the two girls she had been sitting with earlier screamed at the top of their lungs.

"Go, Laney!"

"Wooo-hoooooo! Laney!"

It was glaringly obvious that Laney had won, but the fox and the hunter went on with the charade as they moved down the line of the remaining, now frowning, contestants.

"Looks like we got ourselves a winner!" the hunter proclaimed as he shooed the fox and the losing contestants off the stage.

Lucas smiled. Winner indeed.

Chapter Four

*Who knows when a judge might spy you in a hall-
way, hailing a taxi or at the breakfast buffet? Remember, you must act like you're onstage every moment
of every day.*

Delaney was thrilled that they had presented her win-
nings in the form of cash. The last thing she needed
was to try to negotiate a check from a strip club. Furthermore, no one would be able to recognize her name.
She didn't need all of Austin knowing J.D. Daniels's
wife had just stripped for what used to amount to her
monthly sushi allowance.

*From Miss Teen Texas to Miss Behavin'. Tell me, De-
laney Daniels, what won't you do for a buck?*

"You were really good up there." A voice, low and
husky, tickled her ear.

Delaney didn't immediately turn around, discon-
certed by the proximity of the man standing behind
her, crowding her against the bar. She had the thousand bucks in her purse and she didn't feel like being

polite anymore. Polite had walked out the door after the last dickhead had come up behind her, grabbed her ass and asked if she was in the mood to really misbehave. Unfortunately for him, she was, and he ended up with a groin full of knee before the bouncer tossed the guy out the door. After that performance she decided she needed another drink. Just one more.

Nearly every guy standing at the bar had witnessed her knee-to-the-groin technique and backed off; every guy except this guy who was either: 1) a complete imbecile or, 2) really into pain, which she would be more than happy to accommodate. As she turned to give him what for, her anger was quickly replaced by something slightly less corporal and more carnal. Because standing in front of her was the most beautiful specimen of mankind she had ever seen. The Adonis.

He was tall, 6'4" easy, maybe taller. And dark. Not the metrosexual I-spend-too-much-time-and-money-in-the-tanning-salon dark. But the retrosexual I-spend-every-free-moment-I have-on-my-boat-at-the-lake dark. And handsome. Leading man, if-sex-were-a-drug-I'd-be-addictive handsome.

So what was going to start off as a "Go to hell, loser," came out a (*omigod I actually squeaked!*) "Thanks."

"Let me buy you a drink," he said, moving closer.

She tried to swallow to wet her dry throat. "I think you already did that."

"Then let me buy you another." He leaned in and slid a crisp twenty-dollar bill across the bar.

"Thanks." This time less squeak and more pant, but she hoped it came off as sexy and breathless instead of needy and desperate.

"Where'd you learn to move like that?" he asked.

"I used to dance." She didn't want him to ask where she had studied because then she would have to admit that she hadn't studied at all but spent countless summer hours watching *Solid Gold*, *American Bandstand*, and *Dance Party U.S.A.* She'd have to admit that she had seen *Footloose*, *Fame* and *Flashdance* more times than she could count. And that scene in *Dirty Dancing* where Baby danced up the mountain and across the river and all over the countryside? That would pretty much sum up any semblance of a "hobby" she had had.

"You're very good. The way you move. Very . . . stimulating."

She blinked several times, trying to be certain she had heard him correctly, but his expression was blank. Guys didn't say things like that back when she was dating. Ever. But then she hadn't dated guys like this. Ever.

"Are you trying to pick me up?" she asked.

"Depends. Do you want to be picked up?"

"My friends and I, we came together, we leave together. It's kind of our rule." She motioned to Macy and Phoebe dozens of feet away just as Macy was craning her neck to see who Delaney was talking to. Macy gave Delaney a thumbs-up.

Adonis looked over his shoulder and then returned his attention back to Delaney.

"It looks like your friend approves."

Delaney wanted to throw a rock at Macy. Why didn't she just mind her own business? "She wants to find me," her voice trailed off. What? A lay? A one-night stand? ". . . a boyfriend."

Adonis looked her up and down in that way that told her he would be more than game for a one-night stand. "I can't imagine you having any problems finding a," he cleared his throat, ". . . boyfriend."

"I'm not looking for a boyfriend. I'm not. But she's got it in her head that I need a man."

He raised a brow.

"I don't," she added quickly. A hopeless defense that proved she most certainly did.

She wanted to kick herself. She wasn't the witty one in her crew—that honor definitely belonged to Macy—but usually she wasn't half bad on conversation. On the pageant circuit she had to learn to talk to all kinds of uninteresting people. Now here was this gorgeous guy, the epitome of all things sexy and here she was blubbering—no, worse than blubbering, not saying anything at all—to this Grecian god who, for some reason, pointed his attention to her. She couldn't think of anything to say so she took a deep swallow of her drink.

"So that's why you're here? Looking for a man?"

Delaney nodded. "Yeah." Meaning, of course, looking for Matt, Phoebe's fiancé.

He grinned at her and nodded back. "After that number on stage, I'm sure there's a waiting list a mile long."

She cringed. Thinking but not communicating, because looking at him made it very difficult to do the two simultaneously. He thought *she* was *looking* for a man.

"No, no, no. *I'm* not looking for a man. *We're looking for a guy.*"

His face registered surprise but was quickly blanketed by a sly smile. "Damn! This just gets better and better."

"I'm really goofing here. What I mean to say is we're trying to find my sister's fiancé. She thinks he comes here and spends loads of money from their wedding fund on strippers. So we're trying to catch him in the act. I'm certainly not looking for a *man*." She must have put the emphasis on "man" because his face twisted and he inclined his head toward the fox behind the bar.

"No! I didn't mean that! I just meant . . ." Then she started giggling. Hysterically, because that's what she did when she got nervous. The way he kept looking at her made her a big ball of nervous energy. So she giggled. The drinks didn't help either. She was cutting herself off. Right now. After one more sip. To calm her nerves. And make her stop giggling.

"Am I making you uncomfortable?" he asked, completely comfortable.

"No," she lied. Then giggled. And hiccupped.

He smiled. Full of himself. Impressed that he was rendering her speechless and giggly.

"Okay, maybe a tee tiny bit. Not uncomfortable really . . . just . . ." What was she supposed to say? Horny?

He looked at her again. A full-body ogle as if he'd read her mind. She silently reminded herself that his cavalier leering was supposed to piss her off, but it didn't. It warmed her from the inside out. It had been so long since a man looked at her so appreciatively. She didn't have to say horny because he already knew. She decided to use it to her benefit, wanting him to be as much at a loss for words as she was. She leaned forward to adjust the strap on her sandal that didn't need adjusting, just so he could get an adequate view of her cleavage—in case he needed any help undressing her with his eyes.

She heard him inhale deeply.

"This is no place for a nice girl like you." He managed a straight face while delivering that one.

She cocked an eyebrow. "You're kidding me, right? What kind of line is that?"

He grinned his sexy lopsided Harrison Ford grin. "A good line. I stick with what works."

"Does that usually work?"

"Depends on what I want."

"What do you want?"

"Isn't that the sixty-four-thousand-dollar question?"

"Not much of a question. You seem like the kind of guy who knows what you want."

He paused in consideration. That was exactly the kind of guy he was. He leaned in closer. His lips grazed her ear. She willed her body not to shudder beneath the millions of tingles electrifying her skin.

"What if I want you to give me the full show?" he whispered. His body was pressed against hers. His breath was warm and wet and sending trills up and down her spine. She should have been alarmed but she wasn't. Her body was sounding warning bells, to be sure, but not the *Danger Will Robinson* kind, the *Hello, Mrs. Robinson* kind. Every nerve in her body tingled. She was aroused. Very, very aroused.

This is what happens when you go two years without a man, Delaney Davis Daniels.

"What?"

"I want you to dance."

"I already did that."

"For me. A private dance."

"I'm not going home with you," she said. Even though she was a little buzzed, she wasn't stupid.

"Who said anything about going home with me?" he asked. "Unless you were just thinking you might *want* to go home with me."

"I wasn't thinking anything of the sort. You just look like the type of man who doesn't go home alone often."

"Never," he admitted.

Cocky S.O.B.

"Then I suggest you start hunting down one of these foxes because I'm not going home with you."

"I only asked for you to dance for me. You can do that here."

"Here?" She surveyed the immediate vicinity. Did he mean on top of the bar? On stage again? What? Was she actually *considering* this? *Why* was she actually considering this?

She was sick of always being the girl next door, America's sweetheart. During her entire life she had never done anything off the cuff. She was suffocated by what her friends, her family, the whole state of Texas expected her to be: Delaney Daniels, beauty queen. Perfect and without flaws even though it sometimes seemed the entire world had her under a microscope hunting for them. Macy got to do wild and restless things and blame it on her flame-red hair. When Phoebe did something crazy, everybody shrugged it off, saying "You know how eccentric those brainy types can be." When Delaney did something unexpected . . .

Who was she kidding? She *never* did anything unexpected. She realized she wanted to dance, because she was drowning in everybody else's expectations. And she was sick of it.

Oh, and because she wanted to get laid. Sex with an actual man. Despite the arguments she had made to Macy earlier, her vibrator was becoming a very sore substitute for the real thing. So here was this hot guy, beautiful guy, who could have his pick of any woman in the club and he wanted her. Then she remembered exactly where she was, a strip joint. A nice one, to be sure, but a strip joint all the same, and what if he was some porn-addict whack job who lived in a one-bedroom rat's nest because he spent every dime he mooched off the government on expensive suits and strippers?

He nodded toward the table with the bachelor party. "We rented one of the private rooms in the back. We have it all night."

She was silent for a moment, realizing she was actually contemplating the idea. She shook it off. "Sorry, but I'm not really a stripper or a dancer or whatever they are called these days. I only did it for the money."

"Isn't that what exotic dancers do? Dance for the money?"

"That came out wrong. What I meant was, I'm kind of low on cash right now and I have some really important debts to cover so . . . when the waitress told us about the contest I just figured . . . if I hadn't been desperate for the money I wouldn't have done it at all." Was she trying to dig herself deeper?

"How much?"

"What?"

"Money. How much money would it take to convince you to do a private show for me?"

She chuckled and shook her head. "You're kidding, right? You don't have enough." She hadn't meant to insult him, though when he bristled she knew she had. "I only meant . . ." She stopped and took a long swallow of her (*last!*) bikini martini. She knew she should really stop drinking. Now.

Some people were happy drunks. Some people were sloppy drunks. Delaney was undeniably a sexy drunk. Alcohol made her think things, every once in a while do things, that nice girls from Big Stinking Creek, Texas, didn't think and do. The way this guy was looking right now, she was certainly thinking about doing every one of them.

"You just danced for the entire club for a few hundred bucks . . ."

"A thousand," she interjected. "One thousand dollars." She might be tipsy, but she wasn't cheap. "That's a lot more than a few hundred in my old neighborhood."

"So is that what it would take? A thousand dollars?"

"I didn't say that," she said quickly.

"More?"

"Maybe." *Maybe? Maybe? Not maybe, no. Just say no.*

"Fifteen hundred," he offered.

"I'm not dancing for you for fifteen hundred dollars," she said. Though she meant to say it in a way that stressed the "I'm not dancing for you" part, it came out stressing the "fifteen hundred dollars" part.

"Twenty-five hundred," he countered.

"As in two thousand five hundred?"

"Cash.

She moistened her lips. She needed that money. It would be the remainder of the retainer for her attorney, plus some left over to put in the bank. Forget the bank. She thought about the newest pair of croc (embossed, not real) leather sandals calling her name in the Nordstrom shoe salon. How long had it been since she'd been able just to go buy a pair of really cute shoes without counting cost or weighing consequences? Shoes were her Prozac. And as depressed as she had been the last year, she really needed a good dose of retail therapy by way of an all-leather upper. But she couldn't appear overeager.

"Who carries around twenty-five hundred dollars in cash?" She narrowed her eyes and crossed her arms in front of her.

"Those of us who have it to spend." His tone was casually confident. Almost bored. "I got it legally."

She narrowed her eyes. "So all I have to do is dance?"

"Finish the show," he told her, his tone letting her know that her coy tease act circa 1953 wasn't going to cut it. He wanted her naked.

She glanced over his shoulder at Macy and Phoebe, who were presently distracted from the original "Mission Matt: Seek and Destroy" by a few of the bachelors who had crossed over to their table. Knowing Macy and men, Delaney figured she had a good half hour before they even missed her.

"Okay, but just dancing. Nothing else. Nothing."

"Nothing has to happen that you don't want to happen." He grabbed her arm before she had a chance to change her mind and guided her through the crush of people in the club.

The private room gave credence to every rumor Delaney had ever believed about sin clubs. An eight-by-eight room with tufted velvet walls, low lighting emitting from a quartet of sconces, and heavily perfumed with the heady fragrance of ylang ylang and tuberose. In the center of the room there was a divan laden with oversized overstuffed pillows. It was more decadent than she had imagined it would be. She heard the gentle click of a lock and spun around.

"*No* locks," she demanded.

"Look, I told you, all my buddies pitched in to rent this room for private dances. If we leave it unlocked there's the likely chance we are going to have a visitor or two."

Made sense. "Fine. But I swear if you lay a hand on me . . . Let's just say I know how to take care of myself."

He grinned. "I witnessed your self-preservation with the poor schmuck at the bar." He was removing his suit coat and undoing his cuff links. She wondered about his profession. He worked someplace where image was important, given the high quality of his attire. She could tell that beneath the fine silk blend of his custom-made shirt he was a solid wall of steel. And she realized she was glad the doors were locked.

Why does he have to be so damn sexy?

"And no touching."

He deleted the space between them until their bodies were barely touching. "No hands," he said in a low, suggestive timbre. She didn't miss the fact that he didn't include "no touching."

Chapter Five

If you are playing an instrument, remember, always blow before the show. Woodwinds can behave unpredictably in different climates.

"So dance for me, beauty queen."

"What!" An inexplicable horror came over her face. "What did you call me?"

"Whoooooa!" he said, putting up two hands. "You know . . . Miss Behavin'." He thought he might add that he hoped she would not be behaving tonight, but she was jumpier than a cricket already. One more comment like that and she might bolt.

"Sorry." She brushed a few tendrils of her hair away from her face. "I'm just really nervous. I've never done anything like this before."

Lucas sensed she was having second thoughts. He suppressed a groan. He didn't imagine having to stroke a stripper's ego just to get her to dance for him. But she wasn't a stripper. Riiiight.

"It's just a dance. You don't have to do anything

you don't want to do," he assured her, uncertain of
why she was suddenly freaking out on him.

"Cash up front," she said stepping back and cross-
ing her arms underneath her breasts.

Damn those breasts.

If they weren't real, they were worth every penny.
He could imagine cupping their weight in his hands.
Caressing them. Laving her jewel-hard nipples with
his tongue. He almost groaned audibly with desire.

"Up front?" Now he was the one to sound wary.

"Look, I'm here with my sister and our best friend.
It's not like I'm going to make a mad dash for the
front door or anything. It's just, like I said, I'm not a
stripper or anything, so I don't want you getting any
ideas about not paying up if you're disappointed."

He shook his head. "No way I'm going to be disappointed." He retrieved his sport coat from the coat
hanger and took out a wallet. Real croc from what she
could tell. He opened it and pulled out a wad of hundreds and handed them to her.

"I have to count it."

He shrugged. "Have at it." He watched her shuffle
the money quickly, from hand to hand. The meticulous and quick way she counted, turning all the faces
the same way, told him if she really hadn't done this
before, she probably worked in a bank or retail or
something like that. Her expensive clothes told a different story, which meant she might have some old
rich guy funding her shopping addiction.

Maybe. But she didn't seem the type. She wasn't
especially young, but in some ways she gave off that
fresh-off-the-Greyhound vibe. Maybe ten minutes
off the bus she bumped into some Ewing-come-
lately, complete with a cigar and a pair of Dan Post
shark skins. Maybe he promised he would set her up
like a queen and kept his end of the deal for a few

months before he moved on to the next farm girl. That would certainly explain her desperate need for money.

She was a puzzle, a study in contradictions: one minute she was straight-backed sipping on frilly drinks, then the next minute she was stripping. She was a pretty girl who knew she could get by on her looks but didn't like for people to notice. She was flirtatious and seductive, then with the click of a lock, nervous and unsophisticated.

"It's all here." She moistened her lips again and he couldn't help but stare as her tongue caressed the full pout. The things he wanted to do with her mouth.

"Did you doubt me?"

"I don't know you to doubt you. Or not doubt you. I don't even know your name." The sentiment hung in the air between them. "Maybe I should at least know your name."

"Lucas." Best to keep this on a first-name basis.

"My name is—"

"Laney," he interrupted. "I know."

"Oh?"

"Your friends were calling out your name during your dance and when you won," he reminded her.

"Yeah. I'm Laney. Just plain old Laney." She chewed on her bottom lip.

He scoffed and smiled. "You? Plain? I don't think so."

He watched her as she surveyed the room. She was trying her hardest to look anywhere but at him.

"Still nervous?" he asked. There was almost a hint of genuine concern in his voice. When she didn't respond immediately, he continued, "Look, you can still back out. If this is creeping you out or something." He prayed she wouldn't back out.

"You don't creep me out," she hurriedly responded.

"I can't believe you're going to pay me this much just to dance."

He couldn't tell her that he hoped it wouldn't stop at dancing because that would not only be skirting the illegalities of prostitution but also the highest form of insult. Not to mention, Lucas did not pay for sex. If he were going to screw her, it was damn sure going to be for free. So truly, all he could expect was a dance. To start it off. If things led to something more, well, then . . .

"I'd pay you ten thousand to have you dance for me," he told her.

"Right. You could get anybody to dance for you."

"I'm not interested in just anybody, beauty queen."

"Don't call me that."

"Why?" Her tone piqued his curiosity.

"Just don't. I don't like it."

"Okay then." Lucas was certain there was more to it than just that, but she didn't seem interested in sharing. "Laney. I'm only interested in you, Laney."

"Are you married?" she asked. "Because I shouldn't, we shouldn't . . . you know, if you're married, we shouldn't be messing around."

"Are we messing around?"

"You're skirting the question. Are you married?"

He held up his left hand. "No ring, no telltale tan line." He didn't bother asking her. He had already scoped out her left hand.

She lowered her heavy fringe of honey-colored lashes and then cast him a seductive glance. One that told him she only needed a little cajoling and she was all his.

"We should get started." His voice was raspy, betraying his state of arousal. Her eyes darted below his belt. She gasped at the impressive length that was already straining against his pants.

Instead of throwing her against the wall and taking her right there and then, the way her body was screaming for him to do, he merely turned on the CD player, dropped down on the divan and said, "Dance."

"All right." Delaney unpinned her hair and shook it out. It was long enough to curtain her breasts if she needed it. At first she turned her back in a three-quarters pivot, teasing him. Then when she caught a glimpse of his heated stare, she realized she was spurred forward by desire, not knowing which of them was turning the other on more. She removed each article of clothing piece by piece—her sandals, followed by her halter, slowly she unbuttoned her front-snap skirt—until she stood in front of him with only her thong in place to do a miserable job of soaking up her juicy want.

"Touch yourself," he whispered.

"Lucas . . ." She peered at him from beneath her honey-gold lashes and saw the intense burning desire in his eyes. He was shifting on the divan, likely trying to find a comfortable position to relieve his painfully throbbing erection. She slid one hand up the length of her well-muscled abdomen and dipped her French-manicured index finger into her mouth, sucked on it, then dragged it across her collarbone to caress her stiff nipple. She let the other hand tug on the V of her thong, giving him a peek at her Brazilian bikini wax, her labia swollen and visibly damp. With one hand, she made tiny teasing circles around her nipple; the other stroked her engorged clit.

"What about a lap dance?" he asked. "Does twenty-five hundred dollars buy me a lap dance?"

Her eyes fell to his erection, longer still since the last time she dared to glance at it.

"Do you think it's wise?" she asked.

He crooked his finger, beckoning her forward.

She moved, standing just inches in front of him, and he grabbed her by the waist to pull her down on his lap.

She allowed him to settle her down, straddling him so she fit snugly between the wall of his chest and the stiff tower of his erection. She could feel him poking against her buttocks.

"No hands," she whispered, placing her small hands atop his larger ones. She guided them back behind his head. She had to suppress a moan of satisfaction as her highly sensitized nipples brushed across his crisp shirt. She longed to feel the heat of his bare chest.

She continued to hold his hands behind his head as she leaned the slightest bit forward. He moaned and shifted, creating a delectable friction. Knowing what the motion did for him, she thrust again. Their mouths were just fractions apart.

"I knew if I sat in your lap it would come to this," she murmured.

He grinned. "I wanted you long before you sat down. I wanted you from the moment I saw you sipping on that prissy pink drink."

She blushed. "I've never done this kind of thing before."

She was pulsing, aching to have him inside her.

"A lap dance?"

She shrugged a little and brushed her lips against his cheek. "Or whatever we're doing here." At that point it had gone way past a lap dance.

"Never?" He sounded surprised. She wasn't sure whether to be insulted at the implication or pleased at the compliment.

"Never."

She wriggled on top of him, grinding herself against him and sending gentle shock waves through her body. With that little move she was breathless and on the brink of a long-overdue orgasm.

"If you do that again, we're going to ruin these pants. Then you'd owe me 800 dollars."

"I can't afford that."

"I could get rid of them," he suggested. But too late. She was already fumbling with his belt buckle. Then his zipper. Next sliding her hand into his boxer briefs and stroking him along the length of his sex.

Impressive.

Lucas thought he was going to explode if she kept touching him so delicately. It was taking everything he had not to rip off her thong and bury his cock deep within her. Something about this woman had awakened a jealous possessiveness he thought he was far too jaded to feel. He was thinking in heat, of making her his and his alone.

From somewhere in his lust-hazed fog he heard her say, "I'm going to kiss you because it's been a long time since I kissed a man."

"How long?"

"Two. Long . . ."

She was gyrating and wriggling atop his erection and his pulse was pounding in his ears, drowning out anything that may have followed.

"I'm yours."

She leaned in and first licked and traced his lips with her tongue. Before she could pull away, he caught her mouth with his. He thrust his tongue into her slightly parted lips, mimicking what he wanted to do to another part of her anatomy. At first she tensed, followed almost as quickly by her eager, frenzied return of kisses and using his erection to stroke herself.

Just as he promised, he kept his hands to himself, laced behind his head. She unbuttoned his shirt as they kissed, pushed it opened and rubbed her stiff nipples against the solid wall of his chest. One of them moaned. Laney tensed in ecstasy. He watched her orgasm play across her face until finally she shuddered and wilted against him.

"You could have waited for me," he joked.

She smiled, embarrassed, and shook her head. "That was my first orgasm in two years. I couldn't wait."

It took him a moment to realize what she had said.

Two years! She hadn't said "too long"—she had said two long years.

When it finally registered he felt a primal need to brand her, claim her as his own. Which was ridiculous because she was a perfect stranger he had picked up in, of all places, a strip club. A stranger he would probably never even see again. But his penis was on autopilot because it jumped and throbbed as it tapped against her clit, like it was knocking for entrance.

"What about another?"

"I thought you'd never ask."

He fumbled around in his back pocket for a condom, and a fraction of a second later his hands were all over her, finally settling at the indention of her small waist. He lifted her several inches, enough to press the glistening head of his cock into her tightness. She was drenched in her own juices, so he slid in easily, but when she whimpered he knew he was stretching her to her limits. He paused and started to back out.

"Don't!" she demanded, digging her nails into his shoulder. "I mean . . . keep going . . . it's . . . it's good."

"Are you sure?" he asked. There were still several inches to go.

She nodded and he eased the rest deep within her.

He waited a few seconds for her body to accommodate his size and then began his thrusts slowly, gradually building to a rapid needy drive. She started whimpering again and he slowed almost to a stop.

She began to move herself up and down along the length of him. He heard her moan and guessed he'd found her G-spot. She leaned in again to claim his mouth, encouraging him to resume his previous pace and in less than a minute he was back in the saddle. Then she was coming, juices spilling, tightening around him, sending shock waves through his body.

"God, Laney. Damn, you feel so good."

She was throwing back her head and biting her lip. Her eyes were squeezed shut and her bottom lip trembled beneath the bite of her teeth. He let go of his seed and his violent shudders. He pressed her body tight against his as his cock throbbed, spurting desire down to the last drop. They melted into each other, boneless and weary.

She lay against his shoulder; he stroked her back in a gentle caress.

Like lovers.

This guy paid me and I just slept with him. I don't even know his last name.

Delaney pushed away from him, suddenly embarrassed and ashamed. She could blame it on the liquor; she could blame it on the fact that no man had touched her in any remotely sexual way in the last two years. But the rub of it was that she met a hot guy in a club and she screwed him.

"Hey, hey, hey," he said, attempting to grab her arm and pull her back down onto his lap. "Where's the fire?"

"Look, we made a mistake . . . let's not baste it and bake it, too, okay?"

Her immediate regret took Lucas by surprise. "Am I missing something here? Didn't you enjoy yourself? We had a good time, right?"

"Yeah. Sure. It was fine." She fanned him away and turned her back to him as she frantically grabbed for her clothes.

"Fine? What the hell? It was great." He grabbed her arm, maybe too eagerly.

She shrugged out of his grasp. "Fine . . . good . . . great . . . whatever. Look, this . . . this is the part where things could get really . . . awkward." They already were. She cursed herself for wanting to be Adventurous Delaney, footloose and fancy free with no expectations, because now she didn't really know what was expected of her. She should have just stuck with what she knew.

"It doesn't have to be that way." Was he about to ask her to stay?

"My—my friends are, you know, probably look . . . look . . . looking for me. I have to go," she said, avoiding eye contact. She turned her back to him again, collected her scattered clothes and hastily went about dressing.

He went to stand behind her. He placed his hands on her arms and kissed the top of her head in a gesture that felt more tender than sexual.

"I can take you home. I don't mind," he whispered. "Just stay a little while longer."

She shook her head and shrugged him away, not sure how to react to the intimacy. He was for all intents and purposes a stranger. She was far past the phase of believing in love at first sight. "I told you, my friends and I, we . . . we came together, we leave together."

He ignored her brush-off, wrapped his arms around her waist and pulled her against him. Again she shrugged out of his embrace and turned to face him. "Look, it was nice and all . . . but . . . but I've really got to go."

"Just like that?" He looked so confused that she almost felt sorry for him. "Look, we're both consenting adults. There's absolutely nothing to be ashamed of."

At the word "ashamed," her head shot up. People only said there was nothing to be ashamed of when there was something to be ashamed of.

"It was just supposed to be a dance and I let things go too far. I don't even know anything about you." Her voice was high and squeaky—irrational.

"Then all I'm saying is maybe we can spend some time together, you know, get to know each other—"

"No!"

He wasn't going to beg her to stay or to go home with him. But he could *reason* with her. That wasn't begging. Was it?

"Look, I don't want you to think I planned for . . ." He looked for words to describe what they had done. ". . . this," he finally decided.

"Next you're going to be telling me you're not that type of guy."

He shook his head. "Wrong. I am that type of guy. But you were . . ."

"Different?" Her tone was incredulous.

"Honestly? Yes. There was something about the way you smiled. It wasn't coy, it was almost as if you were embarrassed that I noticed you. Your hair pulled back like you're some kind of librarian, that suit—all of that in this club—you seemed like a doll out of her case."

She tensed in his arms. Had he said something wrong?

"What I'm trying to say is I had one idea of you and

then moments later you were on stage putting on the most erotic dance I've ever seen. I liked what I saw, Laney. And it had nothing to do with your body. You intrigued me. I was eventually going to send my number over to your table but after your dance I had to talk to you. That's why I approached you at the bar. I really wasn't trying to set this up as a one-night thing. I saw the way you looked at me before. Was I way off base?"

Laney shook her head. "No."

Laney chewed on her lip and he could tell she was considering it. Maybe she didn't feel comfortable leaving with him. Despite what they had just shared, he was still a stranger.

"Grab your friends. They can come, too. I know a piano bar not too far away. It's mellow, much more low-key than this place."

She assessed him for a moment and then shook her head. "It's not such a good idea. It's complicated, you know. I was just flirting with you out there and maybe . . . look, this is a really bad time in my life and I'm just not ready to do the dating thing."

She nodded as she pulled the strap of her sandal up her ankle. "Besides, it was just sex, right? Great sex but just sex."

He locked his jaw and glared at her.

Great sex but just sex?

This was one hell of a role reversal. Usually that was his line. How could she be so cavalier? She had definitely lied about never having done anything like that before. The casual way she was making her exit— that was the hallmark of a pro. He should know, he'd done it a hundred times if he'd done it once.

Did she make up the two-year celibacy story to make men uncontrollable with desire for her? Guys were all the same. After hearing something like that they would go mad wanting to be the one to quench her thirst after a drought. That had been how he'd felt, right? Maybe she was one of those girls who needed men panting after her, begging her for every little bit of attention she gave them. Maybe that's what got her off. When she danced for him, she was practically creaming in her thong as she watched him grow longer and longer with desire. Well, he wasn't going to beg. Any woman out in that club would die for the opportunity to go home with him. He wasn't going to play her little games.

His cock was of a different opinion. The longer he watched her dress, the more turned on he got. He wanted to kick himself. He was getting more turned on by her getting dressed than he had gotten when she was getting undressed. Because now he knew. Now he knew that this random woman he barely knew was capable of making him beg! He stifled a groan. He sure as hell wasn't about to beg.

He turned, pacing for a moment with his back to her, and raked his hands through his hair, confused at his need for this girl. He was no stranger to one-nighters. Normally *he* was the one offering half-assed apologies as he made his hasty exit. Now here was this woman who had come and turned the tables on him and he was behaving like a mewling idiot. He was *not* going to beg. No matter how much he wanted her. No matter how beautiful she was. It didn't matter. He was too proud to beg, but he could ask, right?

"Look, at least give me your phone number." He turned to face her but she was gone. The room was empty. "Laney!" He darted to the door and looked both ways down the hall but she was nowhere in sight.

"Shit!" He attempted to slam the door, but he swung it too hard so it just bounced back open. He finished adjusting his clothes, managing to zip his pants over his raging hard-on and was thankful that he had the sport coat to use as a shield as he left the club. He shook his head, trying to shake her from his thoughts and grabbed up his coat. His bundle of large bills—*her bundle of large bills*—fell from underneath the coat and landed at his Italian-designer-clad feet. He shifted the money from hand to hand as he counted it. Twenty-five hundred dollars. He shrugged and headed home.

Alone.

Chapter Six

The only reason your "friends" want you to stay up all night sharing girl talk is so you'll look worse than they do on pageant day.

"You look like shit." Judah, Lucas's best friend, dropped a fat file folder in front of his bowed head. The thud echoed in his head as loud as if somebody had just fired a cannon a foot from his ear.

"Thanks," Lucas said, making sure Judah noted the sarcasm. He had barely survived the morning of Keith Price's constant whining and Mrs. Hamilton's forlorn looks at her estranged husband. All he wanted now was a dark room, a tall glass of cool water and a down mattress sheeted with 800-thread-count Egyptian cotton.

"I heard Ol' Codger Dodger just about read you the riot act in court this morning." Judah chuckled.

"That judge won't cut me a break ever since the incident with his niece."

"You dated her the entire first semester of law

school. With your record, that goes way past 'incident.' You were practically married. You broke her heart when you didn't pop the question."

"I told her from day one I wasn't interested in marriage. Besides, that was more than a decade ago. When's he going to forget about it?"

"There are two things a Texan will never forget: the Alamo and jilted debutantes. To what do you owe the pleasure of your hangover?"

"Alec's bachelor party was last night. You could have shown up." He massaged his temples in a circular pattern.

"So I could look and feel as great as you do now? Nothing doing. I'm a family man." Judah rubbed his hands together and beamed at the thought of his pregnant wife. "No more endless nights at strip clubs for me. Besides, I never really did like the guy. He always thought he had all the answers in law school."

"That's because he did have all the answers. And as I recall you paid through the nose to buy plenty of them. You just hated the fact that he didn't turn them over to you for free."

"Come on. It's not like the jerk needed the money. He was born with a platinum spoon. Charging me for a couple of briefs he could have typed in his sleep when I was working fifty hours a week just to make rent and eat was wrong."

Lucas assessed his friend's demeanor. He had rallied to have Judah as a fourth roommate back during the law school days. The other guys didn't think he would fit in; he graduated from a state school, not a private university, and the closest his family would get to the country club Lucas and the others frequented was by maintaining the grounds or cleaning the restrooms. That said, there was something about Judah that motivated Lucas to be his personal advocate. On more than one occasion Lucas had covered Judah's portion of the rent just because he thought the guy deserved a break or two in life. Judah was right; Alec hadn't been as generous.

Judah chuckled low and shrugged. "Really, who the hell plans a bachelor party on a Thursday night?"

"Last night everyone got into town for the wedding. Tonight we'll be busy all night with the rehearsal dinner. It was the only time we could arrange it." Lucas groaned again and massaged his bloodshot eyes. He had to admit the Thursday night bachelor party was the worst idea in the history of prenuptial parties. He was going to have to get some sleep and try to recover before the rehearsal dinner.

Judah nodded as he steepled his fingers together in front of his mouth. "Something tells me this is more than a headache."

"Really? What tells you that?"

"Twenty-five years of friendship. She must have been one hell of a lay if she kept you up all night long on a school night," Judah mocked.

She was, in fact, one hell of a lay. She had gotten under his skin. He rationalized that it was because she had rejected him. That was a first. And so, of course, that would make her all the more desirable, right? You always want what you can't have? That's what he told himself but deep down he knew that wasn't the case. While the sex was unforgettable, what he remembered most clearly about Laney was her eyes: sad even when she smiled.

That was what attracted his attention at his first glimpse. He remembered wondering what could make somebody seem so sad and isolated. The thought, though fleeting, had haunted him. He was no stranger to isolation.

He had stayed awake all night trying to figure out

how he could get in contact with her. His firm employed top-notch private investigators, but that seemed a little creepy. But there was hope. When he had gone back to the table the night before, he discovered one of his buddies had gotten friendly with the redhead. All night and morning he watched the minutes tick away on his watch, just waiting for an appropriate time to casually call his friend to maybe arrange another casual meeting with Laney. He didn't want to seem too eager. That wasn't reasonable.

He had woken up sometime after eight o'clock and stumbled into the office only to have his secretary remind him he was due in court in less than twenty minutes. Though he had always admired the prestige of his corner office lined with windows, at the moment he was cursing them for allowing the presence of the glaring sun.

"She was," Lucas admitted, finally lifting his head.

"Shake it off, man, because you are going to have to be in prime order for this one." Judah pushed a fat file folder across the desk closer to Lucas.

Lucas tilted his head and read the name on the tab of the folder. James David Daniels. The name sounded familiar, but he couldn't place why.

"This is not one of mine," he said, pushing the folder back to Judah.

"He is now," Judah said in a tone that let Lucas know he was taking the case whether he wanted it or not. Judah picked up the folder and dropped it right next to Lucas's head.

"Fill me in." Lucas groaned and scratched at the stubble of his five o'clock shadow.

"He's one of mine from corporate," Judah began. "Hotshot oil baron and grade-A asshole. He's fired every divorce lawyer he's had this time without cause.

Normally goes through at least three lawyers per divorce."

Lucas raised an inquisitive brow. "Per divorce?"

"He's on number four." Judah held up four fingers for emphasis.

"He's never used our firm for his divorces?"

Judah shook his head. "Apparently doesn't like to mix business with pleasure. But he's gone through just about every reputable attorney in the state. I decided to throw you a bone. Passed your name along. Seems like your name has come up a couple times on the green, very satisfied clients. He wants to hear what you have to say. This guy's got billions. He's a very important client." No matter how Judah tried to spin it, Lucas still felt like the client was being forced down his throat.

"Thanks for the bone, but I am not taking any more clients," Lucas said.

"You have to meet with him."

"Or?"

"No or. No options." Judah shook his head. "If he wants you, you take the case or he could pull all his business from corporate."

"He sounds like a bully. I don't like bullies."

"He's not a bully per se; he's just not used to hearing 'no.' He's a high-dollar client. One of the biggest. If he comes out of this clean, he's promised to bring over everything—estate, trust, the works. You can't turn this guy down. It could mean millions to the firm in billable hours alone."

Lucas sighed heavily. It wasn't that he objected to representing slimeballs; he just didn't like being forced to work for one.

"Who's the wife got?" he asked.

Judah grimaced. "Lawrence."

Lucas muttered an oath under his breath. Lawrence

"My First Name Is Law" Dickerson was, hands down, the best. Lucas knew he was the best because he had been Lucas's mentor when Lucas was still an intern his first year of law school, and later had hired Lucas. Lucas learned everything he knew from Lawrence.

"I can't beat Lawrence." Lawrence's first rule of law: Never take a losing case. Lucas couldn't remember if he ever had. If so, it was certainly a rare occasion.

"Nobody suspects you can, not even the client. He just wants to get out of this paying as little as possible. He probably would have hired Lawrence himself if his old lady hadn't got to him first." Judah said.

"Lawrence wouldn't have taken him." Lawrence *did* object to representing slimeballs, but furthermore, he was a bit partial to the ladies.

"Certainly not after he saw the wife."

"That attractive?" Lucas asked.

"Scale of one to ten? She's a twenty. A former Miss Texas and a dozen or two titles before that. She has enough sashes to cross the state. Apparently, when they got married she had to refashion one of his antique gun cabinets to house all her tiaras. The thing made it through the Alamo, then she marries him and pretties it up with a coat of pink paint and crystal door knobs," Judah said, clearly enjoying spreading his hot bit of gossip.

Lucas had an instant hard-on thinking back to his own beauty queen. Of her eyes . . . he couldn't get them out of his head. He couldn't get *her* out of his head.

Get it together, man, you can't do this. He felt like he was going to lose it. Lose his edge. One of the things that made him such a good lawyer was that he never lost his cool. Lucas Church was always calm, always collected, always reasonable. But it was as if that part of his identity had vanished.

"You know her?" Lucas asked, wondering how Judah was privy to so many details.

"Of her. She used to be in those Texas society mags that Becca is addicted to. Always cutting a ribbon or hosting some charity something, reading to terminally ill kids at the children's hospital. She takes dogs to the nursing home and teaches the old people how to mambo. She even used her husband's money to start up some organization called Through the Looking Glass, some girly group that helps fat girls build confidence. It started as a Junior League project that she took one step further."

"You gotta be kidding me. Is she for real?" Lucas had already had her pegged as some spoiled society type who woke up at noon and complained that the sun rose without her. Just his luck to end up trying to defend Lucifer against Mother Theresa.

Judah shook his head. "She's a damn saint. Of course over the last year, year and a half, she's practically dropped off the radar. Persona non gratis in all the social circles since she's not serving as J.D.'s hood ornament anymore. And that brings us to our present source of contention."

Lucas leaned forward, beckoning for Judah to continue.

"Daniels married her straight out of college. She's half his age, right, only like two months after she's through with the Miss Texas gig. They're married for five years, right, but a year or so ago he kicked her out, bought her a separate house, and moved in his newer, younger honey."

Lucas shrugged. "She might seem like a saint, but she's still holding a pick and a pan digging for gold, in my opinion." Why else would a twenty-something trophy marry a guy over twice her age?

Judah agreed. "Maybe, but if she were in it for the money, you think she'd have her own stud on the side by now. Woman like that has to have needs."

"No evidence of a boyfriend?"

Judah nodded to the folder in front of Lucas. "None that his previous two lawyers could find. One PI followed her night and day for five weeks . . . nothing. And now our client is getting antsy because he's about to have to drop a shit load of money in alimony."

"Wasn't there a pre-nup?" Lucas couldn't imagine anybody with a considerable amount of money to lose going into a marriage without a prenuptial agreement.

Judah flipped open the folder. A prenuptial agreement stared Lucas in the face, a significant portion highlighted for effect.

"Infidelity clause," Lucas muttered as he shook his head. Why did these randy old finicky farts feel the need to include those? It practically guaranteed their young, preying wives a secure future.

"Yep!" bellowed a cowboy hat standing in the doorway. "That bitch has got me by the balls."

He crossed the large office in less than five strides, practically pushing Judah out of his way as he thrust his hand out, offering it to Lucas.

"The name's J.D. Daniels."

As if Lucas needed an introduction.

Chapter Seven

All's fair in love and beauty pageants.

"I might have neglected to mention you're meeting with Mr. Daniels..." Judah glanced down at his watch. "Right now. And Mrs. Daniels and her attorney have a preliminary meeting in less than half an hour."

"Thanks for the notice." Lucas scowled.

"Hey, you're the guy who stumbled into the office late this morning," Judah whispered. "If you'd had been here by six like normal, you would have had plenty of time to prepare."

Lucas didn't bother with faux pleasantries. He merely stuck out his hand and introduced himself. He surveyed his new client and could see why he had an endless plain of younger women at his beck and call. Though Lucas knew J.D. was at least fifty-five, he didn't look a day over forty. Daniels was tall and trim, evidence that he spent at least as much time in the gym as he did in the board room. His clothes were the kind of casual business attire that screamed money without effort.

"Church, huh? I hope you plan on living up to your reputation and not your name, son, because it's going to take one hell of a shovel to dig me outta this shit. And I don't need no freaking choir boy. I need a man with a plan." J.D. dropped down into an oversized leather wingback chair next to Judah.

"Have a seat," Lucas said dryly. "Judah was just telling me the specifics of your case."

"I sure as hell hope you are half as good as I keep hearing you are," J.D. reiterated.

"I'll leave you two to business," Judah said, and quickly made his exit.

"Cut to the chase, Church. Tell me how much I'm going to lose. And if you say fifty percent, I walk right out that door."

Lucas was very tempted to say fifty percent just to get the guy out of his office. But instead he replied, "I'm going to be honest with you, Mr. Daniels. . . ."

"J.D. Mr. Daniels was my father."

"Very well, J.D. I'm going to be honest with you. From just the preliminaries it doesn't look good. You've formed a pattern of behavior, this being your fourth wife. Courts frown on the serial adulterer when it comes to division of property."

"Really? Tell me, just how do they feel about gold-digging tramps?" J.D asked.

"You tell me," Lucas countered. "What has she done?" Whatever he said, it had better be good if he thought to stand a chance of leaving the marriage with anything more than fifty percent of community property. And though Lucas hadn't had time to look at the financials, he followed the market and knew that Daniels Enterprises had more than doubled its assets within the last five years.

"Of course everyone out there thinks she's some kind of saint or something, but I tell you, the woman has another side to her." He stood up and began pacing. "I first met her when she was Miss Texas. We were both there for a ribbon cutting when they opened the new women's and children's wing to the University Hospital."

Lucas nodded, urging him to continue.

"Luke, can I call you Luke?" He didn't wait for a response. "Luke, she zeroed in on me like a naval pilot landing a mig on a deep sea carrier. Within twenty minutes she was asking me to take her out for drinks. Thirty minutes into drinks she's begging me to take her home, and one minute across the threshold of her door she's impaled herself on my dick screwing my brains out. The tramp didn't even bother taking off her sash and crown." He conveniently left out the part where he had begged her to leave them on. "That's not the picture they paint of her in all those society magazines."

"I'm sure it was impossible for you to ward off her advances," Lucas noted.

"You've obviously never had my wife, Mr. Church. She's pretty, she's eager, she's willing, and that all adds up to one hell of a lay."

"Great sex or not, at some point before you said 'I do' you had to realize why she was marrying you. You could have said no."

"She duped me. Caught me while I was vulnerable. I had just gotten divorced from my third wife and broken up with my girlfriend at the exact same time, for chrissakes. Then I met her and she was just so damned sweet. Or so I thought."

"How tragic." Lucas ignored the cross look J.D. shot him and persisted. "You still haven't told me exactly why you married her. Why not just continue to date her, maybe move in together? You had an awful lot to lose by making it official."

"She showed up on my doorstep spouting off about being pregnant. I might be a lot of things, Luke, but a deadbeat dad is not one of them."

"There's a child?" Lucas started to frantically flip through the pages in the folder.

J.D. shook his head. "I said she *told* me there was a child. She conveniently miscarried shortly after the wedding." J.D. emphasized "conveniently" with air quotes.

"But you remained married to her for . . . five years."

J.D. shrugged. "She's a pretty face, good in bed, pleasant enough to talk to. I didn't say I didn't like her, Luke. I've just . . . outgrown her. At least I had the foresight to get her to sign a pre-nup."

Lucas nodded. For all the good it was going to do them. "The pre-nup could be part of the problem. There's the infidelity clause and, from what I understand, you've already started taking applicants for Mrs. Daniels number . . ." Lucas cleared his throat, ". . . five."

J.D. shook his head. "The present Mrs. Daniels is the last Mrs. Daniels. I've learned my lesson. I'm not going back down that road again. I just need to know how much this last trip is going to cost me."

Lucas scanned the contents of the folder. He'd flip a few pages, furrow his brow and rub the stubble on his chin absently. J.D. shifted in his chair. Lucas knew his silence was causing J.D. discomfort, but what the hell was there to say? The current Mrs. Daniels hadn't just been sitting on her pampered, prize-winning ass for the last five years. She'd been busy. It appeared she had acted as an unofficial, unpaid PR liaison between all Daniels's companies and any of the political and charitable organizations they supported. She apparently planned no fewer than fifteen major charitable events a year, not to mention founding and serving as chairperson, counselor, and teacher for the Through the Looking Glass organization—all without pay. Perhaps she hadn't contributed solely and directly to his accumulation of wealth over the last five years, but she had done more than her fair share of working to improve the negative big business image of Daniels and his companies.

Lucas sighed heavily and leaned back in his chair. "She's done quite a bit of PR work for you and Daniels Enterprises in the last five years."

"Cut to the chase. How much?" J.D. insisted.

"I'm not going to lie to you; the alimony is going to hurt. Some judge might get wise and feel you owe her back pay for all the work she did for you. With interest."

J.D. groaned.

"Unless . . ."

"Unless?"

"Unless we can prove that she knowingly and maliciously deceived you by claiming a pregnancy. That will only require a subpoena of her medical records."

"Or?"

"Or if we can prove she similarly violated the prenup. Then you're walking out of this clean as a whistle."

"Infidelity?" J.D. cast a hopeless expression.

"Perhaps there was a relationship you didn't know about . . . the pool boy, guy who delivers the groceries, the termite man . . . anybody?"

"No way in hell. She didn't have any reason to look anywhere else, if you know what I mean."

Lucas ignored the implication. In his experience most women gave more consideration to the operator than to the equipment. "What about after she moved out?"

"She moved out of my bed almost two years ago. Out of my house last year. In all that time she never even smiled sideways at another man. I even hired a PI to follow her for several months. That girl stuck to me like a tick on a hound dog."

"This isn't looking good."

"I chose you, Luke, because she managed to seduce Lawrence Dickerson into believing her. He's the best. She's out for blood. I know you worked with Lawrence and that he has a great deal of respect for you."

"Regardless of our professional relationship, his ultimate responsibility is to his client, your wife. My friendship with Lawrence isn't going to make this ship sail smoothly. You're right, Lawrence is the best. He goes for the jugular every time. This is not going to be an easy fight."

"You're the only attorney I know who can compete in the same ring with him. I'm trusting you to get me out of this jam."

"That's what you pay me for. Everyone has a few skeletons in the closet, J.D. We just have to dig deep and dust hers off."

"Lucas." Claire buzzed in.

"Yeah."

"Mrs. Daniels and her attorney have arrived. They're waiting in conference room three."

"Thanks." He fixed his gaze on J.D. "Are you ready to meet your fate?"

As Delaney got ready for her appointment that morning, she realized two things. First and fortunately, the guy from the night before hadn't recognized her as a former Miss Texas. He didn't know who she was or who she had been and he didn't care. In a club full of beautiful women, he had chosen her.

Second, she had *finally* gotten laid! If she wasn't

mistaken, she had left him begging for more. So she had done something wild and crazy and totally anti-Delaney Daniels, and for what it was worth, she was probably going to get out of this mess she had made for herself without any pain or suffering. She could only hope the same for this divorce with J.D.

She thought about his new attorney, still unbelieving that he had fired two already. She knew from gossip over his previous divorces that this was classic J.D. mode of operation. Start the divorce proceedings, then find five ways to Sunday to slow things down, until eventually the wife and her counsel become so weary of negotiations that they would agree to anything just to be forever free of J.D. Daniels.

She chose her Lilly Pulitzer cotton suit, the one that looked dimpled like a golf ball. Pink, of course, because it was her sincere belief that everybody (even the few brave men who chose to try it) looked a little better in pink, accessorized with her Susan G. Komen Race for the Cure silk scarf because it didn't hurt if J.D.'s new attorney knew she was tied to a cause. Maybe he would have sympathy for her and advise J.D. to settle. She examined herself in the full-length mirror in her dressing area.

"Pleasantly perky and not the least bit bitter." She inhaled deeply. "Delaney Daniels, prepare to meet your fate."

Delaney fisted her hands to prevent herself from chipping away at her Poodle Skirt pink manicure. She had spent twenty dollars that she didn't really have on that manicure, and she was not going to ruin it. The lacquered conference table was so shiny she could see her reflection in it, and checked from time to time to see if her lipstick had smudged or if an errant hair was sticking out sideways from her head. She chewed her lip and looked at her watch for the third time in as many minutes. The meeting with J.D.'s lawyer should have started a quarter of an hour ago.

"Where are they?" She chewed on her bottom lip.

"It's an intimidation technique." Lawrence was calm as he continued to examine the stack of papers in front of him. "Ignore it."

"Lawrence Dickerson," a man said from the doorway behind them.

Delaney didn't know why, but the voice sounded familiar.

"Church, how the hell are you!" Lawrence bellowed as he stood and grasped Lucas by the hand, clapping him firmly on the back with the other.

Delaney followed suit. She stood.

Remember to smile.

She turned.

And then his eyes met hers.

Chapter Eight

When you don't quite hear the question over the audience prattle; when your bathing suit is riding up and your cheeks are hanging out; when you slip and fall flat on your ass, breaking a heel and spraining an ankle . . . just remember to smile.

"This here is Delaney Daniels."

Lucas swallowed and inhaled deeply.

"I see you recognize her," Lawrence continued. "Of course you would. She is hands down the prettiest Miss Texas there ever was."

Lucas read the horror that registered on her face.

"First runner-up, actually," Delaney corrected, never raising her eyes from the floor.

Lawrence furrowed his brow and pushed her forward a little. "Delaney, this here is Lucas Church, the second-finest attorney in the state of Texas."

"Pleased to meet you, Mr. Church."

Lucas hoped Lawrence and J.D. didn't notice the

quiver in her voice. The last thing either of them needed was for the two men standing at their sides to become suspicious.

"Likewise," Lucas said. Cold and crisp. He shook her hand firmly.

"You okay?" Lawrence asked Delaney. All color had drained from her face. She was silent.

Damn, Lucas thought, *she has to pull this off*.

She nodded. "If I could just have a cup of water . . ." She smiled weakly.

"Sure." Lawrence offered her a seat, then crossed to the corner of the room to pour a glass of water from the drink valet.

"Let's get on with this," he said, returning to the table. "I think we could be able to take care of this without getting all messy, and wouldn't you like that?" Lawrence directed his question to J.D. as if he was no more than a seven-year-old being chastised for eating too much candy.

"That depends on what you're asking." Lucas, still not completely collected but doing a better job than Delaney, took his seat directly across from her. She lifted her eyes to meet his for the briefest moment.

"We're just asking for what she's properly due." Lawrence slid his proposal across the table to Lucas, who scanned it for a moment, then pushed it back across to Lawrence.

"Am I correct in my understanding that Mrs. Daniels was never gainfully employed during the duration of the marriage?"

Lawrence nodded. "She was not employed, but she did her fair share of work."

"Certainly she doesn't expect financial compensation for her . . . work. If I'm not mistaken, I don't think that's legal in the great state of Texas." He knew he was playing dirty, but the tactic backfired when vivid images of her long legs and full breasts flooded his memory.

Lawrence shot him a disapproving look. "I was referring to the fact that she practically reinvented this man. Thanks to her, he went from being viewed as a lecherous big-money corporate slug to a goddamn saint. Not to mention, she is entitled to fifty percent of assets acquired during the term of their marriage. According to my records, that's going to include two homes—three if you consider the yacht—several valuable pieces of artwork, the cars, the vacation condo . . ."

"It's moot. The prenuptial agreement signed by your client clearly stipulates . . ."

Lawrence peered across the table over the top of his glasses. "Surely you jest."

"Does your client take issue with the signatures? She signed it, right?"

"My client takes issue with the infidelity clause. The pre-nup clearly stipulates that . . ."

"Let's talk about the infidelity clause," Lucas interrupted.

He heard Delaney's breath catch.

He couldn't read her mind, but her eyes said it all. It was almost the same pleading look she had given him last night just moments before her third orgasm. Unable to maintain his firm determination, he fixed his gaze on Lawrence.

"There's nothing to talk about, Luke. Your client is living with his girlfriend."

"Ward," J.D. insisted. "She's a poor starving college student I took under my wing. There is nothing more to the relationship than that."

"Bull!" Delaney broke in. "You're sleeping with her, and you know it. The entire staff at the house knows it. The whole state of Texas knows it!"

Lucas loved watching the passion sparkling in her eyes.

When J.D. started to protest, Lucas gestured for his silence. "Can you offer any physical proof that might define the relationship in any way other than guardian-ward?" Lucas asked Delaney directly.

"I'm not in the habit of videotaping my husband having sex with other women," Delaney snapped as she raised her eyes to his. This time she held his gaze in challenge.

"I don't think there is a judge in this country who will find it credible that your client has gone two years without engaging in any carnal relations," Lawrence reasoned.

"Come on, Lawrence. You know better than that. You taught me better than that. The first rule of law: It doesn't matter what the truth is; it only matters what you can prove. Besides, I don't know why a judge would doubt the conviction and fortitude of my client in favor of yours. Certainly abstaining from a physical relationship for—what was it, two years—is possible. Unless you're currently admitting to indiscretions on your behalf." Lucas shot Laney a pointed look.

"My client's moral conviction is not in question, Lucas," Lawrence warned.

"J.D. is living with a woman half his age. Any reasonable person can deduce the obvious. . . ." Delaney said.

Lucas leaned forward. "Let me explain a little something about reasonable deductions: They are horribly inaccurate. Take you, for instance. Say you went out for drinks with friends and you're having a good time. Say you dance with a few guys and strike the interest of one of them. He might reasonably deduce that since you are at a club where singles assemble, that since you are not wearing a ring"—he gestured toward her left hand—"that you are single and available to . . . date. So you understand, there is no benefit to making reasonable deductions out or in a court of law. In law, there's the truth and there's what you can prove. And those, Mrs. Daniels, are two very different animals. Wouldn't you agree?"

She continued to meet his cold stare. "Absolutely."

"Damn!" Delaney said as she got to the parking lot.

"Things went well," Lawrence reassured her, clueless to the true reason for her distemper. "Don't let Church intimidate you. Underneath the cold façade he's just a big teddy bear. He's all bark and no bite."

Delaney's mind briefly revisited the previous evening. She could definitely recall a bite or two. She was certain she was blushing furiously.

"No, it's not that. I just left my handbag up there. Look, thanks for everything you tried to do up there. I know you were hoping to get this all settled today. I'm sorry J.D. is being such a pain. If you need more money between now and . . ."

Lawrence smiled. "Don't worry about it. I'll collect my fees when we settle."

Delaney smiled. "Are you sure? You've been more than generous with me so far."

"Positive. And trust me, I wouldn't be saying that if there wasn't a healthy settlement on the horizon." He patted her shoulder and she returned his kind gesture with a hug.

"You're the best." Her eyes were glistening with tears.

Lucas clenched his jaw as he watched Delaney and Lawrence in the parking lot five stories below. They embraced briefly, causing him to mutter an oath. He pushed away from the window and paced the length of the table. The first interesting woman he'd met in ten years and she was married to his client. He cursed again, this time louder.

Chapter Nine

Keep your chin up, your shoulders back and walk with a straight spine. It helps to imagine the generous weight of a crown on top of your head.

Delaney opened the door to the conference room. His back was to the door, but it was him. It was definitely him. Grateful that the door hadn't squeaked when she opened it, grateful the room was carpeted and the *click-clack* of her sandals would not betray her, she tiptoed to the conference desk and squatted to retrieve the bag.

He turned just as she was certain her getaway was clean.

"You weren't going to sneak in and leave without saying anything, were you?" His cold tone hit her back. She pivoted in a manner she hoped was Lauren Bacall casual. "I forgot." He slapped his forehead. "Stealthy exits are your strong suit."

"I think we covered everything during our meeting."

"I can think of one very important thing that wasn't said last night. You didn't say you were married."

"First, I don't consider myself married. J.D. and I haven't been matrimonially bound for . . ."

"Two years?" J.D. had at least corroborated that part of her story.

Her face turned so hot she was certain the shade of pink rivaled her suit. "If you had asked about my marital status, I would have been honest. But I suspect even if you had known I was kind of married, it wouldn't have made much difference, Mr. Church."

"Mr. Church? So formal all of a sudden? After everything that happened last night, I'm pretty sure we can dispense with the formalities. Call me Lucas."

Delaney wanted nothing more than to forget. She offered him her pageant-winning smile. "Good day, *Mr. Church.*" She turned her back to him—if she could just make it to the door.

"Of course now I understand the quick escape," Lucas taunted as she started to leave.

She stopped and turned on her heel so smoothly she looked like she was standing atop a turnstile. "What exactly is that supposed to mean?"

"There's a lot of money riding on your picture-perfect image. A lot more than twenty-five hundred dollars."

"My divorce settlement has nothing to do with why I left last night."

"No? Then please enlighten me."

"As I told you last night, I realized I made a mistake and regretted that I had let things get . . . out of hand."

"Not a moment too soon."

"Just what are you implying?" she demanded.

He shrugged. "You left when you left. But you stuck

around just long enough to squeeze in an extra orgasm or two."

Delaney's mouth dropped open. "Of all the . . ."
Her voice was raised slightly.

"Is everything okay, Mr. Church?" His secretary
appeared in the door.

"Yes. Just fine, Claire. I'll just need another moment
or two." He winked and flashed her a grin and
watched her fluster away as he closed the door.

At the click of the latch, Delaney instantly thought
of the locking door last night. Her libido flared as she
imagined the things they could do in the locked conference room. She shook her head.

You are not that girl, she reminded herself.

"You could have said something." He interrupted
her thoughts.

"What exactly would you have me say? You didn't
seem all that interested in conversation last night, if I
remember correctly," she countered.

"A simple 'hate to screw and run but I'm married to
one of the richest men in Texas' would have sufficed."

"I do not, as you so crudely put it, 'screw and run.'
Besides, my marital status was none of your business.
And heavenly days, please stop saying I'm married
to him."

"Perhaps not, but it would at least explain the dis-
appearing act. Had I known your marital situation, I
wouldn't have had to spend an entire night nursing
my bruised ego."

"You with a bruised ego? Honestly, Mr. Church, I
didn't think they bruised once they got that big."

He chuckled. "Funny. I'm not egotistical. I don't
have to be. I just know I'm good at what I do."

Delaney rolled her eyes. "I couldn't care less about
how good you are." Lie one. "Furthermore, I don't

care what you do or who you do it with." Lie two. "As long as you don't even think about doing it with me!" Lie three. It was nothing short of a miracle that she didn't find her nose growing four feet long.

"Don't worry. I can hardly afford you."

"What!" She knew her face went from hot pink to cherry red.

"Considering J.D.'s precarious monetary obligations to you. Not to mention it cost me twenty-five hundred dollars just to—"

Uncertain what was coming out of his mouth next, she quickly interjected, "I gave that money back to you. I'd appreciate you not bringing it up again. As for J.D., I'm not asking for anything more than I deserve for staying married to that creep for five years."

"He wasn't so creepy when you jumped into bed with him on your first date." He almost sounded like a jealous boyfriend.

She closed her eyes for a moment and inhaled deeply. "Is that what he told you?

"Attorney-client privilege," Lucas replied dryly.

"That's not how it happened."

Lucas closed in on her. He was close enough to smell her perfume—a clean spring scent of honeysuckle and gardenia. He was close enough to wrap his hands around her tiny waist. He was close enough to kiss her. His eyes dropped to her bottom lip. It was trembling. Out of . . . anger? . . . desire? He didn't care. All he could think about was his need to take it into his mouth and taste it, suckle it.

"Then tell me how it did happen." His voice was husky and he knew it was betraying his carnal desire for her. He tried to rein in his runaway senses. He couldn't allow his thoughts to go off in that direction. He didn't want to want her and he certainly didn't want to care, but if she was offering explanations, he certainly wanted to hear them.

A remote part of him *needed* to hear her explanation. Finding out how she and J.D. started dating infuriated him. It wasn't that he believed he was her first or only casual hook-up, it was that he didn't want to be a casual hook-up. J.D. was a grade-A asshole and notorious for his philandering and yet she hadn't only given him a second chance; she *married* the ass. And yet, last night she couldn't wait to get away from Lucas. What did J.D. have that he didn't?

"I was just a kid from Big Stinking Creek, Texas. Do you even know where that is, Mr. Church? No, of course not. You've probably never even heard of it, which tells you exactly how big it is. I had just finished competing in the Miss Texas pageant. When the other girl was asked to step down and I was suddenly Miss Texas . . . all the parties and the people and the big city. It was very easy for me to get caught up in it all. One night, I had a little too much to drink, like . . ."

"Last night?" he filled in, said what she was obviously uncomfortable saying.

"Unfortunately, very much like last night." Delaney nodded, bowing her head and chewing her lip. "J.D. was attractive and attracted to me and so very . . ."

"Rich?" he finished.

He regretted it the minute he said it. Delaney tried not to appear hurt, but her eyes were shining with tears and her bottom lip, the one he couldn't take his eyes off the night before, was quivering.

But she didn't cry. She straightened her shoulders, lifted her chin and said, "I'll see you in court, Mr. Church. Have a good day."

Chapter Ten

Thou shall not soothe thy preliminary round lowest score sorrows with pints of Ben & Jerry's. Häagen Dazs is much more satisfying.

"It's the worst possible thing that could happen." Delaney sniffled through her telephone conversation with Macy.

"It can't be all that bad. Just relax and tell me what happened."

"You know that guy you were asking me about? That one I was talking to at the bar for a while last night?"

"You're hot for him. I knew it."

Delaney wished that was all there was to the problem.

"I wasn't exactly truthful with you and Phebes. I mean something might've kind of happened."

"When you disappeared? You made out with him, didn't you?" Macy's voice was charged with electricity. "I knew it, I knew it. When you disappeared, I told

Phebes you were out somewhere making out with the hottie."

Delaney didn't respond.

"So did you . . . you know?" Macy giggled.

Delaney chewed on her bottom lip, unable to fill the telltale silence.

"Delaney?" Macy stopped laughing. "Oh. My. God. You slept with him, didn't you?" Macy was unable to regulate the shock in her tone.

Delaney took a deep breath and relayed the details of what transpired Thursday and Friday.

"You know what happens to me when I drink. You should never leave me to my own devices when I'm drinking. The last time I got that drunk I wound up hitched to J.D."

"Sorry, sweetie. I was on Matt patrol last night. I thought you could handle yourself. Besides, they barely put any alcohol at all in those girly drinks you prefer. You weren't drunk. You seemed barely buzzed."

"It was surreal. I was like another person with him." Delaney wasn't certain how she felt about that person. She should have been ashamed, and she had been that night, but after seeing him in the conference room of the law firm, she just wanted to be the one who drove Lucas crazy with passion every night.

"So do you think he's going to spill the beans?"

"I don't know. I don't think so. It's pretty obvious he hasn't said anything yet. I figure he doesn't want J.D. to find out any more than I do. I mean, can you imagine? Lucas is his lawyer, for goodness's sakes."

"It wasn't like either one of you knew who the other one was when you—"

"Don't say it!" Delaney rubbed her forehead. "I still can't believe I actually did that. And, trust me, it would matter little to J.D. what we knew of each other. J.D. could ruin him. He *would* ruin him."

"So maybe this Church guy is discriminating enough to figure that out."

Poor choice of words, Delaney thought. Lucas was nobody's "church guy." The things he made her think, *feel*, would keep even the most devout home on Sundays.

"Don't worry, he probably isn't going to say anything," Macy assured her.

Delaney blew out a deep breath. "The one time I've ever done something purely selfish and self-gratifying and I practically destroy my entire life." She sniffled.

Macy paused. "Is that the only reason you're upset?"

Macy always could see straight to the heart of the matter. They had been best friends since freshman year of undergrad. There wasn't anything the two of them hadn't been through.

"I think I might have really really liked him. I mean, I might have been able to really like him if I had gotten the chance to get to know him. He's funny, you know? And even though there wasn't much conversation the other night, he didn't talk down to me."

"There you go, Delaney. Falling for a guy you barely know. I mean, that's how you got into the mess with J.D. in the first place."

"I know. I sound like an idiot. There's no such thing as love at first . . ." She stopped. She didn't know exactly what to call what they had done.

"You're only feeling this way because he's the first man who's made you feel like a woman in a long time. You've got to get out more. No more sitting around the house eating your sorrows away."

"I'm not eating," Delaney lied, dropping her spoon into the now empty pint of ice cream and putting them in the empty sink.

"Really? How many pints of Häagen Dazs have you destroyed?" Macy asked.

"Two," Delaney admitted. What was the point of

lying? Macy could read her every move as if she were watching her on hidden video.

"This calls for immediate intervention. Why don't you go to this wedding with me tonight? It will do you some good to get out of the house."

"God, no. I don't think I could tolerate anybody's marital bliss right now,"

"Come on. There's supposed to be a live band and an open bar at the reception. It will be more like a really huge party. You know how I hate going to these things alone. And I already said I would come and I am, predictably, short my plus one."

"I don't think so. Take Phebes. She'd be much better company,"

Macy laughed. "She's in Matthew heaven right now."

"All's forgiven since she didn't see him at the club the other night?"

"You know how they are," Macy said. "Come to the wedding. It will be fun. Besides, there is no better place to pick up a guy."

"That's what y'all said Thursday, and look where it landed me."

"Then you'll help me pick up a guy. You see, we'll be the two cuties in the corner. Only you will be the incredibly-beautiful-beauty-queen unattainable one and I will be the girl-next-door-reminds-me-of my-best-friend's-sister approachable one."

Delaney smiled. "Mace . . ."

"Please?"

"I have a pint of Häagen Dazs left," Delaney said, eyeing the freezer.

"Please!"

And of course, she went.

You know that sick feeling you get in the pit of your stomach just minutes before you recline in the dentist chair to have a root canal? Well, that was the feeling Delaney had at the moment she noticed the 6'4", raven-haired, cerulean-blue-eyed Hollywood type walking down the aisle in his perfect-fit-Oscar-night black tux.

Lucas.

Either the stars were aligned against her or Allen Funt was hiding somewhere in the garden with a video phone waiting to jump out and scream "Surprise! You're on *Candid Camera*!" Even though she knew the quartet was playing a very soothing *"Canon in D"* all she could hear was the theme music to *The Magnificent Seven. Da! Da da da da. Da! Da! Da da da da!* Her heart thumping in time with the beat. He was soooo magnificent.

And the only thing that saved her from passing out right then and there was that he was not, in fact, the groom.

"Mace!" Delaney shot daggers at her friend.

Macy grinned widely. "Laney, it's fate. It's karma. It's—"

"It is the single most uncomfortable moment of my life. How?"

"When you and Lucas were . . . umm . . . otherwise occupied at Foxy's, I got friendly with one of the groomsmen—the blond on the far right."

"Why didn't you say something?"

"Would you have come if I did?" Macy asked.

"Of course not!"

"There you have it."

Delaney desperately wished she could click her stilettos and be miraculously delivered to the warmth and comfort of her overstuffed couch and what remained of the ice cream in her freezer. Wishing the lady up front wearing the orange hat with the wide brim and peacock feathers were sitting six rows back and a little to the left so Delaney didn't have to absorb Luke's heated glare. But at her present position, she had a direct view. As the wedding party made the endless journey to the front of the church, never once did he break his stare. Not even when Delaney checked over her left shoulder to make sure there wasn't some escaped circus troupe performing behind her.

Once during the ceremony, the preacher had to clear his throat because it was time for Lucas to give the groom the ring. Lucas reacted half a moment too late, causing the groom and a few others in the wedding party to crane their necks, trying to determine what on the left side of the church had him so entranced. That's when Delaney looked down and pretended to engrossed in the wedding program. She looked back up just in time to see Lucas grin apologetically at the groom, that sideways Harrison Ford grin that made Delaney turn all gooey inside, and her body (her treacherous, needy body) betrayed her better judgment and rioted against her common sense. She was supposed to be angry at him. She *was* angry at him. But for all her righteous vindictiveness, she couldn't help but be wildly attracted to him. For the next forty-five minutes all she could think about was wrapping her legs around his waist.

Chapter Eleven

When you get married, you're queen for the day.
When you win a pageant, you're queen for the whole
year.

"I'm beginning to think you're stalking me."

Delaney didn't need to turn around; she knew exactly who it was.

"Maybe it's you stalking me."

Inhale, exhale. Inhale, exhale.

"Perhaps. Except I have the tux. I held the ring. I actually had an invitation to this wedding. I doubt you even know the happy couple's name."

She didn't.

"I came with a friend," she said, hoping she was ambiguous enough to make him believe she was with the gray-haired guy who sat on the other side of her on the pew. Of course, he looked like the original charter president of the AARP but, hey, she was known to date men a few years older.

"The redhead?" he asked.

Delaney raised a brow, then remembered he had seen Macy at the club. With her striking red hair and spring-green eyes, she was hard to forget.

"Is she friends with Jane?"

Delaney gave him a blank look.

"The bride—you know, the one in all white who looked incredibly happy and cried through the whole ceremony."

She bit her lip, then gave in and broke a smile. "Actually she became fast friends with one of the groomsmen Thursday night. The blond—you know, the one who looked incredibly bored and yawned through the whole ceremony."

"You should do that more often," he leaned in to whisper.

"What?"

"Joke. Smile. You're pretty anyway, but when you smile . . . you're downright breathtaking. I bet all you had to do was crack that smile, flaunt your dimples and the judges handed you your crowns on velvet pillows."

Okay, so he was handsome, he was smart, and now, detrimentally, he was charming.

No, he isn't charming. He's a pigheaded jerk who all but called you a gold digger.

Conviction renewed, she smiled broadly, blatantly flaunting her dimples. "And you should do that more often."

"What's that?"

"Stand up straight like that. You know, so your knuckles aren't dragging on the ground. That Neanderthal look did nothing for you." She spun on her heel and turned to the champagne fountain.

"Wait." He sighed. He had suffered through the wedding, dry roast and over-steamed green beans, just to have the chance to say something to her. Now that he had her engaged in conversation, he didn't want to lose her so quickly. After the comments he'd made yesterday, she had every right to be upset with him. He just hoped there was still time to repair the damage. He grabbed her arm as discreetly as he could and pulled her out to the country club patio.

"Let go of me." She pulled back from his grasp.

"There's something I want to say to you."

"Then I think it most appropriate if you say it to my lawyer." She attempted to make her way back to the party.

"I need to say this to you. One on one."

Her eyes widened and Lucas wondered whether she, too, was thinking about when they'd been one on one three days ago.

"As far as I am concerned, there's nothing else to talk about."

"I want to apologize."

She immediately stopped trying to escape. "Apologize?"

"For the things I said yesterday. In the conference room. For what I said just now. It was rude and disrespectful, and I had no right to say those things to you."

He met her eyes and saw her face soften.

"I know what I said was hurtful. I'm sorry. I didn't mean to hurt you."

"Then why did you?"

He closed his eyes. "I was a little bit . . . caught off guard by the whole situation. I don't like not being in full control . . . and it's just like you said. I'm a Neanderthal." He held up his knuckles that still had scars from a skateboard wipeout when he was ten. "See, my knuckles are scarred from dragging on the ground."

She smiled, then laughed. God, she was beautiful when she laughed.

"Fine. Apology accepted." She moved to go back inside. Apparently his transgressions had been forgiven but not quite forgotten.

"Is my company truly so unpleasant that you can't spend a few minutes alone with me?"

She didn't want to admit that she found being in his company immensely pleasant. That when she was alone with him she found herself remembering how the contour of his hard body had felt beneath her hands. That she inhaled deeply, as if her breaths were numbered, so she could recall his scent when he departed. That if she spent another five minutes with him being so considerate and honorable she was going to find herself being very inconsiderate and dishonorable by throwing him into the bushes and ravishing him.

"You're not all that unpleasant," she admitted. "I just think it probably isn't appropriate for us to be out here. Alone. Giving consideration to who you are and who I am and what we've already done and what we can't do again because of who we are."

He shifted, shuffling his feet again the cobbled terrace floor.

"Not that you even want to . . ." she continued. "Do it again, I mean."

"Do *you* want to?"

Just the thought of doing it again made her flush. She raked her teeth across her bottom lip and looked at him from beneath her lashes. Even without that seductive glance, her silence was answer enough.

He cleared his throat and rocked back on his heels. "Me too."

There was silence for a moment.

"But we can't, right? I mean there's probably some law or something against doing what we want to do. Considering you are J.D.'s lawyer."

"It could be considered highly unethical."

"And you could get disbarred, right? For engaging in a relationship that might be considered unethical."

He nodded. "Worst-case scenario? Yes."

She fixed her gaze on the garden gazebo. "As much as I would like for J.D. to find a less accomplished attorney . . . and as much as I would love to explore things between us . . . I don't want to see you disbarred."

He leaned down until their faces were only inches apart. "Of course, that would only happen if somebody found out. What the Texas Bar Association doesn't know . . ." He traced her lips with his thumb.

Don't do it, she told herself. Unfortunately she was talking to the same self who never listened. She wanted to kiss him. Just kiss him. She hardly ever did anything just for her. She was always thinking of others. Not that that wasn't a good thing. It was, but damn if it wasn't exhausting living up to everyone's expectations. If she kissed Lucas, just this once, what would it hurt? They both knew the potential costs. They were consenting adults. Heavenly days, she just wanted him to kiss her like he had Thursday night.

She leaned in and brought her mouth to his. She pressed her lips against his, exerting gentle pressure. She had barely parted her lips, but when she did his tongue darted into her mouth, tasting her. He pulled her in closer, pressing her against his body. She moaned against his mouth, and felt his hips press against hers. Just when she felt like she was going to fall into oblivion, she got hold of herself and pushed away. She brought her hand to her lips, bruised and burning from the heat of their passionate kiss.

". . . can't hurt us," he finished.

"I wish I could believe that, but considering the circumstances, I'm afraid that one of us would end up very hurt." Chances were it would be her. She had to get away. Put some space between them. Unfortunately, there wasn't enough space in all of Texas right now. "It's a lovely night so I'm going to go for a walk."

He watched her sashay toward the gazebo. With every step she took, he ticked off a reason why following her would be foolish.

Three years of law school, ten years building a career . . . all down the drain if you're disbarred.

Yet each protest was rationalized.

Who cares about practice? The real money is in corporate consultation fees. No hassles, no worries.

She's just another piece of ass.

Like you've never had before.

Her husband is one of the most powerful men in Texas. He would ruin you.

If he found out.

He'll find out.

I'm smarter than he is. He won't find out.

This could all be a trick. She could be using you so you have to step down as J.D.'s attorney.

Think about the way she used you the other night.

He groaned thinking about it. He rubbed his hands over his face and tossed back the rest of the champagne punch.

Chapter Twelve

There are only three million people watching you . . .
No pressure.

She felt the heat of his presence before he even said anything.

"You shouldn't have followed me out here," she said to the black of night.

"You knew that I would." He crossed the gazebo and stood directly behind her.

"I wanted you to, but I didn't know that you would."

He wrapped his arms around her waist and she instinctively tilted her head, allowing him to caress her neck with kisses. "Hmmm. God, you smell so good." He was practically moaning.

"This is foolish. You could lose your job."

"I'm resourceful. I would find another one." His kisses trailed upward to her ear. He nibbled on her lobe, causing a sharp intake of breath. Every inch of her body tingled.

"Not . . . not in this . . . state. If J.D . . . found out he . . . he would destroy you."

"For you, I'm willing to take my chances." She thanked the fashion gods that strapless dresses had come back in style as his hands moved up from her waist to cup her breasts. He tugged on the top of her dress until he freed her breasts. She wasn't wearing a bra and loved the contrast between his warm hands and the cool breeze caressing her skin. She could feel her nipples were already firm and erect. He pressed his own erection against her bottom, letting her know that the feeling was reciprocated. With his thumbs he traced teeny circles across her nipples. One hand dropped from her breasts and worked at lifting her skirt. He pushed aside the scrap of material that was supposed to cover her sex and sighed as he stroked her dewy cleft.

"Brazilian waxes drive me crazy," he groaned hoarsely as he parted her labia and fondled her clit until she shook. He must have sensed the weakness in her knees because he pushed her forward a step so she could brace herself against the railing as he dipped two fingers deep inside her honeyed sex.

"Can you take three?"

She nodded, wanting him to continue so badly she wouldn't have said no to anything. He thrust again and again, driving her mad with ecstasy. She gripped the railing until her knuckles went white and bit back a moan.

"Why are you holding back?" he whispered in her ear.

"I'm . . . I'm not," she said through measured pants.

"Yes. You are. You're trying not to make a sound. You did that the other night."

"I'm not . . . I'm not." She swallowed, trying hard to find the words to complete her sentence. But she couldn't. She couldn't think at all with the things he was doing to her. "Idontscream." The words rushed out of her mouth as one before she forgot them again.

"I want you to scream for me." He dropped his hand and fumbled with his pants, freeing his huge erection. He slid his hand along her spine, indicating that she should bend over.

"Is this okay?" he asked. He pressed the tip of his penis against her, sliding the head partially inside her.

How was she supposed to say no to that? She briefly nodded her acquiescence.

"You're so tight. You're so wet." He eased further inside her. She couldn't stifle her moan as she took him to the hilt.

He placed one hand on her hips to brace himself and continued to pet her clit with the other one. Then he began to thrust. Again. And again. And again. She bit her lip until it bled, squeezed her eyes so tightly together.

She was still holding back, and he seemed to know it. He drove hard. Hard. Harder.

"I. Want. You. To. Scream," he demanded.

She could barely manage a sentence as she felt her climax building. "I. Don't. Screeeeee . . ."

She didn't even recognize it as her own voice she heard screaming. And once she started she couldn't stop until the orgasm crested and crashed, leaving her a boneless, breathless, voiceless, and sated, oh so sated heap.

Chapter Thirteen

*During the interview, you don't want to appear too
smart . . . it simply isn't sexy.*

Delaney repaired what she could of her disheveled appearance in the reflection of a window of a European
sedan before reentering the grand ballroom of the country club. She said a silent prayer of thanks to the fashion
goddess for the unkempt look being all the rage this
season. She found Macy, quite predictably, in the center
of a circle of what had to be every single and available
man in the room.

"There you are!" Macy flashed her cast of suitors an
apologetic smile as she shimmied Delaney toward the
door. "I've been looking for you for the last hour.
Where did you disappear to?"

Delaney shrugged. "I just went for a walk."

Macy's face creased in a frown.

"I think I'm going to cut out. I'm beat," Delaney
told her.

"You didn't drive. How are you going to get home?"

"Yeah, I think I can find a ride." She tried to sound casual, but her voice was dripping with uncertainty and nervousness. She chewed on her bottom lip and twisted a lock of hair, refusing to make eye contact with Macy.

Macy surveyed Delaney's appearance carefully.

"Excuse us, fellas." She flashed a smile and then dragged Delaney by the elbow to a quiet corner. "The best man, what did you say his name was? Lucas? He was conspicuously AWOL for the last hour, too."

Delaney flushed. "Mace . . ." Her sigh and her tone told Macy all she needed to hear.

"Are you sure you know what you are getting into?" Macy asked. "I mean I know I told you that you had nothing to be ashamed of, and I still don't believe that you do, but, hon, that was when we were talking one-night stand. Señor Adios. You can't actually *date* J.D.'s attorney. I mean, don't you think you'll get found out? Do you really know what you're doing?"

The answer, of course, was no. Not only did she not know what she was getting into, but she couldn't explain her unappeasable attraction to Lucas. Sure he was drop-dead gorgeous, but that was nothing new. She had never been one to date anything less. But there was something more with Lucas. Something that could only be described as . . . magnetic. She was drawn to him in a way that she had never been drawn to a man before. And the things she did with him, it was as if she were a completely different person altogether.

"I don't want to talk about it." Her head pounded and her brain smarted with the effort to sort through all her inexpressible emotions. She was tired of living up to everyone's expectations of who she should be.

Yet the more she thought about the events of the last three days, she wasn't even sure of who she was.

Macy sighed heavily. "I'm not going to get preachy on you. You know I'm the first one to go out there and have a good time, but just . . . be careful. The only one who can get hurt in all this is . . . you."

"You're awfully quiet," Lucas said to Delaney as he drove her home.

Delaney forced a smile. "I have a headache."

"Excuses already? It's only three days into our relationship," he joked.

Our relationship. The words hung heavy in the space between them

"I only meant . . ." he started, but didn't know how to finish. He didn't know what to say. So he didn't say anything. He just let the words sit there and followed her succinct directions to her house. When they arrived, he hurried out of the car and circled around the front to open her passenger-side door.

"Nice place," he said.

"Thanks. It's one of J.D.'s developments."

He nodded and followed her up the path to her front door. She fumbled several minutes with the wrong keys before finally finding the right one.

"Would you like to come in for a drink or something?" she asked.

Definitely "or something."

But the way she said it, so seemingly unsure, caused Lucas to hesitate.

"You aren't obligated to invite me in. We could just say good night."

"No, I know. I just . . ."

"If you aren't one hundred percent certain about what we're doing here, then I can leave. I don't want you to feel pressured."

"I'm not really certain about anything right now," she told him honestly. "But this house is really big and it's been a really long time since I've had company. . . ."

He understood that what she needed more than anything else right now was a friend. He inclined his head to the side and lifted his knuckle to brush the back of her cheek.

"If you wanted to come in, we could just . . . talk."

"I'd love to."

"Coffee? Hot chocolate? Tea or beer?" Delaney called from her kitchen.

"A beer would be good." He sat down on her leather couch and took in the furnishings. They were sparse, but he could tell every piece she owned had been chosen with time and care.

"I'm just going to change," she said, bringing him the beer.

He nodded and tried to block out the mental image of Delaney fully naked. He took a long sip of beer in an attempt to quench his mounting desire, reminding himself over and over he was just here for a drink and conversation.

She returned, visibly more comfortable. Lucas was sure she thought she appeared completely asexual in her yoga pants and tee with her face freshly scrubbed and hair knotted haplessly atop her head, but to him she looked incredibly enticing, just comfortable enough to curl up next to all night long.

He was staring at the infamous modified gun cabinet full of tiaras and crowns.

"I didn't know it was an antique when I renovated it. It was his great great great—well, I'm not so sure how many greats but it survived the Revolution, the Alamo and the Civil War," Delaney said with a twinge of guilt.

"Then you go and paint it pink. Travis is rolling over in his grave."

"That was during my DIY TV phase. We had just gotten married, and J.D. didn't spend a lot of time at home, and that was before I had the community center."

"A desperate housewife plus do-it-yourself television." Lucas chuckled. "Definitely the recipe for disaster and pink gun cabinets, apparently. You really won all of these?" he asked, hypnotized by the flashes of ruby, violet and emerald that danced between the crystals in the crowns and the carefully chosen lighting in the cabinet. There must have been fifty crowns in there, each with a neatly penned place card describing the year and the title.

"Hard to imagine that somebody could spend that much time on the pageant circuit, huh?"

"Not really. I mean you're beautiful. Really, really beautiful. It's just you don't seem to fit the bill. You live in an ordinary house with an ordinary car and everyday, ordinary problems. You're just ordinary."

"You flatter me!" She laughed.

"No . . . no . . . that's not . . . I only meant . . ." This was going all wrong. He wanted to kick himself because he was never awestruck by women. He never said the wrong thing. He was never speechless. Delaney was changing all the rules. He wasn't sure he knew how to play this game.

She let him off the hook. "I know what you meant. I was just kidding. Actually it was a compliment. Nobody's ever realized that I'm just a plain old Jane Doe."

"I wouldn't go *that* far." She was a long drive from Plainsville.

"What I mean is, when people hear that you've won a title, especially a big one, like a state title, they imagine there is this glamorous life that goes with it, jets and cruises and trips around the world. When I had the crown, I would wake up, put on a full face of makeup and four-inch heels to go fill my tank with gas because what if, heaven forbid, somebody saw Miss Texas without her makeup? But I'd be willing to bet that there are a whole lot more girls out there just like me. In real life not all beauty queens end up as international movie stars. Halle Berry, Vanessa Williams, they're two in a million. The rest of us are mothers, and doctors and lawyers and writers and . . ."

"Billion-dollar oil baronesses turned amateur strippers?"

Delaney laughed. "So maybe not just like me. But you know, regular people with regular problems," she said, ducking into the kitchen for a moment. "Ice cream?" She returned and offered to share a pint of Moose Tracks with him.

He needed to cool down, but he held up the beer. "Maybe later."

She plopped down on the couch dangerously close to him, tucking her legs underneath her. He thought about scooting closer to the arm of the couch to put some space between them, but quickly determined she might interpret it the wrong way. He took a very long swallow of beer instead.

"So how long have you been practicing law?" she asked him, propping her head up with her fist as she leaned her elbow against the back of the couch.

"I graduated ten years ago."

"Have you been with the same firm ever since?"

He shook his head. "I worked for Lawrence, for a short time."

"Both your egos couldn't fit in the same firm, I suppose."

He smiled. "Actually, he wanted to make me one of the partners, but then there was this incident with the daughter of one of the other partners. Before that I was a public defender. I thought I was going to save the world."

"How wonderful." In her line of work she had seen fantastic defenders save her girls from some really ugly places. "Why did you leave?"

"It's a high burnout job. I mean, sure, every now and then I would get the one guy I knew in my gut was clean as a whistle but the ninety-nine I had to defend to get to him . . ." He shook his head. He'd had to defend everything from rapists to bank robbers, using his powers of persuasion to work out deals to put the assholes back on the street in as short a time as possible. "After a couple of years, I figured if I was going to defend the scum of the earth . . . might as well profit from it. That's when I went to work for Lawrence."

"Lawrence really respects you."

"I respect him, too. Everything I know, I learned from Lawrence. Not just law. Everything. He's more like a father to me."

"Is that why you ultimately left? Too much like working for your parents?"

"Yeah. He's great, but it was *exactly* like working for a parent," Lucas explained. "He started trying to groom me for mayor. He had my whole political life plotted out in his Franklin Covey. Mayor at twenty-eight, governor at thirty-six, president at forty. I think at one point he even had me on a curfew. He set me up with the partner's daughter. If she wasn't the next Jackie O., nobody was. The entire firm thought we were going to get married . . . until I dumped her."

Delaney feigned horror. "You jilted Jackie O.?"

"Hey, in my defense, I told her from the beginning I wasn't interested in marriage." The words tumbled out before he could stop them. He waited for Delaney to react, but other than slightly raising her brows, she didn't get all ruffled like other women did. "What about you? What did you do before you were Miss Texas?"

"I worked in Momma and Daddy's soda fountain until the day I left for college."

"Dairy queen turned beauty queen?"

She laughed a deep laugh. The kind where you smile so hard your cheeks hurt. "The Texas version of the American dream. Can you believe it?"

"So how'd you get into pageant life?"

"Momma entered me in my first pageant when I was eight just to prove to one of our neighbors that they did not have the most beautiful child in the world. She had a year's worth of free chocolate malts riding on my head. I wore a secondhand Easter dress and tapped my heart out to the most pathetic rendition of "On the Good Ship Lollipop." I won. It's been downhill ever since."

"So I take it you don't miss it? Competing?"

"Goodness no!" she answered quickly enough to reveal how she really felt about the pageant circuit.

"You didn't like competing in pageants?" It surprised Lucas, especially sitting across from an oversized curio cabinet crammed with crowns and scepters. "I thought being Miss America was every girl's dream."

"Like scrubbing toilets and mopping floors."

"Then why did you . . . I mean you competed in a lot of pageants. Why, if you hated it so much?"

Delaney considered the question. Why *had* she done it? The first dozen pageants had just been for fun. She got to get out of the house on weekend trips with her mother. She got to dress up and put on makeup and use her mother's hot rollers in the oversized lavender train case. She loved to sing and dance and people clapped and whistled when she did. It was like she actually was Shirley Temple or somebody. She wasn't just the oldest of the long string of Davis girls. She was Delaney Davis, Little Miss This or Junior Miss That. She stood out. She was *somebody*.

Then being somebody became less of a hobby and more of a chore. From a chore it became a definition. It followed her name like a lost puppy. "Hey, aren't you Delaney Davis, Miss Rio Grande?" "Look, I think that's Delaney Davis, Miss Longhorn." "Guess who I saw in the 7-Eleven at eleven o'clock at night in blue-light-special flip flops and no makeup? Delaney Davis, Miss Texas."

There was never the time and opportunity for her to be anything less than picture perfect. She feared the occasional zit the way some feared nuclear war. She smiled so much she was certain her face would permanently freeze in that position. Her corpse would be laid out in her coffin, bathed in tears of passersby and she'd still be wearing that ridiculous smile.

Nobody saw her for who she was. Nobody cared that she watched reruns on Nick at Nite until her eyes crossed. Nobody cared that she stocked ice cream in her freezer like it was the end of the world. Nobody knew that after J.D. started cheating on her she woke up *every* morning searching *every* inch of her body, trying to determine why he had lost interest. Nobody knew that because when they looked at her, they didn't see her. They saw Miss Beauty Queen.

She shrugged. "Why do people get up and go to work every day at a job they hate? I guess I didn't really hate it in the beginning. When I first started out, it was kind of fun to get all dressed up and have people taking my picture all the time.

"But one pageant turned into five turned into fifty. They were neverending. The only thing Texas values more than a Cowboys game is a beauty pageant. I was Miss Random Shopping Mall, Miss All-Beef Hotdog, Miss Excuse Me Can You Wear this Sash for the Grand Opening of My Car Wash. I can't remember a time when I was just Delaney."

She thought about the first night they had met. He had referred to her as a doll. That's how he had seen her until she was up on the stage having a little fun and, of course, in the private dance room with him. That was the first time in a long time she could be herself. He didn't know who she was supposed to be and he liked who she actually was.

"The prizes went from plastic tiaras with paste gems to cars and cruises and lots and lots of money. And sometimes that money came in handy if the dairy bar had a bad year, but most of it has been invested. Not that Momma and Daddy would have ever made me participate if they knew how I started to feel, but I never really told them. Momma wasn't one of those awful pageant moms you see on daytime talk shows or anything. There were a lot of us girls and believe it or not, there's a lot of money to be made winning beauty pageants. I kind of felt I was doing my part. Besides, I didn't really hate it as much as I viewed it all as a chore. Phoebe washed dishes, Brooke kept the laundry, Tyler vacuumed and dusted . . . I did pageants. After a while it was just . . . expected.

"Then when I got to high school, I knew it was the only way I was going to get any scholarship money. I certainly wasn't going to college on an academic scholarship."

"You're very smart," Lucas protested.

She slid another spoonful of ice cream into her mouth.

"I've read a lot about you in the last two days. You couldn't do the work you do if you weren't smart."

"What made you approach me Thursday night, Lucas? My brains or my beauty? I wasn't on stage calculating the square root of 87.6. You were attracted to me because of the way I look."

"That's true with anything. The car you drive. Your favorite flower. Anything. It doesn't negate the fact that a beautiful car can be a performance machine or that a beautiful flower smells just as good as another."

"But you didn't know anything about me when you propositioned me. Would you have even taken a second glance if I didn't match your idea of attractive?"

Delaney shifted uncomfortably, wanting to kick herself for having said that aloud. It wasn't fair to take out her frustration on him. The longer the question hung in the air, the more she wanted the answer. Then again, she already knew the answer. So the minute it looked like he was going to open his mouth to respond, she changed the subject. "Have you ever been married?"

He shook his head.

"Have you ever been close?"

Another negative.

"I guess being a divorce lawyer kind of sours you on marriage, huh?"

"It certainly makes me a more prudent decision maker when it comes to affairs of the heart." He considered for a moment how ridiculous that sounded, considering he was sitting in the home of his client's soon-to-be-ex wife, straining against his will to not have sex with her. Again. He read the same curiosity in her brown eyes. "Normally I am, anyway," he continued. "But marriage is not much more than a contract. I believe that if two people work hard, they can live together amicably and have a mutually satisfying union."

"Marriage is a contract?" Delaney asked, incredulous.

"More or less. That's how I see it anyway. I don't see any reason to confuse things with unrealistic ideals like love and romance. I believe marriage is two people working together to live together to build something together."

"Not me. I want the same red-hot romance that my parents have. Even after almost thirty years, they're still madly in love."

"My parents were mad all right, but not for each other . . . at each other."

"Tell me about your parents," she said.

The only person who knew anything about his upbringing was Judah, and that was because he had been there through most of it. Everybody else just assumed Lucas had lived the charmed life. It didn't matter to him. He let people think whatever they wanted, even if it was usually wrong.

But this time he didn't hesitate to answer. Something about Delaney made her incredibly easy to talk to. "Not much to tell. I had a mother who regretted every minute she was married to my father and a father who I only saw on Sundays that were too rainy to golf. He was a well-respected physician and surgeon who had the picture-perfect family."

"That's it . . . that's your life?" Delaney questioned.

"My family wasn't as loving as yours seems. I can't remember one solitary conversation between my dad and my mom and me. Father was, ironically enough, a cardiologist. On the doors to his clinic and on all the pamphlets and brochures was his motto: Mending broken hearts. I say, *Physician heal thyself*. When my dad died, I think the staff of nurses shed more tears than my mother or I."

"If he was so cold, why did she marry him?"

"She was poor, he was rich. Her parents had drummed into her head that marrying into money would solve all her problems. She must have loved him immensely at one time; otherwise I don't think she would have been so deeply affected when things started to go wrong. She thought she'd have the perfect life together. It was far from perfect."

"Why did she stay married? When she realized it wasn't what she wanted?"

He met her eyes. "Why does anyone stay married to a person they don't love?"

She savored a spoonful of ice cream as she rolled the question around in her head. "I suppose it's better than being single and lonely."

"For my mother it was worse. She was married and lonely. I'm sure she told herself she would stick around in the marriage until I grew up. Of course, by that time, she thought it was too late to start over."

Lucas thought about how growing up in that cold, sterile environment had defined him. He thought about how his father's patients needed him so much more than his family. How his mother spent hours, sometimes even days, locked in her bedroom and when she did come out, red and puffy-eyed, she was just a shell of the mother he should have known. How in a house full of staff, he felt abandoned and alone. How he had never allowed himself to grow truly close to another person other than his surrogate brother, Judah. Especially not a woman. He had seen up close and personal what love and marriage did to a person and he made it his personal goal to avoid that pain and heartbreak at all costs.

To Lucas, women had been little more than objects of desire and sex, an outlet for tension. He hadn't learned the art of caring for another or allowing another person to care for him. He never gave it enough time. Lucas was always out the door before the sun rose and the sheets cooled. He had a speech for every exit occasion. She's crying? Take advantage of her sensitive side. She's angry? Turn the tables on her. She's just as happy to see you go? Don't look a gift horse in the mouth . . . just run! Yep. Lucas was a leaver. He could teach a seminar on escaping the uncomfortable "morning after."

Leave them before they leave you.

It was for this reason that he didn't understand why he couldn't leave Delaney. Why he felt drawn to her like a magnet. Why, for the first time in his life, he was looking for an excuse to . . . stay.

"Are you wondering why I didn't divorce J.D. sooner?" Delaney asked, breaking the uncomfortable silence.

"Actually, I'm wondering why you married him in the first place."

Delaney looked down for a moment. Aside from her family and Macy, she hadn't shared that story with anyone. She wasn't ashamed of what had transpired, but it was still painful to talk about. She didn't want Lucas to believe her relationship had anything to do with J.D.'s money.

"There were circumstances that led me to believe it was the best decision."

He cocked an eyebrow. "Prenatal circumstances?"

"So he told you then?" She shook her head in disbelief.

"I'm his lawyer. I can't fulfill my obligations to J.D.

without knowing all the circumstances involved. I asked him to be wholly honest with me regarding all matters," Lucas said, skirting the question.

"I suppose he led you to believe I made the whole thing up." She could only imagine the venom J.D. had spouted. Even after a long, grueling, miserable night in the emergency room, J.D. never truly believed Delaney had been pregnant. He was so paranoid he actually accused her of staging some complicated charade to which every doctor, nurse and aide in the E.R. was privy.

Lucas shrugged. "I make my own decisions about what I believe."

"I didn't. Make it all up. I was pregnant and had a wastebasket full of little pink lines to prove it. It's in my medical chart."

"You're young and healthy, so what happened?" She was relieved that he sounded genuinely concerned.

"Who knows? You know doctors say something like twenty-five percent of all first pregnancies end up as early-term miscarriages. Some women don't even know they are pregnant when it happens. I know stress can do it, and I was really stressed out those first few weeks after we got married."

"Why? Those are supposed to be the happiest days of your life."

"J.D. went from Prince Charming to the Prince of Darkness in like ten days. He cheated on me on our honeymoon, did he tell you that? I had horrible morning sickness and one day couldn't even crawl out of bed until four in the afternoon. When I went looking for J.D., I found him, with a girl who worked at the hotel, in a compromising position in the hot tub."

Lucas looked disgusted. "Honestly, Delaney, why didn't you fly home right then and file for an annulment?"

"I was twenty-two. Young and dumb. He told me he had too much to drink and that the girl didn't mean anything. I was pregnant. Like your mother, I guess I thought I was doing the right thing for the baby. Then a couple of months down the road when I miscarried, well, I was too depressed to even get out of bed and brush my teeth, much less do the legwork toward getting a divorce. I wanted that baby. I've always wanted a minivan full of kids, so I was just devastated. At first J.D. was really sweet, but after I didn't just snap out of it, he started right in on me about how I faked the whole thing. I could have handled that. I mean he just married some dirt-poor kid from Big Stinking Creek. He had every right to question my honesty. What hurt me the most was that he seemed . . . relieved. He didn't want the baby and what I realized too late is that he didn't really want me. He was infatuated by my crown. He had the ultimate trophy wife—a beauty queen."

"That's one of the reasons you hate being identified that way."

Delaney nodded. "Sometimes you just want people to want you for you."

"But you stayed with him?"

"After a while we became amicable; we were friends who sometimes enjoyed sex with each other. Then we kind of fell into a numb groove of married life. I shouldn't say that . . . I was actually having a good time. I was doing a lot of charity events for his corporations, shining up his image and all. People actually took me seriously. They started to ask for my opinion instead of my autograph. He wasn't all bad all the time. He had flashes of humanity. He bought Momma and Daddy a real nice house in Abilene. Helped them start a nicer restaurant—half old-fashioned soda shoppe, half artsy café. He helped Phebes, my sister, through college. He poured hundreds of thousands of dollars into my outreach program. And I'm not going to lie to you; I kind of got accustomed to the lifestyle. The house, the parties, the clothes, the shoes. It's fun being rich. A lot more fun than a weekend full of making chocolate cherry sodas back home. But that doesn't make me a gold-digger." Her eyes darted up, challenging him.

"I've apologized for that. I swear I didn't mean it."

"Then why did you say it?" She was of the philosophy that everything you said had some basis in reality.

"What if I told you I was jealous?" he said.

"Jealous?"

"It's not a secret. I'm really attracted to you. It's crazy. I know you had a life with J.D. before we ever met, but . . . I started letting myself picture you with J.D. . . . you with Lawrence . . ."

"With Lawrence!" Her mouth dropped open in shock.

"I said it's crazy. That's just how I am. If there's something I really want, it makes me crazy thinking about somebody else having it."

When their eyes met, the passion between them raged. Lucas was the first to look away. He cleared his throat. "So what was the proverbial straw? Between you and J.D., I mean."

"We went to a golf tournament at the club one weekend. I wasn't supposed to be in town that weekend, but Mace and Phebes canceled our girls' weekend, so I thought I would surprise him. Turns out, the surprise was on me. I get to the club and the whole ladies' tea was all abuzz about J.D.'s hot new honey and sure enough, there she was in the middle of the room, county fair blue-ribbon pretty. So I march right up and introduce myself. I say 'Hello, I'm Delaney Daniels, as in Mrs. James David Daniels.' And you know what she has the gall to say?"

He shook his head but smiled, beckoning her to continue.

"She had the nerve to ask me to leave so I please wouldn't ruin *her* weekend with *my* husband. Then she called me out as a fraud and a phony. She announced to the whole room that I was nothing more than trailer park trash playing like country club Barbie."

"What did you do?"

"I told her that Misty was a stupid name."

He raised a brow.

"I was angry and it was all I had. Then I left. I went straight back to the ranch and moved everything I owned to the guest quarters. Once J.D.'s real estate company broke ground on this development I moved into the first spec house that was completed. And now you know the rest of the story."

She glanced up to see that he was grinning broadly.

"What's so funny?"

"You. Your accent. I hadn't noticed it before. You practice hiding it, don't you? Why?"

"Come on. I'm a 5'8" walking stereotype. Blond hair, big boobs, tiara. So of course I must be dumb as dirt, right? When people hear my accent it just gives them more fuel for the fire. After I won my first pageant, when I was ten, I watched *All My Children* every day and practiced my Erica Kane speak. I got so good to where I hardly slip. Unless I'm at home and comfortable. Then sometimes I revert."

"I like that."

"The accent?"

He nodded. "And that you feel comfortable with me."

She raked her teeth across the bottom of her lip. She

hadn't meant to imply that he was making her feel comfortable. He was, but that was absolutely none of his business at this point.

"And you're not dumb as dirt. When I first read the client file on your marriage, I was amazed at everything you have been able to accomplish with your work toward charitable organizations. Pretty impressive."

"Thanks. Coming from you I'll accept that as a true compliment."

Chapter Fourteen

If it can't be fixed with hair spray, nail glue or hem-orrhoid cream, it can't be fixed at all.

They had been talking for over two hours. They talked about everything from their favorite colors to who should win the Indy 500. In that time, Delaney brought him two additional beers, another spoon so he could share her ice cream and a half-full bag of chips that were stale but neither of them noticed. He told her about his family, but the story was short since his father and mother had passed away ten and five years ago, respectively. He still had a brother he saw occasionally, mostly on holidays, but Asa was in the FBI and his work kept him undercover and incognito a lot.

"That's interesting that you both chose occupations in the legal system," Delaney said.

"He finds the bad guys, and I put them away."

"You don't talk to him much?"

"No. He's quite a bit younger than I am . . . five

years. . . . I love him, of course, more than anything, but we don't have all that much in common. Actually I'm closer to Judah than I am to Asa."

She nodded. She was amazed to hear about his relationship with his only family. How he talked to his brother only a few times a year. She couldn't imagine it. Right then, her answering machine's red light was blinking furiously, which meant the tape was loaded with calls, more than likely from Phebes or one of her other four sisters.

"Five sisters?" Lucas asked incredulously.

"Yep. Daddy just had to keep trying for a boy. Momma finally put her foot down."

"Tell me about them."

"Really?" Delaney was both surprised and impressed. In the five years she had been married to J.D. he had never shown any interest in her family. Quite the contrary. He would tell her not to go spouting off about her life in Big Stinking Creek at the club since it made her sound like a country bumpkin. So, to most people, she was from Abilene or Lubbock, whichever popped into her head first, until J.D. actually bought them a house in Abilene, and then she was just from Abilene. She told them she had one sister, Phoebe. And a respectable mom and dad, who were retired ranchers, not live-off-the-land farmers.

It felt good to talk about the rest of the family for once. Phoebe was the brainy one. She had her bachelor's, her master's, and was halfway through her Ph.D. all at the ripe old age of twenty-six. She was a biochemical engineer and Delaney was certain she was going to find the cure for cancer or something. In New York, there was Brooke, the artsy one. She had an apartment in Soho and a healthy contract with some gallery. All she ever did was make stuff out of old retired Texas flags, license plates and longhorns, not pretty landscapes and still-lifes, but she was the hottest ticket right now. There was Tyler, named for the city of her conception, who had branched out to Hollywood to be an actress. Right now, she played a maid on a popular soap, but in just two months she had gone from smiling and nodding to one-liners to now giving her reel employer love advice on occasion. Fan mail poured in for her.

"Just give her ten years and she'll be winning Oscars," Delaney proclaimed with pride.

There were two more left at home. Sixteen-year-old Evelyn, Evie for short, was the athlete. Blue ribbon for anything she ever competed in, but it was swimming that was going to take her to the Olympics.

"Don't tell me she practiced in the big stinking creek," Lucas joked.

Delaney laughed. Normally she got defensive when people made jokes about her town, if it could be called that. But with Lucas it was just like he was one of them, even though they had grown up in very different environments. She just felt . . . connected.

And finally there was five-year-old Ashleigh.

"Five?"

"Momma's last stance, Daddy's last chance. He really wanted to try for a boy." Delaney told him the family joke.

"I guess Ashleigh has yet to demonstrate her talent."

Delaney nodded. "She has a little of all of us in her, I guess. A face carved by angels, smart as a whip. When Daddy's after her with the switch she's the drama queen. She can turn on the waterworks like that." Delaney snapped her fingers. "She lives for sports. You'll find her in Daddy's lap watching games or outside playing catch. But turn around two hours later and she's helping Momma bake cookies. She's a great kid." She looked up to find him staring at her. Again. Every time she looked up he was staring.

"What?"

"I can't get over how beautiful you are." He glanced at his watch. He couldn't believe the time. They had been talking all night long. Lucas Church had gone home with a beautiful woman and . . . talked.

"It's getting late," he said for no apparent reason at all. He didn't want her to realize the time. He didn't want to leave.

"I suppose you have to go."

"I should go. Now," he said, but didn't make a move to leave the couch.

She took his empty beer bottle from his hand. "You've been drinking. Do you really think you'll be okay to drive?"

Something in her eyes told him what she wanted his answer to be. "You're right. I shouldn't drive." He remained silent. He didn't trust the words that might come spilling out of his mouth. When it came to Delaney his brain was unpredictably unpredictable.

"You could call a cab, but then that'd be stupid because you'd have to pay another fare all the way back out here tomorrow just to get your car," she reasoned.

"You're right." He realized if he didn't say something she would continue gushing without end.

"Or . . ."

Her "or" was suggestive, but he couldn't tell what was about to come out of her mouth.

"You could . . ." She was concentrating severely on the task of picking something, lint presumably, from the chenille throw that blanketed her legs, but if there was lint, it was invisible.

"Stay here." She finally finished her statement in a quick rush of breath.

Lucas concentrated on her statement, on her demeanor, on her face. She refused to make eye contact. "Are you sure? I'd hate to put you out."

"No, it'll be fine. I'm afraid I don't have any furniture in the guest bedrooms yet. Ever since this whole split has turned ugly, J.D. hasn't exactly been generous with his financial help."

Lucas nodded.

"There's the couch, but it wouldn't be very comfortable," she said. "With you being so tall, your legs would dangle off."

He nodded. "Sounds like we're running out of places for me to crash."

"There's my bed. It's huge. A California king. I never even realized it was so big until I had to change the sheets on it by myself. Do you know how hard it is to change sheets on a bed that big all by yourself?"

She was rambling again, indicating her nervousness.

"So we'd have plenty of room. I mean you could have your side and I could have my side. And we wouldn't even know the other one was there. I'm real still when I sleep."

He rubbed his hands across his face. She was practically begging him to spend the night with her. And he wanted to stay more than anything. But he didn't want to hurt her any further. He knew this couldn't go anywhere after tonight. He didn't date to mate. He didn't even date. He met girls, had sex with them and moved on. Tomorrow he should be moving on. But could he?

"Delaney . . ."

She looked down quickly and turned a furious shade of red. "It was a dumb idea. You probably need to get home."

He lifted her chin with his thumb and index finger. "That's not it. It's just . . . We've been playing with fire as it is. I'd love to stay here tonight but if I do, it'll have to be on the couch. I can't sleep with you."

She swallowed and began to lower her chin, but his resistance was too great.

"I meant that. I can't sleep with you ... meaning *sleep*. If I get in the same bed with you ..." He couldn't even utter the words without a challenge from his penis. "I can't control myself when I'm with you. I won't be able to keep my hands off you. These last couple of hours have been torture enough." He chose that moment to shift, to give himself extra room in his pants, releasing the straining pressure.

Her eyes shifted downward, noting his raging hard-on. She chewed on her bottom lip.

"Even now, all I can think about is how badly I want you." His voice went raspy and hoarse. He raked his hands through his hair.

"I want you, too," she said. She leaned in and kissed him lightly on the mouth. He responded immediately and way too eagerly. He cupped the back of her head and pulled her in to deepen the kiss. Suddenly her hands were everywhere: in his hair, caressing his chest, tugging at his belt. He pulled away, cursing under his breath.

"Did I do something wrong?" she asked, her eyes heavily lidded with passion.

"I don't want you to think this is the only reason I brought you home tonight."

"Shhh."

And before he could pull away again, she was crawling into his lap and wrapping her limbs around him, kissing him with desperate ferocity. She wasn't going to make it easy for him to walk away. She fisted her hands in his waves of black hair and moaned as she scooted higher on his lap in her attempt to obliterate any remaining space between their bodies. He realized how perfectly their bodies fit. As if she were that one long-lost puzzle piece he had finally found.

His hands were exploring the soft curves of her body. He was fascinated by how truly exquisitely she was made. He brushed lightly against her hardened nipple, and when she bucked he moaned low and deep into her mouth. As their kisses began to build, he realized she had unbuttoned his tuxedo shirt and her small hands were hot and smooth as they explored the wall of his chest. She sighed as she traced her kisses from his mouth to his ear, down his neck, across his chest, following the trail of silken black hair as it disappeared into his waistband. She was fumbling with his zipper and he couldn't speak or watch her as she attended him, knowing he would spill if he did. He threw his head back and reclined against the back of the couch as she searched for his sex, finding it and holding him firmly.

Without even looking he knew what she planned to do.

"You . . . you don't . . . have . . ."

She squeezed him gently as if she were prepping him for the event. Her tongue tested him first and he bucked, then fisted his hand in her hair, making it impossible to change her mind. Not that she was going to.

He knew it would be nearly impossible for her to take him whole in her mouth but she seemed to swallow his length, inch by inch, using one hand to stroke his balls and the other one at the base of his penis, squeezing and stroking. Her mouth was so hot, he wanted the sensation to last forever. But, at best, he had about two minutes before he wouldn't be able to hold back any longer.

"Ummmmm," she moaned in satisfaction, as if she was savoring the most decadent dessert. He almost lost it.

"Laney . . ."

She sucked harder.

"Laney, baby, you've got to stop." He was panting now, the words barely escaping his mouth.

"If you don't stop I'm going to come." He was never one to look a gift blow job in the mouth and therefore made certain to always give plenty of fair warning, but it was as if she hadn't heard a word he said. He grabbed the fabric of the couch, bracing himself as he felt the first crest rise.

"Laney!" She still didn't pull away and then it was too late. He was spilling into her mouth, his body shaking. He let out a loud guttural growl, so loud it even surprised him. He relaxed, senseless, loosening his grip, now raking her silky tendrils with his fingers.

She smiled mischievously. "One screaming orgasm deserves another."

"You didn't have to do that."

"I wanted to." She crawled back up the length of his body, nestling in his lap.

"Thank you."

"No thanks needed. My intentions were purely selfish."

He raised a questioning brow.

"I want you all night long, Mr. Church. I want you to be at prime operating level for me."

"It's going to take me a few minutes," he said.

"You've got five."

Chapter Fifteen

If you wake up and you're still wearing the crown, you know it wasn't just a dream.

Lucas awoke the next morning to the smell of bacon. He inhaled deeply and rubbed the empty side of the bed where Laney hadn't slept all night. After they had finally exhausted themselves, she had curled next to him so closely the two of them could have been accommodated by a twin bed with space to spare. At the foot of the bed she had laid out a pair of jeans, a shirt, and some shoes. He checked the sizes and they were close to perfect. All the clothes appeared new. Had she gone out shopping? Where did she find open stores on Sunday morning?

He grabbed a quick shower and was still drying his hair as he ambled into the kitchen. He leaned against the door jamb and watched her as she practically skipped around the kitchen. She was wearing a low-rise terry track suit that had "Juicy" stamped across her butt. His penis started to rise to RSVP to the invitation. He groaned, low, but it must have been loud enough for her to hear because she turned around and smiled.

"Good morning, sleeping beauty. Or should I say afternoon?"

He looked at his watch, realizing it was almost noon.

"You shouldn't have let me sleep in so late. How long have you been up?"

"Since six."

He found that pretty amazing considering they hadn't gone to sleep until after three, and she didn't seem to be missing an ounce of energy. She was even preparing him a full breakfast. Freshly squeezed orange juice included.

"I got up and went jogging and grabbed a shower and went grocery shopping. And made you breakfast." She seemed proud of her accomplishments.

"I have my groceries delivered. I didn't know the market was selling designer jeans and Italian leather loafers nowadays." A more polite, less jealous guy might have just assumed there was a perfectly natural reason for a woman to have a spare set of clothes on hand for the man who spent the night. But he wasn't polite. And he was very jealous, no matter how irrational.

She smiled nervously. "I bought those for J.D. right before we split up. I didn't even realize I still had them until I went scrounging around in my closet for something for you to put on. You guys are about the same size."

The exact same size, evidently.

And there was his jealous streak again. Wanting to be something different, wanting to stand out in Delaney's life. Wanting to be her one and only.

She must have sensed his darkening mood because she hurriedly continued, "They're brand new, though.

I showed them to him and he hated them. He thought I was trying to make him look younger or some nonsense."

Lucas nodded.

"I only thought they would be more comfortable than the tux. That's the only reason I brought them out. You don't have to wear them."

She was rambling again. Lucas smiled apologetically for his reaction. "They are much better."

"Breakfast?" she asked, holding out a plate laden with three eggs over medium, a stack of waffles and five strips of bacon. He grinned at her handiwork. She was obviously used to cooking for the breakfast crowd in Big Stinking Creek.

"Is it too much food? I figured you might have worked up an appetite with all that . . . last night."

"I'm famished," he said, sitting down at the breakfast bar and digging in. "I love my eggs over medium. They're my favorite."

She cleaned the dishes while he finished his breakfast and he had to stop himself at least ten times from imagining her in his kitchen, in his bedroom, in his home every day doing this . . . as his . . . and he wouldn't even let the word form as a thought because it was impossible.

Impossible because she was still married to another man—if only by a shoestring. Even though she would be divorced soon, she would need time to recover. Although he wasn't in this for the long haul, he didn't want to be a rebound relationship. Even if he wanted to explore something longer term, which he was certain he didn't, he couldn't unless they planned on moving very far away. There wouldn't be enough time to let J.D. "recover" from the idea that his ex-wife and lawyer were an item. So he should just let this ride out for what it was: two people who spent a couple of days filling the intense physical needs of each other. He decided he would walk out her front door and the next time he would see her would be in court.

That's what he had reasoned but he said something entirely different.

"Why don't we go for a picnic?" Lucas asked.

"A picnic?" Delaney raised an eyebrow. Her gaze was wary. "Do you really think it would be wise?"

He nodded. "There's this little park I know about. Always empty. Come on. The weather is beautiful. We should spend it outside."

"I don't know." Delaney chewed on her bottom lip.

"Nobody will see us. It's way out of the way," he persisted.

"Well . . ." She turned her attention back to the sink.

"We'll grab some sandwiches and maybe some wine. Nothing fancy."

She smiled. "I'd love to."

Chapter Sixteen

So what if it came straight from a deodorant commercial? It's the best advice a girl can get: Never let them see you sweat.

"Lucas. Lucas!" When Lucas heard his name he knew immediately who it was. At first he tried to quicken his gait and pretend he didn't hear Judah calling him from across the pasture, but as the voice grew louder he knew Judah was actively pursuing him.

"Whatever you do, don't take off the sunglasses," he warned Delaney as they slowed down.

Delaney shot him a curious look before lowering her shades but complied.

"Hey!" Judah greeted them. "What are you doing? Training for the marathon?"

Lucas shifted his position and stood mostly in front of Delaney. "Hey, Jude. Becca," he greeted them as Becca waddled from behind Judah. "I didn't know you guys hung out around here."

"You're out of your neck of the woods, too." Judah

inclined his head to peer around Lucas's shoulder. "You going to introduce us?"

Judah hadn't been at the meeting two days before, and Lucas was grateful for that, but it was still going to take a small miracle for Rebecca to not recognize Delaney. She never forgot a face. But with the shades, her hair up in a ponytail, the casual attire, maybe Delaney wouldn't be recognized. She wasn't exactly the picture of a former Texas beauty queen.

"This is Elaine," he said, thinking quickly on his feet. "Elaine, this is my best friend and colleague, Judah, and his wife, Rebecca. Judah works with me at the firm."

Delaney looked unsure for a moment but then smiled her prize-winning smile. "Good to meet you." She offered her hand to the couple.

"You, too. Boy, you look familiar."

Delaney nodded. "Yeah, I have one of those faces."

Rebecca shook her head. "I never forget a face. I know you from somewhere. Do you work out at Ms. Fit?"

Delaney shook her head. "Really, people are always getting me confused with the grocery checkout girl or their kids' swim instructor."

"Maybe." Rebecca frowned. "I usually never forget a face." She was clearly mulling over where she might have seen Delaney before.

"You should join us on our picnic." Judah raised their picnic basket and nodded at the one Lucas carried.

"Well, actually we were just leaving."

"Come on. I just saw you guys unload your trunk. You don't want to join us?" Judah sounded hurt. Lucas weighed how long he could keep Delaney's identity under wraps. Judah would certainly grow more suspicious if they ran out. If they dined together for an hour or so, perhaps Delaney could feign a headache and Judah and Rebecca would be none the wiser.

He looked to Delaney for approval. She shrugged, no more certain of how to get out of the sticky situation.

"Sure," Lucas finally, though reluctantly, agreed.

Lunch was pleasant and Lucas managed to steer the conversation toward the approaching birth of the twins, which kept Rebecca talking instead of thinking. His date was noticeably quiet and conspicuously never removed her dark sunglasses. Judah kept glancing from her face to Lucas's. When the sandwiches and beverages were finally consumed, Judah suggested Lucas's friend escort Rebecca a lap or two around the pond.

"She'll drag me around, otherwise. Bad knee." He rubbed the ball of his knee for emphasis.

As soon as the two women were out of earshot, Judah blurted, "There are only two right answers here, Luke. Either that is some apparition over there walking with my wife or Delaney Daniels has an identical twin."

Luke sipped his lukewarm beer, taking his time to swallow. "Then you recognized her."

"She doesn't exactly have the face or the body you would quickly forget."

"I didn't know you had seen her the other day."

"In passing."

Judah shook his head, thinking about the advice he was about to offer Lucas. Ever since Lucas had met Judah in the fifth grade they had been best friends—closer than brothers. Life hadn't been easy for Judah. While Lucas seemed to be handed dreams and opportunity on a silver platter, Judah had had to fight for every dime he earned.

Judah had been poorer than poor. His father was a deadbeat and an alcoholic, his mother a crack addict who turned tricks for hits. In junior high, the only true meals Judah ate were the ones provided at Lucas's table and, thankfully, those were many.

A strange twist of fate landed them in the same detention during the first week of fifth grade and they were fast and forever friends. Their lives followed each other up to this point. They both lettered in football and went on to attend Rice University where they pledged the same fraternity. Judah knew he had only successfully crossed the pledge line because he was Lucas's best friend. After undergrad, they both chose law as a career path.

They met Rebecca in law school. Both were hitting on her at the pool hall one night, but, for a change of pace, Judah was the one in whom she showed genuine interest. He had fallen instantly and head over heels in love with her and asked her to marry him within the month. The dynamic duo became the terrific trio. Lucas found there wasn't anything he couldn't share with either of them. They were the two people in the world who knew Lucas better than anyone else. They worked together, they took vacations together, they were indivisible.

Judah hated to see Lucas throw away everything he had worked for on a woman or a relationship that was bound to go nowhere.

"Do you know what you're doing?" Judah asked finally.

Lucas ignored the question and slid the Frisbee they were tossing back to Judah.

A wide grin spread across Judah's face. "Wait a minute. I know what's going on here," he said. "This is just like *State of Texas v. Peterson*, right?"

Lucas groaned. He had worked on the case when he was a defense attorney straight out of college. Peterson was a wealthy architect who had walked in on his wife going down on the pool boy one afternoon.

He left the room, went down the hall, retrieved a base-ball bat and came back swinging. He beat up the kid, a senior in college, pretty bad, but the only permanent damage was a scar above his brow and occasional short-term memory loss. The kid was lucky. Peterson, not so lucky. The state had acquired overwhelming evidence of Peterson's uncontrollable temper, all ruled admissible.

Lucas had only one card to play: the ADA, Chris-tine Nicholson. She was a better than attractive red-head, a few years older than Lucas and not shy about letting him know she was interested in getting to know more of him. They met up one night at The Bar, a joint so named because of its proximity to the court-house. She pretended to put him off for a couple of hours until her libido overtook her common sense and she took him home.

Somewhere in between her last orgasm and the verdict, Christine had fallen hard for Lucas. The rest of the trial was his for the taking. All he had to do was give her a wink and her brain turned to gelatin. Her questioning was off focus. She totally forgot to introduce three critical pieces of evidence. Before the jury came back with the verdict, she was willing to plea down to probation on aggravated assault. Lucas had never told anyone of the situation and God knew the ADA hadn't, but the sexual tension in the court-room during the trial was unmistakable, and the fact that Lucas was never (never!) paired with another fe-male DA while he was working Criminal was lost on no one.

Lawrence had been Peterson's divorce lawyer at the time and had taken a quick liking to the young attor-ney. Divorce was the real golden egg, he told Lucas. Lucas, trapped in a dead-end job, envious of the excit-ing cases Judah and Rebecca had, took Lawrence up on his offer. He'd worked with him a few years until he couldn't take the paternal dictation any longer, and, like a child leaving a mom-and-pop business for the big city, he went to work at the same firm as Judah and Rebecca.

"That's urban legend," Lucas lied, frustrated and angry that his past should pick this opportunity to rear its ugly head. "Besides, I wouldn't use Delaney like that."

"Then what are you doing with her?"

"I don't know . . . having a good time."

Judah hesitated, noting Lucas's assertion. "With your client's wife."

Lucas shrugged. "They're almost divorced."

"Are you falling for this girl?"

Lucas didn't answer, which was answer enough. Judah could read Lucas like a book.

"How'd this happen? What? You're arguing over who gets the toaster oven during division of property and what? You look up and you fall in love?" Judah asked.

"One, nobody's talking love here. We're just hanging out having a good time. I met her before . . . before I knew who she was."

"How? When?"

Lucas blew out a long deep breath. "Do you remember the girl I told you about? The girl from Foxy's?"

"*She's* the girl from Foxy's? She's moonlighting as a stripper?" Judah whispered.

"No. It was amateur night or something. She didn't even strip. She danced. And she only did it because she needed the money to give to Lawrence. She won. I went to congratulate her and one thing led to another."

Judah had spent more than a few nights out with Lucas in their two and a half decades of friendship. With Lucas, one thing always led to another.

Lucas continued, "I had no idea. I didn't know who she was until she walked into that conference room on Friday."

"So this is Sunday. How does it come about that you're still playing blind date with your client's spouse two days after the fact? Once you knew who she was you should have dumped her."

"I know. I know. But she happened to be at that wedding last night. We started talking and . . ."

"And one thing led to another?" Judah repeated for him.

Lucas nodded. "I don't know what I'm doing," he admitted.

"Do you know what's at stake here, man? Your job. More than just your job. Your career. How do you think you are going to remain objective throughout the proceedings if you're sleeping with your client's ex-wife? You could be brought before the ethics committee. Disbarred even."

"Don't you think I've thought about all that? I have. I just can't get her out of my system. When I woke up this morning, I fully planned to walk out her door and out of her life. Good-bye. Sayonara. Adios. Aloha."

Judah smirked. "Freudian slip? Doesn't aloha mean 'hello'?"

Lucas winced. "It also means good-bye."

"Depends on the context." Judah jerked his head in the direction of their abandoned picnic baskets. "In this context I think it definitely means hello."

"I meant good-bye. I really did. But we were having breakfast this morning, then next thing I know I'm asking her to go on a freaking picnic. I don't understand it."

Judah understood. He understood perfectly. As only a married man could.

"Look, it's not just your job. It could be your life, too.

J.D. Daniels is nobody to mess around with." Judah shook his head as he skipped a rock across the pond.

"He's a bully. He doesn't scare me. I'm just worried about what he would do to Delaney if he found out."

"You're my best friend. I don't want to see you go down in this mess. Take my advice; just take her home and walk away. This is not the time to play the bad ass, Lucas."

Lucas's expression hardened. "Look, even if I didn't give a rat's ass about myself, I'm wild about Delaney. I'm not going to let J.D. Daniels or anyone else do anything that could hurt her."

"Wild about her? You've only known her three days. Don't confuse lust with the real thing. You've been overworked lately and I know this girl provides some much needed R and R but that's all it is, Lucas. Remember that."

Lucas knew Judah was right. He hadn't even thought the words before they came spilling out of his mouth. He didn't know that much about Delaney except that she made him feel things in bed that he had never felt before. It didn't change the fact that he'd only known her a few days.

But it felt like a lifetime.

"So you and Lucas, huh?" Rebecca asked, nudging Delaney with her elbow. Rebecca was a pretty brunette with naturally golden bronzed skin and eyes blacker than her hair, hinting at her Latina genes.

Delaney nodded.

"How long have you known each other?

This sounded ridiculous. "Three days."

"Three days? Wow. Well, hang on for the ride because when these guys fall, they fall hard. Judah proposed to me in less than a month."

Proposal? Delaney shook her head. "I don't think

that's exactly where we're going with this thing. We're just kind of, you know. Hanging out."

Rebecca shook her head. "I've known Lucas for a long time. You're the first girl I've seen him take out on a date . . . ever."

"This isn't a date . . ." Delaney started.

"No, it's just a romantic picnic in a picturesque park with expensive wine and a gourmet picnic lunch from the most expensive caterer in Texas. You're right, that sounds nothing like a date." Rebecca giggled.

"He doesn't date?" Delaney asked after a few moments of silence. "I got the impression he dated often."

"Not in the conventional way. He sees people, of course, but mostly at night and it never carries much past the next morning, if you get my drift."

"Oh."

"He's Mr. Commitmentphobe himself. If you've managed to keep his interest for three days, it's just a matter of time." She waggled her brows knowingly and patted her stomach.

Delaney smiled politely but knew she would ignore Rebecca's suggestion. It seemed once married people got married they found ways to squeeze every one of their friends into their mold. Delaney had been guilty of it herself soon after she married J.D. She was constantly harassing Macy or Phoebe to settle down.

The sun was starting to go down and dusk was setting in over the park. Delaney shifted her shades to the top of her head. "Really, I think you're way off base. . . ."

"Wait a minute! I just realized where I know you from," Rebecca interrupted. "You're Delaney Daniels."

"Um . . ."

"I guess you have to go by Elaine to be incognito." Rebecca grinned like Delaney was the president, vice president and secretary of the most secret organization in the world. "Your secret is safe with me."

"Secret?" Delaney felt like she had to throw up.

"I know how fans can be. The paparazzi. Geesh! They find out we have a former Miss Texas right here, live and in person, picnicking at the park and it will be a total mob. I'll keep my voice low. Wow, I can't believe I actually had lunch with Miss Texas."

"Former. And first runner-up, really. I mean, I didn't really win. It was more by default."

Rebecca continued as if Delaney hadn't said a word. "Judah said he passed your divorce case on to Lucas, but for some reason I assumed he was talking about your husband. Wait until I tell the girls in Lamaze. You're practically a celebrity."

Delaney really didn't see the purpose in lying. Rebecca already knew who she was. If she knew the whole situation, she might be less likely to accidentally spill the beans.

"Um, they *are* representing my husband."

Rebecca stopped abruptly, opened her mouth to protest, but then shut it again quickly and shifted her glance from Delaney to Lucas, who was standing just across the pond next to her husband skipping rocks. She looked back to Delaney and a chill blanketed the air, causing Delaney's skin to pimple like raw chicken.

"Oh," Rebecca whispered. They walked a few paces in silence before Rebecca quickened her pace, seemingly in an effort to get away from Delaney. She moved awful fast for a woman so far along in her pregnancy but Delaney kept up, determined not to be out-trotted by someone eight months pregnant with twins.

Rebecca, known for many things, was not known for holding her tongue. "Let me get this straight. You're sleeping with the man representing your husband in your divorce settlement?"

Under any other circumstance, Delaney might have considered herself righteously offended. Might have denied the physical relationship between herself and Lucas. Might have even told Rebecca to mind her own business. But defensiveness seemed pointless.

"I don't really have any explanations," Delaney said, her voice low and her head hung.

Rebecca shrugged. "You don't owe me any." But her tone told Delaney that she had expected one.

"We didn't know who the other one was when we . . . got involved. Then, one thing led to another and . . . look, I would like to make this sound like everything is just grand, but I know that it is not. Can we trust you to be . . . discreet?"

"I would never do or say anything that would harm Lucas. Do you know what could happen? If somebody else found out? I mean, you're picnicking in public. You're semi-famous. What if somebody snapped a picture of you two? He could lose everything."

"I've thought about that."

"Have you? Have you really thought about it?"

Delaney didn't know how to proceed. She had stayed up all night thinking about it. She had awakened that morning certain she was going to tell him that it was over. To go home and that the next time she saw him it was going to be in court. She had told herself all of that and as the sun rose she had convinced herself that was the best course of action. Then she had looked at his glorious features and remembered the tenderness with which he kissed her, held her, caressed her, and she forgot all about her lofty goals. Instead she had beat the sun up making him breakfast and playing house.

"I don't mean to come down hard on you. It's just . . . Lucas is like a brother to us. He's really special. Just don't hurt him, okay?"

"I wouldn't dream of it," Delaney rushed, surprised at the gravity of the warning.

"Dream of what?" Lucas asked as the two neared.

"Nothing," Rebecca offered quickly. "Just girl talk." She turned to Judah. "We should go."

Without a word or sign, Judah and Lucas knew that Rebecca knew.

"Why don't you make your way to the car? There's something I have to say to Judah and Rebecca," he told Delaney.

Delaney nodded. "Nice meeting you."

"You, too," Judah said. Rebecca returned the courtesy with an ice-cold stare.

"I know what you must be thinking," Lucas said as he watched Delaney get into his car.

"Good, then we don't have to tell you what an idiot you are." Rebecca, true to form, was no holds barred.

"I need your vow of confidentiality here," he said.

"I could lose my job." Judah seemed worried. "I need my job."

"I wouldn't let that happen. I'm going to work things out with this. I just need to know that you aren't going to say anything before I get a chance to figure out what to do next."

Judah stared at his lifelong friend for several heartbeats before finally acquiescing with a nod.

Lucas's eyes darted to Rebecca's dark expression. "Rebecca?"

"I think you're crazy for getting involved with her." Her words were clipped.

"We're not involved."

"A romantic picnic on a Sunday afternoon? That's what I do with random strangers, too."

"Look, I know it's not the ideal situation, but it's not like I'm marrying her. We're just . . ." He didn't have a definition. Truth be told at this point, they were just sleeping together. "You gotta help me out here. Judah, you owe me."

Lucas had saved his ass on more than one occasion. If it weren't for Lucas, Judah would have never made it through college, much less law school. Lucas had also covered for him during a brief indiscretion right before Judah and Rebecca were married. Lucas hated to say it. It wasn't a card he had ever drawn before.

"We won't say anything," Judah said.

Rebecca was less committed. "But . . ."

"We owe him. We won't say anything." Judah turned his attention back to Lucas. "But I won't cover your ass if this goes public. Get rid of her."

"She's not right for you," Rebecca added.

"You don't even know her," Lucas protested.

"I know she's using you."

"That's ridiculous. You couldn't possibly know that. You don't know what you're talking about."

"I know she's married to one of your biggest clients. I know in the two years they have been very publicly separated, he's been seen with teems of women and she's been seen with *nobody*. I know all of a sudden she's interested in dating again and it just happens to be—guess who? Her husband's lawyer. I know that's one hell of a coincidence. The only reason she's with you is so that you can screw up the divorce and she can walk her pampered ass away with a truckload of money."

"Is that what you think, too?" Lucas asked Judah.

Judah nodded. "She might have a point."

"You don't know her."

"*You* don't even know her, not really," Rebecca retorted.

"You want to know what I know? I know she's not like that."

"Correction. You *believe* she's not like that. I'm never wrong about the women you choose."

"Well, I *believe* you're wrong about her."

"Until you lose your job and she moves on to her next millionaire."

"I'm not having this discussion with you guys. Judah, I'll see you in the morning." Lucas turned on a heel and left.

"Luke!" Rebecca called after him.

But he wasn't listening.

Chapter Seventeen

The second best advice you can get from a commercial? Just Say NO!

"You're awfully quiet," Lucas said on the drive back home. "Talk to me."

Delaney had spent the bulk of the trip looking out the window. "Does Judah know about you and Rebecca?"

Lucas was surprised he didn't end up with whiplash, as fast as his head snapped. "Do *I* know about me and Rebecca?"

"The whole picnic she was acting like a jealous girlfriend."

"No. She was acting like an overprotective big sister. *You're* acting like a jealous girlfriend."

"So there's nothing between you two? Now or ever."

"When we first met, yes, I was slightly attracted to her. She's a beautiful woman; who wouldn't be? But she made it clear from day one she was only interested in Judah. We're just friends and that's all we've ever been. Now do you want to tell me what this is really about?"

Delaney sighed and pushed her head against the leather headrest. "Your friends hate me," she said without breaking her gaze from the landscape whizzing by her window.

"They don't hate you."

"Rebecca hates me."

"She doesn't hate you."

"She doesn't like me."

That he couldn't argue. "She's just worried about . . . about the consequences of what we're doing."

There was that uncomfortable silence again.

"What are we doing?" Delaney finally asked.

"I don't know." Lucas pulled into her driveway and shut off the ignition. He crossed at the front of the car to open Delaney's door and walked her up the path.

At the door, she turned and extended her hand. "Thanks. Despite it all, I really did have a good time today. You probably have a long day tomorrow, so you should be going."

It was a clear un-invite inside. Lucas tried to hide his surprise and disappointment. He had been waiting all afternoon to get his hands on Delaney, and now she was turning him away with a handshake. A handshake? Not even a kiss.

"So this is good night?" he asked.

"Yeah, this is good night."

"Look." He pulled her against his body and nuzzled his face against her neck, kissing her lightly from her collarbone to her ear. "Why don't we talk about this inside?"

"Because if we go inside we aren't going to talk. We both know what's going to happen."

"Nothing has to happen."

"This is stupid and selfish. You could lose your job."

"Why is everybody all of a sudden worried about my job? The operative word in all this is *my*. Screw my job. I don't care about my job. I have plenty of money; I don't need that job. But I do need you." He pressed forward.

"Well, you might care tomorrow. Or in fifteen minutes when you're not as . . . distracted."

Fifteen minutes was generous. With his high level of arousal he'd be lucky if he lasted five. "Delaney, *please*."

"One of us has got to stop this." She avoided making eye contact. "Good night, Luke."

"But I need you"?

Smooth, Luke, real smooth.

He started down her path, stopped, then retraced his steps back toward her door. He stopped halfway back, turned again, and then headed back to his car. He was not going to let this girl make him lose it. So they had a good conversation one night? So what?

So it was more than Lucas shared with most people. The only other person who knew about the isolation and loneliness he felt was Judah, because he had felt the same thing growing up. Lucas hadn't ever taken the time to get to know many women, but Delaney was the kind one could feel comfortable talking to about anything.

Most women had a gaggle of friends that they felt these deep inner connections with, but it was clear after their all-night conversation that Delaney shared things with him that she hadn't even shared with some of her sisters. Didn't she see what she was throwing away?

He laughed at himself. Of course she saw it. She was being perfectly logical. It was he who wasn't seeing things clearly. He was the one letting some ephemeral idea of a connection make him lose all reason and rationality. He couldn't believe he was letting some girl make him behave irrationally enough to risk his career. He was just about willing to give up everything for . . . what? A chance at the kind of relationship Judah and Rebecca had? That was a crap shoot. Dumb luck. He was a divorce lawyer, for heaven's sake! He *knew* the odds. Most people who gave up everything for love ended up like his parents; ghosts in a lifeless marriage.

Pretty girls litter Texas, buddy. She's no different, he told himself.

Now if only he could make himself believe it.

He sat in his dark car, shadowed by trees, and watched them. It wasn't the first time he had watched her. He liked to know all the players before he entered a game, so there had been several nights that he sat camouflaged by night, just watching her. Her routine was so predictable he had even grown bored with her. But now all of a sudden she was acting completely out of character. This was the second night in a row she had come home with him. The watcher hadn't factored in a boyfriend. He worried, but only slightly, that it could be a problem. He could handle the boyfriend, but he was happy to see them arguing under her porch light. Maybe this wouldn't be quite the wrinkle he thought it would be. If the boyfriend had sense, he'd walk away. No need trying to save what's already lost.

Chapter Eighteen

You win some . . . you lose more.

Judah entered the office without knocking, just as he always did, but this particular morning he was met with a dark, angry glare instead of Lucas's normal friendly hello.

"Don't you ever knock?" Lucas asked.

Judah didn't even look fazed. "No, as a matter of fact, I don't. Which you well know after twenty years."

"Screw you," Lucas said returning his focus to his laptop. "Next time knock."

"Wow. No wonder the secretaries said you're in a foul-ass mood this morning."

"I'll make sure the partners know that the clerical staff has way too much free time on their hands. Maybe if they have a bit more work, they'll spend less time at the water cooler gossiping. Don't you have some work to do? Oh I forgot, you don't actually *work* up there in corporate. You pass it along to your assistants while you kiss ass on the greens and hobnob during three-hour lunches."

"Don't take it out on me. Or them. It's not our fault."

"What exactly would 'it' be?"

"Apparently your plans to do whatever you consider yourself doing with Delaney last night went awry. It's not fair for you to take it out on the staff just because you didn't get laid last night."

"You don't know what the hell you're talking about." Lucas was growing angrier by the second.

"Don't I? Come on, Luke, I've been in your position more times than I can count. I'm more than familiar with all the telltale signs. As a matter of fact, the only guy in this world who's never been there before is . . . you. Until now, that is. Welcome to the real world—where you don't get laid every time you buy a pretty girl a drink."

Lucas's anger started to diffuse. Judah was, of course, right. He hadn't gotten fifteen consecutive minutes of sleep the night before. Every time he started to dream it was about Delaney. And the things they had done together. And the things he wanted to do with her. He'd wake up with a boner so hard he couldn't lie flat on his stomach. He had spent practically the entire evening under the cold rush of his showerhead. Still, Lucas wasn't going to admit as much.

"Don't you have some work to do?" he asked, but this time in a much kinder voice.

"Got some good news, Church," J.D.'s voice boomed on the other line of the phone.

The only good news Lucas could imagine coming from J.D. was that he had found somebody else to handle his divorce. Of course, he couldn't say that.

"What is that, Mr. Daniels?"

"Now, I told you to call me J.D., son. Anyway, it looks like Little Miss Priss has gone and mud wrestled in some shit. . . ."

Lucas tensed. What did he know? He mentally slapped himself for being stupid enough to have gone out in public with her. What if J.D. was still having her followed?

"Really?" He tried to keep his voice even. *Calm*, he told himself, *remain calm*.

"A good buddy of mine I golf with says he saw her last week at some downtown titty bar, Foxes or something."

Lucas cleared his throat and played it cool. "Foxy's. I know the place. What exactly did your friend see?" Lucas didn't want to sound too eager.

"Said she was dancing."

"Dancing? It's a club. That's not so unusual."

"Up on the stage. Shaking her ass for the whole state of Texas."

"From what you described of your wife, and from what I observed, it doesn't exactly seem like anything she would do. Did he mention anything else?" Lucas skipped a breath waiting for the answer.

"What the hell more is there to say? It was Delaney on stage getting bare-ass naked for a crowd full of drunk men."

Bingo!

"Did he actually say she got naked?"

J.D. hesitated, no doubt wondering how Lucas knew all the right questions. "Hell, no wonder I'm paying you a small fortune. You're smarter than Columbo. No, as a matter of fact, he said she left him with a goddamn raging hard-on with some *Moulin Rouge* cock-tease show."

"Then maybe she was just in a bar dancing and letting off some steam," Lucas said.

"A seedy strip club. She was dancing in a strip club. Whose lawyer are you? This is something we can use."

"Yours. And as your lawyer I don't think we should go making wild accusations about your wife when we don't know if what you are describing even happened. I fight hard but I fight clean. I'm not going to slander your wife at a cheap attempt to get a leg up on her. If we can't substantiate it, we won't use it."

"Yeah, but—"

"Your friend was drinking, I assume. Probably more than a little drunk."

"Yeah. So?"

"So could he swear, on a Bible, in a court of law, that it was Delaney?"

"You saw my wife, Luke. She's the kind who stands out in a crowd."

"Even so, Foxy's is far from seedy. It's one of the premier gentlemen's clubs of the city. Every woman who dances there is cover-girl beautiful. And while I'll admit your wife is very striking, pretty blondes in Texas are more common than sinners in hell."

J.D. scoffed and Lucas knew that he was mulling it all over. J.D. was swallowing this hook, line and sinker.

Lucas proceeded cautiously. "The lights in those places are low. Your friend was drinking. He could have been mistaken."

"Doesn't matter much. The son of a bitch owes me money. He'd swear to whatever I told him to swear to."

"That's illegal, J.D. It's called coercion. Lawrence will come up with a dozen waitresses all to testify that they served your friend drinks. Probably several of them. An eyewitness who was under the influence, substantial influence, does not make a good witness."

"So you're saying we've got nothing." It was more of a statement than a question.

"I'm saying I like to fight clean. We'll keep our eyes open."

"What about a PI?"

"You've been down that road already. Save your money. Anything we uncover about your wife at this point is still after the fact. Your extracurricular activities are already well documented, so it would just appear malicious. If we start slinging mud, the judge won't look positively on that."

"What the hell am I supposed to do? Hand her a blank check? I don't think so."

"I don't have any hat tricks. You're signing a check one way or another. It's my job to make sure you are putting as few zeroes on that check as possible."

J.D. clucked an ambiguous agreement and went on for a few minutes about his financials. "One more thing. I forgot to bring it up last week."

"What's that?"

"I want her out of that girl-power playhouse."

"What?"

"That little organization of hers where she pretties up dog-face fatties and sends them to charm school. I want control transferred to me through my corporate emissaries."

"Through the Looking Glass?"

"What?" It took a minute for the familiarity to kick in and Lucas realized J.D. didn't even know the name of the organization he was insistent on having. "Yeah, that's the one."

"Why? It's a nonprofit organization . . . what could you possibly want with it?"

"She used my funds to start it. It belongs to me."

Lucas stopped breathing. "Come on, J.D., that's our one real bargaining chip. It's the only thing she really wants. If we give her that, in all likelihood she'll compromise on everything else."

"Nothing doing." J.D. was firm.

"That organization is her life's work. If you take it, you're taking everything." Lucas hoped his eagerness wasn't betraying his cool and calm façade.

"You going soft on me, son? If she wants to start up another group through the Junior League or something, let her. But that organization has my name stamped on the bottom of the stationery, and that's the way it's going to stay. Do you have a problem with that?"

Lucas realized he had sounded too adamant. "No. I'm just not sure we want to go after her that way. It would look like we were deliberately trying to hurt her."

"To be perfectly honest, I don't care how it looks."

"With all due respect, is that why you want it? To hurt her?"

J.D. guffawed. "Hell no! I want the club because it makes me look good. Makes me look like I care about the community. Giving back and all that shit. Helps keep the government out of my pockets. Not to mention, it's my money that started that little powder-puff club. My name that's on the door as funder and founder. So you call her lawyer and you tell him that Daniels Enterprises will remain in control of the Look Good Club or whatever the hell it's called."

"Through. The. Looking. Glass," Lucas corrected before hanging up without saying good-bye.

Lucas was only certain of one thing. There was nothing good-looking about the immediate future. This was war. And this was ugly.

Chapter Nineteen

All that glitters . . . is probably Aurora Borealis Swarovski crystals.

At the same time, Delaney was across town on the phone with dozens of people regarding the annual Girls Night In! lock-in/sleepover hosted by Through the Looking Glass. It was a lot to organize: dancing and karaoke, motivational speakers and image consultants, college and career counselors. They had even hired a staff of masseuses. All services and time were donated and volunteered. The evening was free to whoever could demonstrate need, and dirt cheap to everyone else.

Delaney reclined in her chair and massaged her scalp. Every year she promised she would take on more help during the planning stages and every year, though the event had grown from twenty-four students to two hundred forty, she didn't.

"Headache?" asked Shannon, her assistant.

Delaney nodded. "I can't wait for this to all be over."

Shannon sat in the bright orange chair across from Delaney. "The event planning or the divorce?"

"Both," Delaney said, forcing a smile. "Do you have the accounts reports I asked you for?"

Shannon shook her head and looked down. "No, I haven't gotten them from J.D.'s—I mean, Mr. Daniels's—accountant yet."

"We need to get those, Shannon. You know we can be audited at any time. I would feel more comfortable having the records here. Just until we can find an independent accountant who is not associated with J.D." Delaney wanted as much of her organization away from J.D. as possible.

"Wouldn't it be best, for the organization, I mean, to just let Mr. Daniels worry about all the money and records and stuff?" She sounded nervous. Delaney was certain Shannon was worried about her job security. J.D. might be a jerk, but he was a jerk with the Midas touch. As long as the organization was funded by him, they wouldn't have to worry where the next paycheck was coming from.

"Look, the harsh reality is that J.D. and I are getting a divorce. Once we're split, the last thing he is going to want is to continue to pour money and funding into the club. I'm surprised he hasn't cut us off already. So we have to look at doing some additional fundraisers and sticking our hands in a few of the other well-lined pockets in the great state of Texas."

"I don't know."

"We can do it. We've made a real difference in this community. I've spoken with some of the teachers in the local schools and the confidence the girls are developing is starting to show in their grades and in their social interaction. There are many more around Austin that could use a community center like this one."

"It's just J.D.—I mean, Mr. Daniels—has the best accountants, the best connections, the best of everything that money can buy. I don't know where we'll find anybody as good willing to work for peanuts."

For the most part, Shannon was right. Running the center took money, lots of it. Not just for supplies and events but all the behind-the-scenes stuff that, up until now, a check signed or a phone call made by J.D. and, presto!, it happened. He had accountants who did the books every month. Lawyers who crossed *t*'s and dotted *i*'s. He had a marketing group that came up with logos and ads and a graphics company that printed their ideas. Delaney had not thought about how much work it would take to coordinate all those individuals, much less convince them to do the work for nothing or something right next to it. When the organization was tied to J.D., they were on his payroll, so they just did it. She would have to hire additional help because she suspected that over the next few weeks, she was going to spend a lot of time making phone calls. The only problem was, there was no money in the coffers to pay for that additional help. It would have to be on a strictly volunteer basis. Her headache was compounding.

She pasted on her pageant smile and said in her best interview voice, "I didn't say it was going to be easy. But this is a good organization and we do important work. Look how many girls have come to us and told us about the life-changing decisions they have made because we showed them how.

"Look at how many women can protect themselves on college campuses because of our self-defense classes. And look how many girls, who once thought they weren't worth the time of day, have gone on to graduate with honors and win tournaments because they have more confidence.

"Look, I know people drive by our Pepto-pink storefront and laugh. And I know it has taken a while for people to take us seriously. But we have made some real progress and we can keep it up even without J.D.'s money." The last thing Delaney needed was Shannon walking out on her, too. Maybe she could make it all happen, but she couldn't do it alone.

Shannon's mouth had dropped open through Delaney's impassioned speech. "You really believe in what we do," she said quietly.

"I do. And you have to believe in us, too. That is the only way we are going to be able to make it without having a cushion stuffed with millions to fall back on."

Shannon nodded. "I do . . . it's just . . . well, I'm a little anxious. I mean, I have college to pay for and rent and . . ."

"Shannon, I'm saying this to you as a promise: We will make this work."

"I'll get those financial reports as soon as possible," she said, rising from the chair and leaving the office.

"Thanks," Delaney said as she picked up the ringing phone. "Through the Looking Glass," she answered with a smile.

Lucas's stomach turned somersaults. "Good morning, Delaney."

His voice was warm and soothing like a mug of spiced cider on a cold winter's day. "Uh. Hi. I didn't think you would call."

"I wasn't going to . . ."

"But?"

He should have told her the truth. That he thought about her all night. That he couldn't stop thinking about her. He would have liked to tell her that he wanted to hear the sound of her voice. He would have liked to tell her that he couldn't go another night without her in his arms. He could have told her that a woman had never made him feel the way she had made him feel. He could have told her that for the first time in his life he wanted to do what was right, not just what was right for Lucas. But he was Lucas Church. And Lucas Church may have been called many disreputable things, but he wasn't about to add "whipped" to the list.

"There's something we need to talk about."

"I think we said everything that needed to be said last night. There really isn't any way we can go forward with whatever it was that we were doing. A clean break, I think that's best."

"This is not about us."

"Oh?"

"I wanted to give you a heads-up."

"Does this have anything to do with the divorce?"

"Yes."

"Then I think you probably shouldn't. I mean, isn't this privileged?"

"No. I've been instructed to relay the information to Lawrence. I'm just taking a shortcut." But he knew it wouldn't have mattered. Privileged or not, he probably would have told her anyway because he had bent ethics enough in defense of the scum of the earth; he was more than willing to cross the line for her.

Cross the line.

The thought rendered him speechless. At that very moment he realized he had crossed the line. It wasn't the first time he had fallen a little short of ethical. But this time he stood nothing to gain. Even worse, he could lose . . . everything.

"Lucas?"

"Huh?" He wondered how long he had been silent. How long his revelation had left his voice frozen in his throat.

"What is it you wanted to tell me?"

"It's about his intentions toward your organization."

"He doesn't have any intentions . . . Wait a minute, what is he planning to do?"

"I hate to tell you this, Delaney, but he wants to replace you as director with somebody who works directly for him and Daniels Enterprises. He wants me to contact Lawrence and draw up a conversion plan."

"Is that legalese for he's planning to steal my center right from underneath me?"

"Legally it belongs to him. With the exception of a few outside donations, its operation is funded almost wholly by Daniels Enterprises."

"It's my brainchild. I'm the one who brought up the concept with the Junior League. I'm the one who took it from a one-time spring event to a full-time job. I'm the one who's done all the work for the last three years. I'm the one who leased the building and painted the walls and scrubbed the floors and made the calls."

"And he's the one who paid for it. Mostly. Like I said, the other donations are negligible, really, when you compare it to how much money Daniels Enterprises has given."

"Then I'll pay him back. Every dime."

"It's not that simple. When he put in all that money, it was considered a charitable donation. You can't pay him back. You'd have to transfer the articles of organization and—"

"How?" Delaney cut him off.

"It is very complicated and it requires the complete cooperation of all parties involved."

"And he's not going to cooperate, is he?"

"He is adamant. He wants Daniels Enterprises to retain control of the group. He won't budge."

"Why?"

"He believes Daniels Enterprises should retain the organization for philanthropic reasons."

"Bull! There are millions of philanthropic organizations he could pour his money into. There are at least half a dozen others he funds in part."

"He's insistent on maintaining control of this one in particular."

"Well, then maybe he's using it as leverage. Maybe if I just walk away from the divorce, then . . ."

Lucas cleared his throat. "As I said, Delaney, he's adamant. He wants to retain control, regardless of what it might cost him down the line."

"He's doing this to hurt me."

He couldn't stand the sound of hurt in her voice. He gripped the pencil in his hand so tightly it left indentions on his skin.

"I've put everything I had into this organization and now you expect me to hand it over on a silver platter. I don't think so."

"There's nothing else you can do." Lucas tried to sound reasonable. He hated sounding reasonable. His father had sounded reasonable. He wasn't his father. He wasn't cold and uncaring. There was nothing else he could do. A passionate uproar would just further instigate Delaney, and J.D. had been adamant about his intentions toward the organization.

"He doesn't care about the organization. He doesn't care about these girls or what happens to them. The only person he cares about is himself. He's a slimy, repulsive monster, and I can't believe you have the audacity to represent him. But I guess the lawyer is only as good as the client he represents."

So it had come to that, had it? Lucas was not surprised. He hadn't expected any other outcome. It wasn't possible for the two of them to carry on the way they had been without his employment becoming a factor in one way or another.

"It's my job, Delaney. I don't have a choice." He tried to keep his tone measured.

"This is America, Lucas. You always have a choice."

"You're not being reasonable. What do you expect me to do? Tell J.D. to shove it? And when he asks, why don't I tell him? Hell, why don't I walk right up to the ethics committee and spill the beans? Tell them everything. Let me see, what should I say? I know. I'll say I'm refusing to further represent my client because he hurt his wife's feelings. Oh, and yeah, by the way, I forgot to mention I'm screwing his wife. Is that what you expect?"

"I expected you to be the man I thought you were."

"You don't know what you're asking me to do. The center will be fine. Lawrence and I might figure out a way to keep you on staff even if you're not the director."

"Good-bye, Lucas.

He feared this time it truly was good-bye.

Chapter Twenty

Vanessa Williams is infamous for the crown she lost, not the crown she won.

He could have sent a clerk. He *should* have sent a clerk. If he had been thinking rationally he would have sent a clerk. But Lucas Church hadn't had a rational thought with respect to Delaney Daniels since the night he met her. That was how he found himself in the lobby of Through the Looking Glass, smiling down at a plump brunette with corkscrew curls that passionately disobeyed the laws of nature.

"I've never seen so much pink in my whole life," Lucas said with a grin.

He must have startled her because at the sound of his voice she jumped and almost knocked over a can of Diet Coke and a tumbler of pens and pencils. "Hello?"

Lucas gestured around the room. The walls were peony, the leather sofa was bubblegum, the Lucite desk that protected the corkscrew brunette was rose.

Everywhere he looked it was pink. But it worked. Even all the dozens of shades, from the palest almost white to the deepest almost red, it worked.

The receptionist blushed a pretty shade that almost did her desk injustice. "Can I help you?" She batted her lengthy lashes from behind her trendy frameless glasses.

Oh yeah, he was in the right place. She had definitely studied under the tutorship of Mrs. Delaney Daniels.

"Yes. I'm Lucas." He didn't offer his last name just in case Delaney had referred to him in reference to J.D. "And I'm looking for Delaney Daniels."

"Oh." She seemed disappointed. No telling how long she had sat behind that desk waiting for her knight in worsted wool. She shrugged and returned to furiously pecking on her keyboard.

Lucas cleared his throat, reminding her of his presence. "Is she here?"

"Oh yeah, of course. But she's with a class right now. In the back. They should be out in . . . oh, about five minutes. You're welcome to go wait if you'd like."

He nodded. "I'd like."

He followed the sound of preteen giggles to a large empty room that looked very much like a dance studio. He was able to get a full view of the room from the door without disturbing the class. Delaney stood in front of a line of mismatched ten- to twelve-year-olds in a pink ballet leotard with one of those sexy, filmy skirt things tied around her waist. She demonstrated a twirl that ended with stretching one leg and Lucas stifled a groan, remembering those legs wrapped tightly around his waist.

"Practice your pirouettes, Penny," she told a stocky redhead.

Lucas winced. Who in their right mind named a

girl with copper hair Penny? Penny obediently pirou-
etted, or attempted to, since Lucas determined that
nothing that looked so bad could have a name as
beautiful and dignified as *pirouette*. She tried a second
and third time, landing on her butt each time.

Poor pudgy Penny.

"Good job. You just get better and better every day."
Delaney smiled and sounded so damn genuine that
Lucas wondered whether she would reward him with
a similar smile if he got out there and made an equally
bad attempt at a twirl.

Delaney's hair was pulled back with loose tendrils
framing her face. She was . . . beautiful. No, she was
more than beautiful—she was art. The painting *De-
spues del Baile* by Royo came to mind. Once he thought
of Royo, he thought of his Madonna pictures, *Caricia*
and *Genesis*. Once he thought of that, he started thinking of her, of Delaney, with a baby in her arms, at her
breast. His baby. Their baby. And as their baby grew,
she would love her and cuddle her and praise her as
she was doing for these girls right now. And they
would have a houseful of little Delaneys just as her
parents had and he would keep trying for a boy even
though he didn't give one eyelash what baby he had
as long as it represented their union. Then he shook
his head because he couldn't believe that in a span of
thirty seconds he had them married with children in a
four-bedroom, three-and-a-half bath brick façade
cookie cutter somewhere in the suburbs.

His friends had warned him about baby lust. As his
inner circle of friends stopped drinking and partying
and settled down to start families, he had had infrequent flashes of a prison he promised himself he
would never want. Over the last week those flashes
weren't as infrequent as they had previously been.

"You heard me! What are you doing here?" Delaney hissed.

He hadn't heard a word she said.

"What?" he asked, shaking himself out of his daydream. The girls had scattered across the room and were stuffing ballet slippers in various backpacks and duffels and tying hoodies around their waists.

"What. Are. You. Doing. Here?" She enunciated each word, but managed to keep her voice hushed so as not to rouse the interest of the eager little eyes.

"Bye, Miss Delaney."

"Bye. See ya next week, Miss Laney."

Each girl said good-bye as she scurried past Delaney and Lucas, shooting him metal smiles and freckled smirks.

"Good-bye, girls. Be careful," she called out after them.

"Cute kids," Lucas said, grinning.

"How long have you been standing here watching?" she asked.

"Long enough to know that you are really good with these girls."

"These girls . . . this center . . . is my life."

Lucas nodded. "I can't imagine anyone else doing what you do here."

"Are you saying that you are going to talk J.D. out of his plans?"

"You know I can't do that." Truth be told, he wanted to feed J.D. a knuckle sandwich and tell him to take his divorce, his corporate law contracts and his mansions full of money and go to hell. But he couldn't do that. Lucas understood why Judah had given him Daniels as a client. Judah and Rebecca were swimming, no, more like sinking, in thousands of dollars of student loan debt. If Lucas could pull a hat trick with this case, he knew that all parties involved would reap the reward. With the twins coming along and Rebecca off the job, Judah had even taken a part-time research job at a university just to make ends meet. If Lucas bungled this case, he was not only risking his reputation but also Judah's livelihood, and he couldn't do that. Lucas didn't want to betray Judah by making Delaney privy to his friend's financial distress.

"Shirking my responsibilities in this case won't do either of us any good. I could recuse myself, and maybe I should, but at this point there would a lot of questions asked. You have to trust me on this. It will hurt you more in the long run. And I don't want to see you hurt."

"Then why are you here? Exactly?" She eyed the envelope he was nervously shifting from hand to hand.

He gave it to her. "Some preliminary numbers."

"Why didn't you just courier them to Lawrence? Or send a clerk?" She folded her arms across her chest.

Lucas shrugged. "So sue me, I wanted to see you."

As far as she was concerned, she was less tempted to sue him and more tempted to kiss him. She forced herself not to smile because she didn't want to be happy with the fact that he was standing in front of her. She didn't want to care that he had made a special trip to see her. She didn't want to admit to herself that she wanted to see him just as badly. She didn't have to admit it because he had been all she was able to think about for the last four days. The more she thought about him the more she wanted to be with him. Underneath him. Writhing. And moaning. And screaming. Oh God, how he had made her scream.

She raked her teeth across her bottom lip and in nanoseconds ticked off reasons she shouldn't kiss him and dozens of reasons why she should. In fact, she wanted to do more than kiss. Much *much* more. Several seconds passed between them, looking at each other. Wanting each other. So she did it. She grabbed him by the lapels and pulled him to her and swore to herself, *Just one kiss.*

After a split second, his mouth opened on top of hers, his tongue plunging into her mouth. He pulled her in closer.

She wasn't sure how long they had been kissing when they first heard the snicker, but she was certain they both heard it at the same time, their lips frozen together. He quickly broke off and glanced over his shoulder.

"Hi . . . uh, Penny, is it?"

Delaney groaned. Of all the girls it had to be Penny. Penny, who had the propensity to repeat everything she saw and heard.

The girl nodded; red ringlets rebounded and recoiled around her face. Delaney turned to face Penny and started to move away, but Lucas kept a firm grip on her arm, immobilizing her.

She looked up with questioning eyes and when he raised his brows and widened his eyes she understood she shielded his very noticeable hard-on.

"Are you Miss Delaney's boyfriend?"

"Uh . . . no . . . Delaney and I are just friends."

"Friends don't kiss friends like that. 'Cause I'm friends with Hunter Campbell and he won't even hold my hand. Princes kiss princesses like that, like Cinderella and Snow White and Jasmine, and Lil' Mermaid . . ."

Delaney stifled a groan. Penny was very likely to cover fifty years of Disney animation. "Penny?" she interrupted with a pleasant smile.

". . . right before they get married. Are you getting married?"

"No!" Lucas quickly answered.

"Everyone loves Miss Delaney," Penny continued. "So if you don't you're a meanie or a dummy. Or both."

Delaney caught the rising giggles in her throat.

Lucas elbowed her to the side. The coast was clear now, and he bent to meet Penny eye to eye. "I think you're right." He tousled her copper curls. "And I'll tell you what. If I ever wise up and decide to marry Delaney, you'll be the first to know."

Penny nodded and threw her duffel over one shoulder. "Deal," she said, extending her hand.

"Deal." Lucas returned the shake.

In that moment, Delaney realized what a wonderful father Lucas would make. She shook the thought out of her head practically the second it entered. She should not be thinking about this man fathering children because it made her wish he was fathering *her* children and that just wasn't practical or possible.

Penny marched out of the room.

"Penny is . . . precocious," Delaney informed Lucas.

"That's the understatement of the year. But she's cute, you know."

"I can't wait to have a load of my own," Delaney said wistfully.

"I think you will be very happy with them."

"Kids?" Delaney asked, confused.

"The preliminaries. J.D. has already agreed to almost everything you and Lawrence asked. I'm sure you'll be very happy with the final numbers." He shuffled his feet against the wood floor.

She opened the envelope and took her time as she examined the pages. Her ire elevated with each line she considered. To think, just moments ago she had been kissing him. She shook her head and then stuffed the papers back into the envelope.

"Not interested."

"What? How are you not interested? We were very, *very* generous. Overly generous. Insanely generous."

"Oh, you're insane all right, if you think you can buy my cooperation." She shoved the envelope at his chest. "You want me to hand over the directorship like a good little beauty queen and fly off to my new vacation home in Antigua and order up a froo-froo umbrella drink and a pedicure. Well, it ain't happening. No way. This is my organization and these girls need me. I'm not going to walk out on them like everybody else has in their lives."

"You gotta be kidding me. You're kidding me, right? You know what? You aren't looking at this with a clear head. Why don't you just take this, let Lawrence look over it. He'll tell you that you couldn't ask for better if you had written that settlement yourself." He tried to pass the envelope back to her.

"Listen carefully. I'll talk real slow and use small words. No. Dice. I won't consider anything that doesn't allow me to maintain my position here. You go back and you tell J.D. to take his 1.5 million per year and shove it."

"So you're turning us down?" Lucas said.

"That's right. I'm turning you down."

Delaney breezed past Lucas, leaving him alone. Again.

Chapter Twenty-one

Don't grow up to be the beauty queen whose sole objective in life is to find love on The Bachelor *or become the next "Barker's Beauty."*

Delaney hurried to the bank. She couldn't believe she had let herself get all worked up over Lucas again. She had promised herself he was strictly hands-off. There was something about him. He was her forbidden fruit. Her personal Pandora's box. Every time he showed up in her life, something bad was certain to happen. Unfortunately, when it came to Lucas, she didn't learn from experience.

"Get it together, sister," she told her reflection as she fanned her bangs from her forehead in the rearview mirror. She couldn't allow herself to lose track of what was important. The center was important. The girls at the center were important. Splendid, enchanting, intoxicating sex with Lucas Church was . . . less important. Because it was just sex. Even if he made her mouth dry and her heart race at wicked speeds. Even if he rendered her speechless. Even though he was the first and only man on the planet who actually looked inside her instead of just *at* her. Even with all that, it all boiled down to simply great sex. At least that's what she coached herself into thinking. She wasn't ready to consider the alternative.

Besides, she had more important issues to think about now that J.D. had set the wheels in motion to take over the center. She needed to find financial backers, but in order to woo those backers, she needed to know exactly where the organization stood. No company was going to hand them money if they didn't know exactly how it would be spent. She would have to get the bank records, have their accountant prepare financial statements, and come up with a prospectus. She didn't have much time.

"How are things going, Adriana?" Delaney asked the pretty young teller.

Adriana had been one of the first girls to visit the center. At the time, she had been overly shy and introverted, still a senior in high school. Delaney suspected abuse from alcoholic parents had turned Adriana into a shrinking violet. Adriana had had absolutely zero self-confidence the first day Delaney went to the high school to speak to the girls about an alternative to after-school video games and mall crawling. As Delaney had discussed the activities, such as learning second or third languages, dance lessons, etiquette, Adriana's face lit up. Delaney had managed to work her out of her shell and, when Adriana graduated, helped her get a job as a teller at the bank and enroll in community college. Now, just under three years later, she had an associate's degree, she had been recently promoted to teller supervisor, and she was making plans to attend a four-year university to work on her bachelor's degree. Sadness pierced Delaney's heart to think that she wouldn't be able to help more girls like Adriana.

Stop it! Don't be defeatist! He hasn't won yet and he's not going to. Not without a fight.

"You made it just before closing." Adriana smiled at Delaney.

"Sorry. Do you mind?" Delaney asked, passing Adriana a large stack of checks.

"Of course not." She processed the transaction quickly and thanked Delaney.

"Um, I'll need a receipt," Delaney gently reminded her.

"Oh. Well, I can mail one to the address on the account, but I can't give you the receipt since it has the account balance on it."

Delaney didn't really understand her reasoning. "You've always given me the receipts before, Addy."

"Yeah, but that was when you were on the account." Adriana blushed furiously. Adriana hated saying no to the one person in the world who had told her yes, but the rules were rules and the privacy policy was not one that could be bent.

"You must be mistaken. I'm the director, Addy. Of course I'm on the account."

Even though Delaney didn't think it was possible, Addy turned three shades redder. Addy looked at the computer monitor, pecked several keys on the keyboard, then returned her gaze to Delaney. "Not anymore. I'm sorry, but your name has been removed."

"By whose order? I never signed anything authorizing my name to be removed," Delaney said.

Addy shrugged. "I can't say exactly who did it, but normally on business accounts they only have to have a letter signed by all the officers to add or remove names. That would be the president, V.P., secretary and treasurer. You being director, that's a real important job and all, but if you're not an officer of the organization, it simply doesn't matter."

"So now you can't give me any information on the account."

"No, ma'am."

"But I can continue to make deposits."

"Yes, ma'am."

Delaney rubbed her temples.

Damn J.D.!

He was doing everything in his power to rip the center right out from under her. Her head pounded.

"Ms. Daniels?"

"I'm sorry. I know you're closing." Delaney started to gather her stuff from the teller counter.

"No, I was just going to say that probably whoever changed the names on the account might not know anything about the Internet banking you set up last year."

Delaney gave her a questioning glance. She could tell Adriana was thinking carefully about her phraseology so as not to violate any bank policy.

"What?"

"I mean, changing the names is just a branch function. Just a contract that tells us who can do what. But it doesn't change the status of the account. Or any of the features that might have been added to the account. And unless we are instructed to do so, it is not the course of normal business for us to make any changes to the Web banking account. We would leave those sign-ons and passwords intact unless the customer told us to change them. Everyone always forgets to change those when they make other changes on the account. Usually."

Delaney nodded understanding. She had access to

everything online! J.D. wouldn't imagine that she had set up an Internet banking account. He thought she was too dumb to know how to turn on the computer.

"Thank you, Adriana."

"Not a problem. I owed you one." She winked and pushed her shiny brown hair away from her face as she walked Delaney to the door. "Have a nice day!" Adriana called out as Delaney left.

Delaney sat over stacks of the center's monthly statements that she had printed from the online banking option. She was beginning to seriously regret that she had never taken any time to examine the records before now. Playing catch-up after three years was almost impossible. After several hours of trying to decipher some of the large deposits and wire transfers, she called Shannon.

"I'm sorry to bother you so late, Shannon, but I was going over some of the statements for the center."

"Statements?" Shannon asked.

"Yes. Did you ever look over these when they came in the mail?"

"Um . . . no. I just handed them right over to the accountant. Is . . . is there something the matter?" Delaney could hear the alarm in Shannon's voice and wanted to put her at ease, but she wasn't certain herself if ease would be appropriate.

"No. Yes. Well, really, I don't know. It seems like the deposits made after our fund drives are . . . larger than I remember. Then there are several wire transfers to banks I've never heard of. . . . Does any of this sound familiar?"

"No, ma'am . . . but . . . but I'm not on the account so I never really bothered checking the statements."

Neither am I.

"So I really wouldn't know what happened," Shannon continued.

"I know, but you made the deposits, right? Would you remember any of these numbers if I showed you the statements?"

"I don't know . . . I make a lot of deposits. A lot. It would be hard, really hard for me to remember anything specific if it wasn't recently."

"Of course. It's just . . . I really don't remember ever raising this much money at any of the events."

"Well, you know how it can be. Sometimes people can go home and then decide to mail in a check later. I used to get a lot of checks in the mail that I would add to our deposits. Maybe that's what happened."

"Maybe." Delaney chewed on her bottom lip. She wished there was a way to get copies of the deposited items. She should know who was donating the funds to the club so she could write them thank-you letters. And even though some very wealthy people donated strictly out of altruism, surely at least one of them wanted a receipt or something for tax purposes. There was little chance of her being able to request any research now that she had been removed from the account.

"What about the wire transfers? Do you know anything about them? Why would we be transferring money out of our account and where is it going?"

"Really, Delaney, I wouldn't know."

Delaney sighed. "Of course not. I'm sorry. I don't mean to be giving you the third degree or anything."

"Maybe these are all questions for J.D. Or the accounting firm.

"You're right."

I just don't think I'll be getting any answers.

"Will you set up an appointment for me, please, with Mr. Schuyler? As soon as possible."

"No problem. Oh and while you're there, maybe you can ask him about our retirement plans."

"What about them?"

"Haven't you opened your statements?" Shannon inquired.

Delaney shook her head and thought about the pile of mail sitting on her computer desk. She didn't go to her mailbox often, much less actually open her mail. It seemed her mailbox had become roost to every bill collector in Texas. Opening an envelope these days was like playing financial Russian roulette.

"I don't know. There's just some weird stuff I don't quite understand. Last year it looked like I could retire a multi-millionaire at forty. But over the last six months my balances have really dropped. And there are a lot of trade transactions I don't really understand. Anyway, every time I call the program administrator I get the runaround, so maybe Mr. Schuyler knows of some safer investing options."

Delaney nodded, unsure. "I'll be sure to ask him when we meet."

"Oh, by the way, J.D. will be at the benefit tonight."

"The benefit?" Delaney shuffled through some of the mail. There were half a dozen unopened fat invitation-sized envelopes.

"The Heart Ball. For the American Heart Association. You're still planning on attending, right? Because when the office didn't receive your RSVP they called to verify that you would be there since you and J.D. have always been such big supporters. I told them you would. I thought I reminded you a few weeks ago."

Delaney nodded. With the events of the last several days, the Heart Ball had slipped her mind entirely. She would be receiving an award *with* J.D.—Mr. and Mrs. James David Daniels, courtesy sponsors of the Austin Heart Walk. She sighed. They weren't even together when J.D. had made that donation, but her name was on the check and so the award was being presented jointly. They would have seats together, no doubt.

"Yes, I plan on going. I guess it just slipped my mind. Maybe I'll ask J.D. about this when I get there. Thanks, Shannon."

Chapter Twenty-two

Grown men don't stay up all hours of the night to watch a talent competition.

All the men were strutting around in their designer Italian tuxedos and the belles were sparkling and glittery in their crimson, cherry and ruby sequins. Except for Delaney, who had donned her signature pink, a brilliant watermelon shade.

She and J.D. had come in separate vehicles, but as she suspected, their table was together, front and center. She said a silent prayer of thanks when she realized he had not brought Misty. Delaney wondered what extravagant bauble had appeased her this time.

"Hello, James." He *hated* being called James.

"Delaney."

"I hardly recognized you without your girlfriend in tow."

"She couldn't make it."

"Awww . . . too bad. Past her curfew?"

"Cute. I see you're here with an empty arm as well.

Though that doesn't surprise me. Barbie dumped Ken. You with a date? Why, he might actually try to kiss you and smudge your perfect lipstick." He assessed her dress, the plunging neckline in the front, the deep V that darted and arrowed to the small of her back. She looked good, and she knew it. "Of course with that dress, I'd say you are dressed for the husband hunt. Is that what my money is paying for these days?" he sneered.

So he was going to start right in on her. She felt her ire rise to all-new highs and she welcomed the relative privacy provided by the nearly empty corridor.

"You haven't given me a dime in over six months, and you know it." She wasn't about to tell him she'd had to take a position as an image consultant at an exclusive boutique, although most of the wives at the country club shopped there, so the information had probably already trickled down to J.D.

"Let's try to make it through this evening without the dramatics," J.D. said. The entire time he spoke to her he looked over her head and smiled and waved at familiar faces.

"Fine, but after this is over, we have something important to discuss."

The dinner was expectedly bland, the speakers predictably boring and the awards unsurprisingly long. When it came time for J.D. and Delaney to accept their award, they stood and he raised his arm to wave to the attendees and gallantly helped Delaney up the stage stairs. He wrapped his arm around her waist as the emcee gushed on about Daniels Enterprises' support for the advanced science of cardiology. To anybody who didn't know them, they looked like a happy couple smiling under the blinding white lights of flashbulbs. It was less than a minute, but it felt like hours until Delaney was comfortably back in her seat at her table, and it felt like days until the dinner was over and the group was escorted to a different ballroom for dancing and cocktails.

Delaney pulled on J.D.'s arm before he could escape.

"I didn't know you were that eager to dance with me, filly," J.D. said to her. He pulled her onto the dance floor. He was smiling, his eyes gleaming. Delaney recognized that look. It was the look he always got when he thought he was going to get laid. He was either crazy or drunk if he thought he was taking her to bed tonight, but she followed his lead as they glided across the dance floor. There was no sense in unnecessarily agitating him when she still needed his cooperation.

"We need to talk about the center," she said against his shoulder.

"Then I would advise you to contact my attorney. I pay him well to handle you." His voice was smooth as silk. Absolutely nothing ruffled J.D. Daniels.

Heat flooded Delaney's face and she wondered if she was blushing as brightly as she burned. She couldn't help the way her thoughts wandered to Lucas and the way he touched her. The way he finger combed her hair when he thought she was sleeping. What she wouldn't give to be in his arms right now. But it wasn't possible. Lucas was representing her husband in the ugliest divorce since the *War of the Roses*. Delaney Daniels, the girl with the perfect face and the perfect body had fallen for the most imperfect man in the world.

If only you knew. Advising me to contact your attorney would be the last thing on your agenda.

"This is not about the divorce. This is about the center."

"Again, a matter for our attorneys. Dance with me, filly. Let's leave all this nonsense about divorce outside the door. Just for tonight."

Delaney pressed on. "You've taken my name off the bank accounts."

"I heard you were in somewhat of a financial bind. I didn't know how desperate the situation might become. I've heard that recently you would do just about anything for money." His look was smug.

Delaney's pulse raced. Did he know about her dancing at Foxy's? She couldn't imagine him knowing something like that and not using it immediately to his benefit to hurt her or disparage her name.

She wet her lips, praying he wouldn't discern anything was amiss. "I would never funnel money from the organization. You know that. Besides, there are other things, things I don't understand, on the statements. While I am still director, I have a right to know what's going on, and I need to have access to those accounts."

"You won't be director for long, so don't worry your pretty little head about it. Thank you for making a perfectly pleasant dance an intolerable chore." He made a move to brush past her.

"Do not blow me off! This is important to me." Her voice was slightly raised and seemed even louder as the few clusters of people around them hushed and looked their way.

J.D. smiled and nodded to them. "You are making a spectacle of yourself, Delaney," he hissed. His eyes cruised her body again from head to toe. His tone changed from piss and vinegar to sugar and spice. "If you have something that is that important to talk about, why don't we go back to the ranch and talk about this like civilized adults?" His honeyed words suggested he wanted more than talk.

"You're kidding me, right? I'm *not* going home with you."

"Pity." He trailed a finger down the column of her

throat. He leaned in and whispered against her ear, "I could still be convinced to change my mind, you know. I mean, perhaps you could use some of your talents to persuade me to drop all the nonsense with your little club."

"What are you suggesting?" Her words were cold and clipped.

"Look, I don't know what's going on with the bank accounts. Schuyler mumbled something to me about the center the last time we met. *He's* the one who thought it would be a good idea if Daniels Enterprises maintained directorship of the center for the tax breaks. That organization doesn't mean anything to me. So why don't we just go back to the ranch and figure this all out?"

Delaney pushed away from J.D. and looked into his eyes. They were crystal clear, missing the normal mischievous glint.

"J.D," she warned.

"Chubby preteens in tutus and painting aprons? Come on, you know me better than that."

She had known him better than that. J.D despised the center. He hated going to all the charitable functions Delaney forced him to attend. That was precisely why it had come as such a surprise that he wanted anything at all to do with the center, much less retain exclusive directing of it. His tone was silky smooth but she blamed that on the liquor, on the late evening, on her dress even. . . . She chewed her bottom lip, contemplating the idea. If she could get him to sign something, anything, tonight, he wouldn't be able to go back on his word tomorrow.

"You can follow me in your own car. If we can't come to some sort of agreement . . ." He eyed her full cleavage. "Or if things get too . . . heated . . . for you,

you can go and leave all this nonsense to the attorneys. Surely after five years of marriage . . . the two of us can come to some sort of compromise."

"I'm not going to bed with you," she told him as she let him guide her out of the ballroom.

He chuckled low. "Let's not go making any rash decisions right away. Let's just see where things go."

"Mr. and Mrs. Daniels . . . one more picture?" A photographer stopped them on their way out. As the bulb flashed, for some reason Delaney remembered how people of certain religious beliefs felt a picture stole their soul. An eerie chill crawled along her spine and prickled her flesh. At this moment she understood the sentiment.

"Why don't we just work out a compromise? You'd like that, wouldn't you?" J.D. asked Delaney for what was probably the fiftieth time. Once they had gotten back to the ranch he had turned into Doc Ock, his hands all over Delaney.

"Where's Misty?"

"Gone to her mother's or something. We have the entire place to ourselves. We can do . . . whatever."

"Are you out of your mind? Did you actually think I came back to the ranch to sleep with you? I came back here to talk about a reasonable settlement."

"Lucas presented you with a reasonable settlement already. He said you turned him down flat."

"A reasonable settlement that includes Through the Looking Glass."

"Don't you ever get tired of saying the same thing over and over again?" J.D. sighed heavily. "Why are you being so ornery, filly?"

Delaney hated when he talked down to her like she was a five-year-old. "I'm not going to hand over all my hard work on a silver platter. If I'm going down, I'm going down with a fight." She paced the length of his study.

She and J.D. had been sparring for the better part of an hour and her nerves were wearing thin. She realized now that he hadn't asked her back to the ranch to negotiate anything other than positions in bed.

"You either budge on the center, or I swear I'm going for the jugular on alimony. I'll milk you for every dime you have." She didn't even recognize her own voice uttering the words. Who had she become in the last two weeks? Exotic dancing in strip clubs, sleeping with the enemy and now, heavens to Mary, an alimony shrew? She wasn't even interested in the money.

J.D. chuckled. "You're no match for me, little girl. It is going to take a hell of a lot more than a pretty face, big boobs and a tight ass to go up against me. Take my advice: *Don't* fight me." His voice had an edge to it. Delaney began to realize that he was serious about taking over the organization. She didn't know if he was just doing it to hurt her or if there was another motive, but J.D. had his game face on now and he only wore that when he was taking over a Fortune 500 company and reducing it to a house of cards.

"I'll fight you with my dying breath," Delaney said through clenched teeth.

J.D.'s gray eyes turned cold. Dead. "Drop it. Drop it all. Put your efforts toward finding yourself a rich old man with one foot in the grave. Maybe he won't tire of you before he kicks the bucket."

For the first time ever in her life, Delaney struck another person. She slapped J.D. so hard it stung her hand for several tens of seconds. "Go to hell." As she walked away, she was taunted by his low, vile chuckling.

* * *

"What was that about?" asked Paul, J.D.'s younger brother, as he happened upon the end of the argument.

J.D. passed his brother a flute of champagne. The two men looked enough alike to be identical twins with the same height, build, steel gray eyes and salt-and-pepper hair. Throughout his brother's marriage, J.D. knew Paul had been intrigued with Delaney. He used to lament that had he not been caught in traffic on I-35, *he* would have been the brother representing Daniels Enterprises at the ribbon cutting where Delaney and J.D. had met.

"What are you doing here?" J.D. asked him without an attempt to camouflage his irritation.

"I saw the two of you leave the ball together. Thought it might make for some healthy entertainment when I realized you were coming back here."

"Bullshit. You were following me."

"I just don't want you getting . . . distracted. Or forgetting what's important here."

J.D. laughed low. Sinister. If only Paul knew. He was no more interested in getting Delaney in bed than he was in growing a second penis. But Paul didn't know and that was exactly how J.D. wanted to keep it.

"You never answered my question," Paul said. "What was that about?"

"Nothing. She's just got her feathers ruffled over the Looking Glass account."

Paul's ears burned. "What of it?"

"It's nothing. I removed her name, just like I said I would, and she's upset."

"No, you said she wouldn't even notice."

J.D. shrugged. "I was wrong. Normally that chubby little receptionist of hers makes the deposits and all the statements are sent directly to Schuyler. How was I supposed to know Delaney would start making deposits?"

"So she's suddenly taken an interest in accounting?"

"Apparently she's gotten the idea in her head that

she can secure funding and donations from private sources and thereby remove the center as one of our ventures. She's been calling everybody we know trying to get money. She wants to sever the Looking Glass's alliances from Daniels Enterprises and she thinks if she gets alternative funding she'll have something to fight us with."

"This isn't good. We wouldn't be in this mess at all if it weren't for your greed."

"I got us into this mess, and I'll get us out, little brother."

"But if she's asking questions . . ." Paul insisted.

"It's nothing," J.D. assured him. "Business as usual. We stick to the plan. Understand?"

"I think we should consider a contingency."

"We stick to the plan. No deviations."

"Very well. I trust you know what you're doing," Paul told his brother as he left the house.

J.D. grinned. He knew exactly what he was doing. In time enough, so would everyone else. He retrieved the champagne flute his brother had been drinking from and placed it in a Ziploc bag along with a second one Delaney had used. Dumb blonde had followed him right back to the house under the impression that she could cajole and seduce him into changing his mind. He grinned wider. Little did she know in a matter of days, the directorship of that stupid center would be the least of her problems. He unlocked a drawer of his credenza and placed the flutes alongside one of Delaney's old brushes. Thank goodness she never cleaned her brushes. Her hair was a shade blonder from the summer sun but the detectives would overlook a detail like that. He locked the drawer and leaned back in his executive chair. Regardless of what Paul believed, things were going *exactly* according to plan. His plan.

Chapter Twenty-three

Once you win a major title, there's always a camera somewhere. Get used to it.

It had only been four days since Lucas last saw Delaney, but it felt like four years. He had debates with himself every morning in the shower listing the pros and cons of contacting her, always winding up with more cons than pros. He couldn't explain his attraction to her and was beginning to wonder if it was more than an attraction. There was a magnetism. He was drawn to her. Like flies to honey. He winced. Why did people say always say you could catch more flies with honey?

Twice Lucas had driven by her house, telling himself that if her custom pink convertible was in the drive he'd knock. It wasn't either time. Four times he'd called the center and talked to Shannon, who in her singsong receptionist voice told him that Mrs. Daniels wasn't in and that she was not at liberty to divulge her schedule but that she would be more than happy to take down his name and number, neither of which he offered. Once he'd even gotten desperate enough to call Lawrence's offices to see if he could get her home number. But the matronly sounding receptionist informed him that releasing that information would violate attorney-client privilege. She had absolutely no song in her voice.

He realized he was developing into a borderline stalker, so he took the same stance regarding Delaney as he would any addiction. He quit. Cold turkey. He didn't think about her, or if he did catch himself in random thoughts of her, he didn't allow himself to linger on the thoughts overly long. He timed each thought, ninety seconds to seventy-five to fifty to thirty-three—with each instance devoting less and less time to her until, by day four, it was just brief clips of her eyes, her lips, her smile. . . .

"This is crazy." He ran his hands over his face and pushed them through his hair.

"Tell me you aren't still thinking about that girl," Judah said, entering the office.

Lucas's head shot up and he glared at Judah. "Go. Away." Lucas scowled. "Didn't I ask you to knock?"

"My bad." Judah threw two hands in the air as he backed out of the office. He stopped in the doorway and knocked three times.

Lucas sighed and couldn't help but crack a smile. "Come in."

"You need to get out. Get Delaney off your mind."

"I've been out the last four nights," Lucas said, pretending to be engrossed in a case file he knew nothing about.

"Out someplace other than trolling Delaney's neighborhood," Judah suggested.

"What the hell do you know?" Lucas asked. It was the only response he could gather. It didn't make any sense to attempt a lie; Judah could read the truth on his face as if it were printed in big red letters.

Judah dropped the daily paper on Lucas's desk. "I know if you had been out last night, you might have seen this." He tapped the front page of the society section.

In full color was a picture of Delaney in an incredibly sexy pink dress, arm in arm with none other than J.D. Daniels. Underneath the photo was the caption: "Reconciliation?" The brief blurb beneath the picture described how J.D. and Delaney had attended the annual charity benefit, their first time being seen in public together in over a year.

Together?

The two had arrived separately but eaten together, received a commendation together and were seen chatting it up together. They shared a dance just before Mrs. Daniels quickly exited with Mr. Daniels not too far behind. A second picture of them, in the lobby of the hotel where the ball had been held, showed them exiting. Together.

"So they were at some gig at the same time." Lucas pushed the paper across the desk a little more roughly than he intended.

"Together," Judah said, as if he could hear Lucas's thoughts. "They ate together. They danced together. They left . . ." he paused, ". . . together."

"You don't know that."

"They say a picture is worth a thousand words."

"It's circumstantial. Doesn't mean anything," Lucas argued.

"You're arguing law? This isn't circuit court. I'm your best friend. And I'm looking out for your best interest."

"Shoving this shit in my face is my best interest?"

"Hell yes! How many times have you saved my ass

from making the biggest mistake of my life? I'm just trying to return the favor."

"Do me a favor and stay the hell out of my personal life," Lucas growled.

"I know it's hard for you face the facts. . . . I don't want to see you hurt in this. If you were thinking about your relationship with her going somewhere . . ."

"I'm over her, all right? It was a stupid fling and it's over. I'm not thinking about her at all."

Judah stood to leave, pushing the paper back toward Lucas. "Good idea. If you know what is best for your career, what's best for you . . . you'll forget about her. Forget you ever met her."

For reasons not entirely clear to her, the first person Delaney thought about when she saw the picture and misleading caption in the paper was Lucas Church. She thought about the calls from him she had been avoiding. If Lucas saw that picture of her and J.D. taken at the Heart Ball, their almost intimate pose, he could conclude that they were reconciling when nothing could be further from the truth.

Even though it was against her better judgment, and though it took her the better part of an hour to get up the courage, she finally picked up the phone and called Lucas.

"Church," he answered.

"Lucas?" Her voice was uncertain but she knew by his long pause that he recognized it immediately.

"Yeah?"

"It's me, Delaney."

Longer pause. "Yeah?"

"I was just . . ."

"You finally decided to return my calls." His voice was cold and clipped.

Delaney inhaled deeply, not wanting to be discouraged by his evident anger. "I didn't call you before because I thought we needed a little bit of a . . . cooling-off period."

"Cooling off, huh? Sure you weren't just getting all hot and bothered somewhere else?" he asked.

"I'm not sure what you're talking about." She had a pretty good idea of what he was thinking, but she thought maybe if she rushed into a defense it would just make her look like she had some reason to feel guilty.

"Never mind." He waited for her to proceed. This time her pause was long and meaningful.

"This is kind of awkward."

"Then it should be a cake walk for you . . . you're so good with awkward," he said.

"I don't know if you get the paper . . ."

"Oh, I got it," he said quickly.

"Oh. Okay then. I don't know if you saw the society page . . ."

"Saw it."

"Well, okay. Um . . . I just wanted to call and explain . . ."

"Why you were out painting the town with the soon-to-be ex you claim to despise?"

"Exactly. Well, no, not exactly. We weren't out on the town together. We were just at the same place at the same time." Even to her it sounded stupid.

"Most would call that together."

"But we weren't. Together, I mean. I mean, we were there together but not technically. But we didn't come together."

"But you left together."

"No."

"You didn't?"

"We did . . . but we didn't."

"That makes perfect sense."

"What I mean to say is that we left together but we weren't together. Not really."

"So you didn't come together, you're sure of that. When you got there you were together, but you weren't. You left together . . . but not really?"

"Exactly."

"Rrrright . . . You know what? It doesn't really matter. You can spend your time with whomever you want."

"I know that. I just didn't want you to think . . ."

"Why would you care what I think, Delaney? We aren't anything to each other. Just a one-night stand that lasted a bit too long."

"That's not true and you know it. A lot more happened between us."

"I really can't discuss this at work," he said, lowering his voice.

"Then meet me."

"I don't think that's a good idea either."

"You know you can't believe everything you read."

"No, but a picture is worth a thousand words."

"It's not what it looks like," she insisted. She looked at the picture. J.D.'s arms were wrapped around her waist. He was smiling at Delaney and she beamed back up at him. To anyone else, they would look like a happy couple. But her smile was joyless. It was her pageant smile. Maybe Lucas Church didn't know that smile. It was a smile that had charmed and fooled a thousand pageant judges in her lifetime. It meant Delaney knew she was on stage, knew she was being photographed, knew that she had to look, to *be* perfect. But besides being the perfect smile, it didn't mean anything.

"You don't understand. We . . . not we . . . J.D. and his wife, whoever that might be, have a public persona they have to put on. It is what is expected."

"And you always do exactly what's expected of you, right?"

"Yes. No. I mean . . . sometimes, yes, I do what's expected of me. And J.D. does what's expected of him."

"Did you expect him to have his hands all over you like a cheap wet suit?"

"That was just for the cameras. We can't drag our bitter, nasty divorce to every function with us like it's next season's handbag."

"Why did you leave with him?" he asked, softening a little.

"I thought if I was nice to him he might drop the nonsense with the center." She grimaced the minute the words left her mouth.

"Just how nice?" Lucas's voice went icy again.

"I didn't mean that the way it came out. I just thought if we could discuss things like civil adults, we might come to some sort of agreement."

"I already told you he wasn't willing to budge on that issue. Didn't you believe me?"

"I didn't know what to believe. What I knew for sure is that J.D. is a sucker for a pretty face and a pouty smile. . . . I thought if I flirted with him a little he might remember some of the good times we had and he might not be so intent on taking away the one thing important to me. There's almost nothing I wouldn't do to make sure that I keep my center."

"What is *that* supposed to mean?"

"If that means that if I have to play by his rules, then," she paused, chewing on her words for a moment, ". . . then I'll do whatever it is I have to do."

Uncomfortable silence followed. Delaney wasn't sure how far she was willing to go, but at the moment there were three dozen girls who had never had anybody willing to fight for them. She didn't want to be just another adult in their lives who had given up when the game got tough.

Lucas finally spoke. "If you want to go back to your husband who lied to you, who cheated on you, that's your prerogative. My opinion shouldn't matter to you at all."

Delaney couldn't believe her ears. Lucas was speaking irrationally. "I don't want to be with him. Did you hear that either of us wanted to stop the divorce proceedings?"

"It's a little early yet. I'm guessing I should expect his call closer to noon. I know how a night with you can wear a man out."

"That was just plain rude."

"You could take it as a compliment," he added callously.

"You're acting like a jealous boyfriend," Delaney said.

"Is that it with you two? He got a girlfriend so you decide to one-up him with a boyfriend? Maybe now it gets kinky—watching and swapping? Too bad. Misty really isn't my type."

"You are disgusting. I don't know what I ever saw in you."

"Let me remind you: toe-curling, name-screaming, mind-blowing orgasms. As in multiple."

Delaney slammed down the phone without dignifying his statement with a reply.

Delaney Daniels, you sure can pick 'em.

The watcher smiled down at the photograph that headlined the society page. He couldn't plan this better if he were writing a script. The whole cast were like puppets, dangling and dancing exactly as he wanted, as he needed.

Chapter Twenty-four

There are fifty-one girls on stage, and only one is going home Miss America.
All the others need a plan B.

J.D.'s secretary, Ruby, an overly thin woman in her mid-forties with strong equine features, tapped furiously on the keys of her keyboard. She glanced up occasionally at Delaney and offered a tight, uncomfortable smile.

"I'm sure it will be only a minute more."

Delaney nodded. J.D. was a busy man. She didn't have an appointment and so she hadn't expected she would be able to float right in to speak with him. She had known that if she had attempted to make an appointment, the chances were better that he would refuse to see her. So she had taken her chances, asked Shannon to cover the center and come straight to J.D's office to wait him out. She didn't know how much good it would do to try to appeal to his better senses once again, but now that Lucas wasn't in her corner, she had to try something.

Delaney had hoped that by arriving early she would catch him before the stress of the day made him unreasonable. Unfortunately, at the moment he was in a shouting match behind the heavy mahogany doors. At one point the yelling was so loud that both Delaney and Ruby started a little.

"Should you check on them?" Delaney asked Ruby.

"It is only Paul. You know, sibling rivalry." She didn't bother to look up and continued to peck furiously on her keyboard.

Delaney nodded. It wasn't a secret that there was no love lost between Paul and J.D. Sibling rivalry was an understatement if there ever was one. From the day she had met Paul, she had never known him to share a civil word with J.D. She knew Paul had no kind sentiments regarding their marriage. Delaney always believed that Paul secretly resented J.D. for being the firstborn. Their parents had doted on J.D. throughout childhood and adolescence for no other reason than his being the firstborn and his father's namesake.

Other than their notable good looks, the brothers were as different as up and down. J.D. was the star athlete while Paul was the stellar academic. In the grand old state of Texas, a football always took you further than a textbook. J.D. was a natural charmer, while Paul could most politely be described as a people repellent.

"They seem very angry," Delaney said, hoping that conversation would drown out the angry words soaring in J.D.'s office.

Ruby nodded. "You know those boys. They can never agree on anything."

Glass crashed behind the door and Ruby shot up and hurried toward the office. Before she made it, Paul flung open the heavy doors and stormed out.

"I'll see you in hell first!" Paul yelled at J.D. as he almost crashed into Ruby.

Ruby swallowed. "Is . . . is everything all . . . all right, Mr. Daniels?"

Paul's face twisted in a mocking smirk. "Just fine." His eyes shot toward Delaney.

"H-h-hello, Paul."

"Delaney." His smile didn't reach his eyes.

"I trust everything is going well with you." His cold hard stare sent shivers down her spine.

"Very well," she said.

"Good-bye, Paul." J.D. stood in the doorway. His voice was firm and determined. "What do you want?" he directed to Delaney.

She smiled brightly and tried to remind herself that she was here to appeal to J.D.'s better sense of honor and duty, if he had one.

"May we speak . . . in private?" She cast a spurious smile toward Ruby.

"Fine." He stood aside so Delaney could enter the office.

She hesitated across his threshold as she noticed shattered glass on the marble hearth.

"Paul didn't seem too happy with you." She was merely making small talk, but something in the way J.D. looked at her let her know that the subject was off limits. She wet her dry lips, reminding herself that this was only J.D. They had been married for five years. At some point, she had believed herself in love with him. She should be able to talk to him. She should be able to reason with him.

"You had something you wanted to say?" J.D. pressed after a moment of silence.

"It's about the organization, J.D." She tried to make herself comfortable in an oversized leather wing chair.

J.D. stood up as quickly as he had sat down. "As I said to you before, this is an issue for our attorneys."

"J.D., there has to be a way we can solve this."

"As far as I am concerned, there is nothing to solve."

"We were *married*, for heaven's sake. Think about how much this means to me. If you take away this, you'll be taking away everything."

J.D. clenched his jaw. "We are absolving our relationship, Delaney."

"This is not about me or you. This is about a community full of young women whom I can help. You aren't hurting me, but you are hurting them."

"There will be others to fill your shoes."

"But this is my work. My dream. Nobody will care about the girls the way I do."

"Is that what you think? That nobody can do what you do? You're a beauty queen, Delaney. A pretty face. That's it. You're not reinventing the wheel. You're not changing the world. You can be replaced."

The words stung worse than if J.D. had slapped her. "Is that how you really feel about me? I guess that's one of the reasons we didn't work out. Five years ago I might have believed you. Three years ago, I might have taken those mean words personally. But I'm not the kid you married or the wife you mistreated. I understand now that that is why none of your marriages work."

"So a few classes at the university and now you're a goddamn shrink?" J.D. scoffed.

"I don't have to be a shrink to see who you are. I just needed to open my eyes. And that's what this divorce has been for me, a real eye-opener. You think the people in your life are disposable, that everyone can be replaced with a new and improved version.

And that is why you will never find happiness in your miserable life."

"I'm wounded." J.D. shielded his heart with his hand.

"You know, I came here thinking I would appeal to whatever bit of goodness there was in you. Now I see there isn't any. There are some things in life that are worth fighting for, and the center is one of them. I won't give up on this."

Delaney left asking herself what in the world she had ever seen in the man.

She hammered the steering wheel of her car for several minutes, then shook her head. Anger was such a useless emotion. She'd read somewhere that people who spent most of their lives angry died early. Anger didn't accomplish anything, only wasted time, energy, and precious seconds of life. She didn't want to waste another moment of her life being angry at J.D. She wanted to channel that energy into fighting to keep the center. She knew she was going to need every ounce of energy she had.

Maybe she would have better luck with the accountant. She took out the Post-It on which Shannon had scribbled his name and address: Herman Schuyler. She winced. That sounded like an accountant's name.

"Simon, Simon and Skiiiiiii-lur," a pretty voice answered after Delaney had punched the numbers into her cell.

"Yes, this is Delaney Daniels. May I please speak with Mr. Herman Schuyler?"

"Yes, ma'am. Hold please."

Delaney listened to synthetic pop music for a few minutes before a man's voice answered, deep and gruff.

"Mr. Schuyler?" Delaney asked, for clarification. She didn't know what she expected an accountant to sound like, but she had imagined Barry Manilow more than Barry White, that's for sure.

"Yes?"

"Hello, my name is Delaney Daniels. I'm J.D. Daniels's . . . wife." She never knew how to describe herself. "Soon-to-be ex" sounded so junior high.

"Yes?"

"I'm also the director of Through the Looking Glass. I know you manage all of the Daniels Enterprises portfolio and my organization is just a small part of that package, but perhaps you remember it?"

"Yes." His voice wavered.

"I was wondering if I could set up an appointment to discuss some of the financial statements with you. As you might have heard, Mr. Daniels and I are going through a divorce. My organization is attempting to seek philanthropic funding outside of Daniels Enterprises, and in order to do so I would like to have a prospectus to provide potential donors." She crossed her fingers.

"Mrs. Daniels, you must know that it would be highly irregular for me to share with you any financial statements if you are not an officer of the organization. You aren't, are you?"

Delaney sighed and shook her head as if Schuyler could see the gesture through the phone. "No, I'm afraid I'm not. . . ." Plan B. "But I do have some past bank statements, from when I was still an authorized signer on the account, and I have a lot of questions about some of the transactions I see. . . ."

God, please forgive for the lie I'm about to tell.

". . . I thought maybe you would be able to explain to me what this all means so I wouldn't have to contact my friends at the FBI. A couple of them are forensic accountants so I'm sure they would be able to help me. I just thought that since—" Delaney rambled on with jibberish she had copped from an episode of *Law & Order*. She didn't know what any of it meant exactly, but she did remember the thin accountant had sat down feverishly behind his oversized desk before giving Briscoe everything he wanted.

"Wait!" Now she had Schuyler's attention. She thanked the crime drama gods for credible television.

"There's . . . there's. . . . no reason to go contacting anybody else. Is there?"

"Really? I don't know. It's just all these statements seem soo. . . . confusing." Delaney managed to sound overly sweet. She was never above using the dumb-blonde routine when she really needed something. It had rescued her from dozens of traffic tickets in her life and now, quite possibly, it was going to get her everything she wanted from J.D.

"If you were once an authorized account holder, I'm sure there would be no problem with me talking to you about just that period of time, right?"

"Well, I wouldn't think so. And as I said . . . I do have all the statements. You wouldn't have to give me any *new* information . . . just explain to me the transactions on the statements. You could do that, couldn't you, Mr. Schuyler . . . Herman?"

"Surely . . . surely I could do that."

Yes! She pumped a victorious fist in the air.

"What period of time are we talking about here?"

"From the organization's inception, three years ago . . . May . . . up until last month," she said.

"I'll need a couple of days to get it all together; is that okay?"

"Perfect."

"Then we'll say next Tuesday at noon?"

"It's a date!" Delaney hung up and resisted the

urge to get out of her car and dance around it bumper to bumper. By the time she saw J.D. in court she would have two dozen people interested in financing Through the Looking Glass. She would drag in scrapbooks and videos of the girls she worked with. She would have all the ammunition she needed to fight him *mano a mano*. With God as her witness, she would win.

Chapter Twenty-five

Remember the Alamo!
You gotta go onstage armed and ready.
Anybody who tells you "It's just a pageant," has never competed.
This. Is. War.

Schuyler hung up the phone and wiped the sweat beading above his lip and on his forehead. He immediately picked up the phone again and dialed his colleague.

"Yes?"

"We have a problem."

"Problem?"

"Delaney. She just called."

"What did she want?"

"She's asking all kinds of questions about transactions on the statements."

He had his colleague's attention. "What did you tell her?"

"I made an appointment with her. She said something about going to the feds ... forensic accountants ... I panicked."

"You can't keep that appointment."

"I know, I know." But Schuyler's voice didn't sound as if he knew any such thing.

"You aren't freaking out on me, are you?"

"No ... no ... but she mentioned feds."

"She was just trying to get a rise out of you and you fell for it. Ignore her."

"I'm just thinking ... if ... if *we* go to the feds first ... I mean, won't they cut a deal for us? We could turn state's evidence or something. Get immunity. Or plea. We could get out of this with practically no jail time. I mean, you and me are still clean in this. They give guys like us deals."

"One: I'm not a whistle blower. Two: I'm not interested in spending one minute in jail. And three: If you open your mouth, you're dead."

Schuyler swallowed with difficulty. "Don't ... don't thr ... threaten me."

"Then don't threaten me."

"What are we going to do about Mrs. Daniels?"

"I'll handle Delaney Daniels." The man disconnected the call.

Shannon popped her head into Delaney's office before she left for the day. "J.D. called before you got here this afternoon."

"Really? I just saw him this morning. What did he want?"

"He said he needs you to come and get the rest of your stuff from the ranch."

"Stuff?" She couldn't imagine what "stuff" she had left at the ranch. Sure, she had moved out quickly, but J.D. had given her and Macy and Phoebe one weekend about seven months ago to go back and collect everything she wanted.

"I don't have anything left at the ranch."

"He said there was a box of stuff you packed up and never took with you."

"I wonder why he didn't mention it earlier."

Shannon shrugged. "He said he wants it out of the house."

"That doesn't make sense. Why now?"

The question was more rhetorical than literal, but Shannon answered anyway. "Well, if you really upset him this morning, it would be just like him to react by telling you to come and get your stuff. You know, that's exactly what happened with Carrie and Big . . ."

Delaney nodded as Shannon chatted about an episode of *Sex and the City*, but wasn't really listening. Maybe she had irritated J.D. or maybe that twit, Misty, was redecorating the whole place and wanted Delaney to know exactly how replaced she was.

"When did he say I should come by?" Delaney asked, resigned that she would never understand anything J.D. said or did. Besides, maybe there was something good in the box she could sell. She could use the money.

"Tonight. After six. Oh, and one more thing." Shannon's eyes shifted downward and she doodled hearts and flowers on the top of her pink Post-It pad.

"Yeah?"

"He said it had to be tonight because they're changing the code to the entrance gate and all the locks tomorrow."

"Oh." Delaney swallowed the large lump rising in her throat.

Shannon brought her eyes back up to meet Delaney's. "I'm really sorry, Delaney."

Delaney took a deep yoga inhale and exhale. She would not cry. She knew it was over. It had been over before it even got started. This was just the final nail in the coffin.

Delaney flipped through the mail. "I'm not," she said with resolve. "I'm not sorry at all. This is exactly what I need to shock me back into reality."

"Maybe you could just tell him to have your stuff delivered."

"No. I'll go. There are a few staff members I want to say good-bye to anyway."

The first thing Delaney did was get on a three-way phone call with Macy and Phoebe. She wasn't nervous about going to the estate, but she certainly wanted her best friend and sister to know where she was going to be.

"Do you want us to go with you?" Macy asked.

"No. I'm not sure if J.D. and Misty are going to be there, and I don't want to give the impression that I needed my posse to come along for protection. Things were kind of hostile this morning. It's probably best if I just go and try to do it quietly."

"He's just pissed you didn't go to bed with him last night. You know that, right?" Macy said. She, too, had seen all the pictures in the paper. "The way he was looking at you in those pictures. He thought you were a sure thing. He's just doing this to get back at you."

"Do you think it's safe? I mean, maybe it's better if you just have him deliver the stuff to you," Phoebe suggested.

"He wouldn't do anything to physically hurt me. He's an asshole but he's never been violent. Besides, I want to say good-bye to the staff."

"I can't believe he's changing the freakin' alarm

codes. What does he think you're going to do? Sneak in and steal his precious Cuban cigars?"

"It's perfectly practical. I understand actually. I just didn't expect it. It means that everything is really and truly . . . over. Of course I knew that, but it's kind of like when somebody dies. It's just not real until the funeral, you know?"

"You'd be much better off if it were *his* funeral." Macy's scowl was audible.

"Yeah, J.D. dead . . . problem solved." Delaney chuckled.

"Good riddance!" Phoebe declared.

"We should celebrate with a girls' night out," Macy suggested.

"Ooooooooh no," Delaney said. "Our last girls' night out landed me in a pile so deep I thought I'd never be able to climb out."

"It won't happen again," Phoebe reasoned. "That night you were like a time bomb ready to explode. Now that you've taken the edge off a little . . ."

Delaney could admit to them that she only wanted to do two things: cry and be comforted in the arms of a very off-limits Lucas Church. But she didn't. Thinking of Lucas, of the angry words he had exchanged with her, just reminded her that the last thing he wanted to do was wrap his arms around her and comfort her. She couldn't believe the mess she had made of her life in such a short time.

"I think I'll just sit in and watch a movie. I'll talk to y'all tomorrow."

Chapter Twenty-six

Winning a meaningless title doesn't necessarily mean you're the best. Sometimes it simply means everyone else is worse.

"Knock, knock," Delaney called as she entered the foyer of J.D.'s home. Her voice echoed and bounced off the marble floors and the high, cavernous ceiling. She had rung the doorbell several times and knocked before finally resorting to her key, lest she be accused of breaking and entering.

"Hello?" she called out. The house was eerily quiet. She remembered it was Wednesday, "church night" in the Bible belt, so all the staff had the evening off. So much for saying good-bye.

J.D.'s car was in the drive, not the garage, so surely he was there. Then she recalled that a couple of the girls she used to play tennis with had told her J.D. just splurged on a custom Cadillac for Misty, so maybe they were tooling around town in it.

She fisted her hands on her hips, wondering where

J.D. would leave her box of personals. Her heels clicked against the marble and wood floors as she circled in and out of rooms on the bottom floor, looking for a box conspicuously marked "Delaney." Maybe upstairs in her old room, she thought, as she jogged up the circular staircase. She pushed the door to the room open and, not recognizing it, closed it immediately. She looked down the hall in either direction to make sure she had the second door on the right. It was the same location as her room had been but . . . completely different. Misty had obviously decided to begin her remodeling with this room. *Her* room. Her *old* room. The entire space had been repainted a stark white. One wall was lined with mirrors and the room was crammed with exercise equipment, which was absolutely redundant since there was a gym on the first floor. She rolled her eyes and imagined the idiocy of Misty whining that the gym was just too far away to go work out.

She shrugged. She wasn't here to get angry at Misty. She just wanted her box of stuff. Delaney sighed in frustration. She didn't feel entirely comfortable venturing much past her old room in search of the absent box. She wasn't going to go searching throughout an eight-thousand-square-foot estate looking for one little box. Why hadn't he just left it by the door? It was just further evidence of J.D. thinking that the only person whose time was valuable was him. She determined that she wasn't making a return visit to the ranch. If he wanted her stuff gone, he could just use a fraction of his billions to have her stuff delivered. She stomped down the stairs and attempted to slam the large oak door as she exited, but found it too heavy.

It was perfect. She hadn't even known that she wasn't alone. That she was being watched. She'd done exactly as predicted. Opening the door. Going inside the house. Touching just enough stuff to leave her prints all over the place. Better yet, she'd driven that inane pink convertible of hers and been spotted by at least a dozen other motorists heading toward the ranch. Everything was going just as it should. The plan was working perfectly.

Delaney hadn't gotten two miles down the road that led to the ranch when she passed Misty in her brand new black convertible Caddy. She winced, thinking how similar they were in their affection for convertibles. But J.D. had never been one for originality. He stuck with what worked. Misty did a double take as she passed Delaney and, by the pissed look on her face, Delaney was certain J.D. had not made Misty privy to the fact that she would be visiting. Misty's engine gunned as she sped up, pedal to the metal, trying to get home to find out what the two had been doing.

Delaney grinned. She enjoyed the little frustrations she caused Misty. It would have been especially nice if J.D. had actually been there. Delaney would have liked to hear the fireworks. But Misty would get there, find nothing amiss, and just feel foolish for her irrational jealousy and that she had let Delaney notice her irritation. Delaney smiled, satisfied to have caused at least a ripple.

Chapter Twenty-seven

Bright lights are not always good.

The flashing red and blue lights flooded the street in front of Delaney's house. She hadn't heard the pounding on the door immediately because she was in the shower. She had stepped out just in time to hear them shout, "Mrs. Daniels, open the door right now!" She had hurriedly wrapped a towel around herself and bounded to the front door. Thank God for oversized bath sheets.

"We've been knocking for ten minutes," was their greeting.

"I was in the shower," she told the red-faced detectives standing on her porch.

"May we come in?" asked the tall one with thinning hair.

"I suppose." She looked over her shoulder at the three cop cars in front of her drive. Every one of her neighbors who was home had come out to gawk, not even bothering with the pretense of checking the mail or walking the dog—just standing at the edge of their lawns, arms crossed in front of their chests.

"Do you mind having your uniforms turn off the flashing lights? It's kind of drawing attention."

The attractive African-American detective made a gesture and the two uniformed officers reclining against their cars quickly made way to turn off the lights.

"Thanks." Delaney moved to the side and directed the officers in.

"I'm Detective Wayne, this is Detective Cruz." The bald officer didn't offer his hand but Detective Cruz, who had the most charming smile ever, shook her hand energetically.

"You don't mind if I go put some clothes on, do you?"

"By all means." Detective Wayne nodded. Still no smile. His face was so severe, Delaney wondered if he was capable of smiling.

She returned in a few moments wearing her pink terry Juicy track suit and carrying a brush. She had to brush her long hair before it dried or it was impossible to detangle.

"Do you mind sharing with me the nature of your visit?" She was certain she had heard that line on *Law & Order* or *The Practice*. Her years of etiquette training on the pageant circuit had given her conversation for practically every scenario, but she was certain she didn't know what to say when detectives showed up on her porch. When in doubt, trust prime time.

"It's about your husband."

"Yes?" Was she going to have to pull information from them like rainbow handkerchiefs from a clown's lapel?

"He's dead," Wayne said flatly.

"What?" Her brush thudded against the wood floor when she dropped it. Thank goodness the couch was behind her, because if it hadn't been she would have fallen right on her ass.

Detective Cruz, the "good cop," Delaney had determined, sat down next to her. "He was found at his home by . . . a friend." He was obviously trying to salvage her pride.

"It's okay. It's his girlfriend. I know all about Misty."

"Miss Wells, Misty, found your husband . . . dead. . . ."

"Murdered," Wayne interjected.

Cruz shot him an angry look. He was significantly younger, possibly wiser, definitely kinder than his partner.

"Yes, he was . . . murdered. We are the homicide detectives assigned to the case."

Delaney swallowed. "I don't understand. I mean, I just talked to him a few hours ago. Who would want to kill J.D.?"

The officers traded glances and then returned their gazes to Delaney.

"*Me?*"

"That is what we mean to find out. We need to ask you a few questions."

"Strictly routine," Cruz added.

"Do I need a lawyer?" Delaney asked immediately.

Wayne's eyebrows shot up. "Why would you ask that?"

Why indeed? She shrugged. What was she going to tell him? *Because I always wonder why the criminals start singing like a robin without the advice of counsel on television.* She couldn't say that.

"I don't know. I just . . . I just . . . that's the question they always ask on *CSI*." She couldn't believe she just said that.

Cruz smiled. "If you would feel more comfortable

answering questions with your lawyer present, that is your choice. But we aren't putting you under arrest. We are just starting our investigation and need some information."

"Am I a suspect?" She looked to Cruz because she wanted the truth.

"A spouse is always a person of interest in cases such as these." His answer didn't really tell Delaney what she wanted to know.

Delaney chewed on her lip. "All right. I can tell you what I know. But I don't know much . . . about J.D. or what might have happened or anything."

"Okay. Would you say you have an amicable relationship with your husband?"

"As amicable as any divorcing couple can be."

"So I take that to mean you fought?"

"We were divorcing. . . . We weren't exactly the Huxtables but . . . we didn't hate each other . . . not exactly."

"Can you tell us where you were between the hours of five and eight?"

"At work. And then . . . and then at J.D.'s and then here."

"You were at the deceased's place of residence?"

"Briefly."

"What was the nature of your visit?"

"He called and asked me to pick up some of my remaining personal belongings."

"Was he behaving out of the ordinary when you arrived at his place?"

"I didn't actually speak to him. He left a message with my assistant and when I got to the house he wasn't there."

"He wasn't? What time did you arrive at his home?"

"A little after six, not quite six-fifteen."

"And he wasn't there?"

"No."

The two detectives exchanged meaningful glances. Delaney wanted to know exactly what those looks meant.

"How did you get in?"

"I have a key and alarm codes."

"You were getting divorced but you still had full access to his home?"

Delaney nodded. "I'm not exactly America's most wanted. J.D. never had any reason to distrust me or to believe that I would enter his house without his knowing. Again, it wasn't the most amicable divorce but we remained civil."

"Was the alarm set?"

"Come to think of it, no, it wasn't."

"Would you consider that out of nature, for him to leave his home unsecured?"

"Y-y-yes. He normally makes sure the alarm is set. He's a very wealthy man and that house is filled with valuables. He would never leave it unsecured."

"Misty said he fired an employee once because she forgot to set the alarms. Is that true to his character?"

"Yes."

"But it didn't seem odd to you that when you entered the home you didn't have to disarm the alarm?"

Delaney shrugged. "I just didn't think about it . . . we've been separated for a year. His habits aren't exactly front and center in my life anymore. Besides, I thought he was there waiting for me."

"So when you entered the home, not disabling the alarm would have led you to believe he was home."

"Correct."

"But he wasn't."

"I didn't search the entire house but when I called out, there was no answer, so no, I don't think he was there."

"May we see the box of personal belongings you picked up?"

"I don't have them."

"You don't?"

"When I went inside I looked around on the first floor and in my old bedroom and I didn't see any box, so I was just going to call J.D. and ask him to have the box delivered to me tomorrow."

Wayne and Cruz exchanged meaningful looks. Again. Cruz cleared his throat and looked down as Wayne proceeded with the interview.

"Then what happened?"

"I left. I drove straight home.

"Did you make any phone calls?"

"No. But Misty, she saw me leaving the house."

"Yes, she mentioned it. What time do you think you got home?"

"Sevenish."

"And what did you do when you got home?"

"I worked out and then I took a shower."

"You worked out?"

Delaney nodded.

"Some of your neighbors said they saw you jogging this morning. But you worked out a second time when you got home?"

"You've talked to my neighbors? Why are you questioning my neighbors?"

"Mrs. Daniels. The question," Cruz prompted.

"Yes. I worked out a second time."

"Do you normally exercise twice a day?"

"Not normally, but I had some . . . tension to burn off. . . ."

Again they looked at each other, Cruz nodding and Wayne scribbling furiously.

"Tension?"

"I had a frustrating day. I needed to channel my

anger so I . . . could rest peacefully . . . it's a yoga concept. . . ."

"Mrs. Daniels, do you know of any person who might have a reason to want your husband dead?"

"J.D. was a very wealthy, extremely ruthless businessman. A billionaire. You don't get to that position in life without crushing a few skulls. I'm sure there are hundreds of people who have millions of reasons to want him dead."

"How many millions of reasons do you have to want him dead?" Wayne asked.

"I don't think I understand what you are asking."

"Do you know if you stood to improve your position financially as a result of your husband's death?"

Delaney blinked.

"Mrs. Daniels?"

"I . . . I don't know. And I don't understand why you're asking me these questions if I'm not a suspect."

More looks were exchanged before Cruz explained in the kindest tone imaginable, "Well, we never said you *weren't* a suspect."

"I think . . . I think . . . I need to call my lawyer."

"Yes . . . Yes . . . I understand you're nervous, but you just calm down, sweetie. Don't say another word. I'll be there in half an hour." Lawrence snapped his phone shut and deposited his napkin on his plate. "You'd better come with me."

"Trouble?"

"That was Delaney Daniels."

"She's your client. There's no reason for me to go with you."

Lawrence met the piercing blue eyes staring across the table at him. "Wrong answer, son. It seems your client has just been murdered."

Chapter Twenty-eight

I believe Miss America killed the talent competition for one reason only—lots of pretty girls, very little talent.

Delaney paced the great room as Detectives Wayne and Cruz whispered on the sofa. They had ceased the questioning the minute Delaney requested an attorney present. Instead of comforting her, the reprieve just gave her a greater sense of foreboding.

She jumped when the doorbell rang, not missing that the detectives scribbled furiously in their notepads as she did so.

"Lawrence!" Delaney threw her arms around him. "I'm so worried," she whispered.

"There's nothing to worry about." Lawrence patted her on the back. "We'll get to the bottom of this."

At that moment, Delaney noticed Lucas standing behind Lawrence. "What are you doing here?" Her surprise did not have to be feigned.

"I thought he should come with me," Lawrence explained, "considering his relationship to the deceased."

But he shouldn't be here! Considering his relationship to the suspect.

"And what is your relationship to the deceased?" Wayne asked Lucas. Condescension dripped from his voice.

At least he's an equal opportunity asshole, Delaney thought.

Lucas offered his hand. "Lucas Church. I am ... was Mr. Daniels's divorce attorney. I'm also employed by the firm that handles some of his corporate affairs."

"Thank you for your time and effort, fellas." Lawrence clapped Wayne on the back, nudging him toward the front door. "We'll be seeing you later."

"We're not quite finished here." Detective Wayne stiffened under Lawrence's heavy hand.

"You've already infringed on my client's right to counsel ... what the hell else is left to do?" Lawrence warned.

"There is still the matter of the residue test," Cruz managed. Then he added a charming smile. Delaney winced. Lawrence ate kids like him as afternoon snacks. The seemingly sincere smile that had her singing like a songbird an hour ago wasn't going to melt Lawrence's icy façade.

Lawrence raised his brows. "Is that really necessary?"

"She ... she is a subject of interest in the case. We tested the girlfriend. We'll want a test from the wife, too."

Delaney looked to Lawrence, who nodded.

"And the clothes she was wearing. Where can we find those?" Wayne decided to press their luck.

Delaney chewed her bottom lip until she was certain she had bit right through it.

"I . . . I've already washed them."

"You washed the articles you were wearing tonight?"

Delaney nodded. "I know that probably looks bad."

Cruz sighed heavily. "Honestly, Mrs. Daniels . . . it doesn't look good."

It was early in the morning before the detectives left. Delaney could still feel the residue from the gunpowder test coating her hands. She was tired and emotionally sapped. She wanted just a few hours of solace to consider the events of the evening. Lucas and Lawrence, however, lingered, and Macy and Phoebe had shown up as soon as they heard the breaking news, during which time she explained to them the events of the evening.

Delaney sighed heavily as she contemplated everything she had said and done in the last few days. Her words from just a few hours ago rang in her ears.

"It's like when somebody dies . . . it just doesn't seem real until the funeral."

What had she said after that?

"J.D. dead . . . problem solved."

She winced audibly. Wasn't that exactly the kind of stupid thing the suspect was always saying on *Murder, She Wrote*? And wasn't Delaney always the one who said, "Who *actually says* something stupid like that?"

Delaney knocked the fist of her palm against her forehead. She deserved a real ass-kicking for being such an idiot. She'd practically threatened to kill him on a cell phone to her sister and her best friend. If Phoebe and Macy were questioned about their conversation, they would be obligated to tell the truth.

"Stupid, stupid, stupid." She punctuated her words with the knocks against her forehead.

"Are you okay, Laney?" Phoebe asked.

"I'm probably being charged with murder, so, no, I am most definitely not okay."

Phoebe chewed her nails and looked to Lawrence. "Tell me they are not going to send my big sister to jail. Laney couldn't hurt a bug. Do you know whenever she sees a turtle trying to cross the highway, she gets out of her car and moves him to the shoulder and points him in the right direction?"

"You're preaching to the choir, Phoebe. Nobody here believes Delaney capable of killing J.D."

Delaney's eyes shifted to Lucas, who had been noticeably quiet since they arrived. At that moment he looked up and met her eyes. She wanted, *needed* to know that he believed in her. His eyes didn't have any of the fire she had seen in them previously. They were cold. At that moment she knew that he didn't know what to believe.

"What next?" Delaney asked Lawrence.

"The powder kits will come back negative?"

"Of course they will!"

"It won't help us a bit since you showered and washed your clothes," he told her. "They expect for them to come back negative. But they shouldn't be back to bother you unless they can dig up a motive."

"And if they do?"

"Laney, you can't go getting all defeatist on us," Macy argued.

"It's a real possibility, Mace. We were involved in a very public, very ugly divorce."

Lawrence puffed out a deep breath.

"I want you to level with me. What will they consider a motive?" she asked her lawyer.

"It could go either way." he glanced over his shoulder at Lucas. "Much of it will depend on whether or not he was able to make changes to any of his life insurance policies, investment accounts, his will. In short, they'll weigh and measure how much you stood to lose by the divorce . . . and how much you stood to gain by his death."

Macy, Phoebe and Delaney all shifted their eyes to Lucas.

Lucas pushed his hands through his hair. "What do you want me to say?"

"I'm not asking you to reveal anything privileged. But friend to friend, we need to know if they are going to be able to establish motive. Is there enough money involved for her to look guilty?"

Lucas looked from Lawrence to Delaney. "I can only advise that you stick around. They are going to definitely want to talk to you again. You're probably going to want a really good *criminal* lawyer."

Delaney would have liked to say the incessant ringing of the phone woke her up, but she felt as if she had been lying sleepless all night long. She stretched and turned on the television. The story was headline news.

"Texas billionaire oil man James David Daniels was found dead at his ranch just outside Austin yesterday. J.D., as his friends and family called him, was shot to death as he relaxed at home. Police have not named a suspect but in documents leaked to the press, his estranged wife, former Miss Texas Delaney Davis, is considered a subject of interest. Police would not comment on a specific motive, just that the Daniels couple were involved in a lengthy divorce that is being described as "less than amicable." The Daniels and the Davis families have been unavailable for comment. Funeral arrangements have not been made at the hour of this report."

Rather than show a recent picture of the two, the television stations and newspapers displayed a picture of Delaney being crowned Miss Texas and a picture of J.D. at the inaugural ball flanked by presidents past and present.

"Turn that garbage off." Phoebe crossed the room and clicked off the television.

Delaney looked up at her sister. "I didn't know you were still here."

"Come on . . . you've always been there for me. No way I'm abandoning you. How are you holding up?"

"This is like a bad dream. Only I can't wake up."

"Speaking of waking up, I was starting to worry that you were never going to."

"I slept?" She tried to remember the events of the early morning. She could barely make out pieces. After a short conversation with the detectives, Lawrence had told her exactly how J.D. had died. She remembered thinking she should cry, but she couldn't. She was just numb. Then she remembered that the six of them—herself, Phoebe, Macy, Lawrence, Lucas and Matt—were sitting around, sometimes talking about the Cowboys, sometimes talking about politics and sometimes talking about J.D., the way people do when tragedy strikes. She offered to go get more refreshments. When she opened the refrigerator she remembered seeing a package of Ballpark Franks and she cried. She cried because before J.D., she had hated hot dogs.

J.D. had been a huge Rangers fan and their first date was at a game.

"You can't go to a baseball game and not eat a hot-dog," he'd told her. So she tried it. Not so bad. Later, when he had asked her to marry him at a Texas Rangers game, the very moment she had read the electronic bulletin her face was on the big screen and J.D. was on one

knee in their box seats. Hot dogs became their thing in
the rare moments of tenderness in their marriage. Without even knowing it, she had added them to her grocery
list every once in a while. That unopened package of
franks reminded her that it was over. Their marriage.
His life. It was . . . over.

That was where Macy had found her, curled in a
ball in front of the open refrigerator door, crying,
grieving over everything lost.

Phoebe smiled and nodded. "Matt brought something for you to take. It did the trick though, because
it's almost four in the afternoon. One of the benefits of
being engaged to a physician."

Delaney blinked several times. She felt like the
woman on the Lifetime movie who fell into a coma
and woke up twenty years later.

"Engaged?"

Phoebe nodded and held out her left hand. Her
third finger displayed a European cut in an antique
platinum setting.

"That's beautiful, Phebes. When?"

"Last night." She gave a sheepish smile. "Right before you called actually."

"Great. The night of your engagement will forever
be ruined. Because of me."

"Don't say that. You're my sister. I'd be here for you
no matter what."

"I don't understand . . . just a few days ago you
thought he was a lying sack of shit."

"I finally did what I should have done in the first
place. I just asked him. Those charges on his cards
weren't even his. He gave his brother a card to help
him out with expenses while he was in med school.
Matt never opens his statements; he just calls the bank
for balances. He knew his brother was going through

a lot of money but he had no idea where he was spending it."

Delaney dropped back against the headboard. "That's wonderful, Phebes, really. I feel just awful. I've been so wrapped up in my own messes this last week or so we haven't even had a chance to talk. And now . . . last night should have been about you, not me."

"It's okay. All I'm concerned with right now is getting you out of this mess. I can't plan a wedding without my big sister. I want you to be my maid of honor."

"Thanks. I'd be honored to stand by you." She choked back tears. "Have you talked to Mom and Dad?"

"I called them after you went to sleep. They are worried sick. They, of course, wanted to head directly up here. But I told them not to. The girls don't need that kind of exposure to the press and besides, there's nothing they can do. Right now our biggest concern is getting you out of this house."

"Why?"

"The press have descended." She jerked a thumb toward the window.

"What?"

Phoebe moved to the window. Delaney got on her knees and crawled toward it so that whoever might be outside would not detect any movement behind the sheer curtains. She moved the gauzy fabric just centimeters from the sill in order to peek outside. Her lawn was covered, absolutely covered, with people. Flash bulbs sparked every few seconds even though there was not necessarily anything new to photograph. Men with cameras on their haunches, coiffed reporters talking into lenses, shifting backwards glances toward the house every few minutes. Delaney slumped against the wall.

"Macy and I have figured out a plan."

"Yeah?"

"Well, you and I look enough alike to fool them. We're the same height almost, same weight. If I put on a hat and sunglasses and leave through the front door and get in your car, that'll throw them for a little while. Macy pulled her car inside the garage. The windows in the back are tinted dark enough that if you lie down they shouldn't be able to see you. I'll leave in your car and go to the park or something. I'm sure they'll follow me."

"Where will I go?"

"Well, I can't take you to my place and Macy can't take you to her place because eventually they'll sniff us out. They've already shown up at Lawrence's home and office. There's really nobody else we know well enough. So you'll just have to get a hotel room. Macy will check in under a different name."

Delaney nodded, confused and bewildered. She hadn't had this much attention when she was Miss Texas. The only thing America loved more than a rising star was a fallen star. She sighed and shifted her attention back to the masses camped out on her lawn. She just wanted things to be the way they were a month ago. J.D. was dead and all she could do was wonder when she would get her life back.

The watcher couldn't help smiling. Who the hell did they think they were? This trio probably fancied themselves some kind of Charlie's Angels or something of the sort. But they weren't remotely in the same league as the Hollywood super sleuths. Not even the bikini-clad, mica-lip-gloss, dolled-up versions from the 'seventies. Charlie's girls would have never made hotel reservations without first checking their land line for bugs. Charlie's girls would have noticed the late-model navy Mercedes sedan following them—even though it remained three cars back. And Charlie's girls would have never left another Angel unattended and unprotected. Never.

But they weren't angels, the lot of them. Especially not the beauty queen. People only thought she was perfect. If they only knew. Soon they would. Soon the images of her radiant smile outshining the crystals in her tiara would be replaced with mug shots. Her designer duds with a shocking orange jumpsuit. Her tennis bracelet with handcuffs. Bye, bye Miss American Pie, hello Miss Texas Penal System.

Chapter Twenty-nine

Given the choice between bust and brains—the boobs are going to take the crown every day.

Delaney sank into the generous mattress. She rubbed her temples, trying to erase her pounding headache. Normally she was never comfortable in a hotel bed, but this one felt like a cloud as she sank her head into the pillow. Her thoughts drifted to J.D. and then to his family. Paul! She hadn't even called him to see how he was holding up. True, there was no love lost between him and J.D., but they were brothers. The loss of a sibling must leave a cavernous hole, even if they weren't the best of friends.

She wondered if she should contact Paul and ask if she could assist him with any final touches to the funeral arrangements. Mostly everything was pre-arranged. J.D. had seen to that after a close call parasailing a few years ago. The flowers were chosen, the hymns all picked out. His chosen funeral home even stored the suit in which he wanted to be buried.

It would be no problem for her to just make the phone call. It was all arranged. Right down to the engraved invitations and the guest list. What a wonder. Her "ex" husband's funeral arrangements weren't all that different from their wedding arrangements.

Delaney couldn't help thinking she should call Paul to say . . . something. They were, after all, sort of brother- and sister-in-law. Practically family. She thought of the task of laying J.D. to rest falling wholly on Paul's shoulders. She decided she would call him. And say? Say what? She didn't know. She just knew that she wanted him to know how saddened she was. Her eyelids felt leaden as they pulled downward. She yawned and stretched. She would call him after just a short nap.

Three days later, Delaney sat pressed between family and friends in the large church. It was crowded with at least 1500 of J.D. Daniels's closest friends.

At least 1495 of the observers are only here for curiosity and the spectacle, Delaney thought.

She had arrived at the church, heavily guarded at Lawrence's insistence, early enough to avoid the press skulking outside the church. Her head throbbed at the thought of having to dodge them to make it to the cemetery. Once they got to the gravesite, there was no guarantee that the groundskeeper or off-duty officers could keep the cameras at a respectable distance.

She could feel Cruz and Wayne watching her from the sidelines. They were there, they explained, to determine if there was anything suspicious, to see if anybody acted out of the ordinary, but, the best that she could tell, they never took their eyes off her. She was beginning to believe the "police protection" being offered by the department was less an effort to keep her safe and more an effort to monitor her behavior.

She couldn't let them preoccupy her thoughts. She surveyed the crowded church, making contact with random faces of J.D.'s life. His dentist. The owner of the PGA store at the club. The girl who cut his hair. All with eyes so red you'd imagine they'd lost their best friend.

And there was Paul. He had never returned any of her calls or asked for assistance with the final plans. The funeral was the first she had seen of him since the time at J.D.'s office, the day of the murder. He was perfectly coiffed and pressed, just as he always was. There was something . . . different about his temperament. Delaney hadn't expected him to show an outpouring of grief as Misty had. Not even the occasional sniffle and tear to which she herself had succumbed. Men, especially macho cowboy/oil baron Texans, didn't cry. But Paul seemed even more distant and colder than his normal self. She couldn't put her finger on why. There didn't seem to be a moment during the services when she couldn't feel him watching her. She put her own discomfort aside and approached him after the burial.

"Black doesn't suit you," he said without looking at her. "Nor does being a widow at such a young age, but I guess better widowed than divorced. It has sort of a . . . glamour to it, doesn't it?"

"Considering my relationship with J.D. of late, I don't think I can fairly consider myself his widow," Delaney said, trying to mask her confusion.

"I suppose you have a point." He turned to meet her face to face. "Not actually the grieving widow, but not quite the ex-wife . . ." He shifted his glance to Misty, who was being helped into her car by some unknown. "Not the mistress on the sidelines or in the back pew. Just somewhere in . . . limbo."

"You . . . you can't imagine how sorry I am." She wanted to shift the conversation.

"No, Delaney, I can't." His words were clipped but not quite angry.

"I can't help but feel I'm in some way responsible."

"If you had nothing to do with his murder, you shouldn't feel responsible," Paul noted.

Delaney considered the word "if." Two little letters weighted the sentence more than if he had used the entire alphabet. She assured herself that there wasn't any sinister suggestion of guilt behind the statement. He had just lost his big brother; his one remaining immediate family member had died as a result of a brutal and callous execution . . . he was understandably grief-stricken and he didn't know what he was saying.

"I only meant . . . I wish I had been at the house earlier. Perhaps . . . if the intruder knew that J.D. wasn't alone, perhaps this wouldn't have happened," she said, trying to fill the void.

"Don't be foolish, Delaney," Paul said, overly kind. More chills crept along her spine. Paul had never shared a kind word with her since the day he had met her. He stroked her cheek with his thumb. "If you had been there, we might be mourning the loss of both of you. Besides, that face of yours is far too pretty to be adorned with a silver bullet as a beauty mark." He smiled but the mirth didn't reach the cold steel of his eyes.

"Mrs. Daniels." Detective Cruz tapped Delaney on the shoulder.

"Yes?" Delaney welcomed the interruption.

"We need to speak," Wayne said.

"Is there some further development?"

"Perhaps we should discuss this downtown," Cruz insisted.

"Downtown?"

"At the precinct."

"I'd rather not," Delaney said. They had just buried J.D.! Whatever needed to be discussed could surely wait until the following morning.

"You don't exactly have a choice, Mrs. Daniels," Wayne told her.

"What *exactly* are you saying?"

"We're saying we can leave now in a nice un-marked car that will take you to the station so we can ask you a few questions. Or we can call a black-and-white and uniforms, read you your rights and take you to the station to ask you a few questions."

"Is everything okay?" Macy asked, coming up be-hind Delaney.

"No. I think I'm being placed under arrest."

He watched as she climbed into the car. Though unmarked, it was clearly compliments of Austin's finest. The darkly tinted windows of his own car were barely cracked. Not enough to be seen, just enough to let out the tendrils of smoke from his cigar. He wasn't a smoker. Not much of one anyway, but the Cuban cigars he had recently acquired had become somewhat of a guilty pleasure for him. He only smoked one when he thought there was the occasion for cel-ebration. He was certain Delaney was about to be arrested for the murder of J.D. Daniels. And he couldn't think of a better reason to celebrate than that.

Chapter Thirty

A beauty pageant is just a dog-and-pony show where nobody wants to be the dog.

Delaney rubbed her forehead, trying to massage away the dull ache behind her eyes. She had tried several times to call Lawrence, and she knew Macy and Phoebe were doing their best to locate him. The detectives, while polite, weren't going to release her until they had all the answers. Unfortunately, the only answers she had weren't the ones they wanted.

"I've told you everything I know," she repeated.

"One more time, Mrs. Daniels, perhaps there was something you missed."

Delaney had watched this technique on prime-time crime dramas on more than one occasion. The suspect was alienated from friends and family, sometimes even legal counsel, and asked the same questions repeatedly in the hopes that eventually the fatigue would cause them to trip over their own lies and reveal the truth. But she had nothing more to offer them. She was already telling them the truth.

"I've never seen that insurance contract. I don't know how the champagne flute with my prints wound up near the hot tub. Yes, that is my brush but I haven't seen it in ages. I must have lost that brush two years ago. I was married to J.D. for five years. There must be scads of my stuff around that place."

"Two feet away from a stiffening corpse?"

"I don't know why any of it was there unless somebody wants me to be blamed for this murder."

"Like who? Who would have had access to all these things and also holds a grudge against you?"

"I don't know. Toward the end, our divorce was less than amicable. J.D. hated me."

"So your ex-husband planted these things to incriminate you, then committed suicide by getting in the hot tub and shooting himself in the forehead from six feet away?"

Delaney shook her head. "Maybe . . . maybe the flute is from last weekend. I went to J.D.'s house to . . . work some things out. But I got angry and I left. He must have kept the flute around. As for the brush . . . just look at the color of the strands of hair. . . ." She reached for the brush.

Wayne's hand slapped down over hers. "Don't touch the evidence," he told her with steely gray eyes.

Evidence. *Against her.* The insurance contract they presented her with when she entered the interrogation room, well, that was motive. She swallowed and stiffened.

"I did not kill J.D.," she said with equal determination. "Now charge me or let me go."

"Screw it! Charge her!" Wayne directed Cruz.

"No, Wayne. We're going to give Mrs. Daniels the

opportunity to answer us one more time. Why don't you go get some coffee or something?"

Just great! Now a vigorous round of "Good Cop, Bad Cop" to throw into the mix.

Delaney resisted rolling her eyes as Wayne stormed out of the room and slammed the door. These two had their dog-and-pony show down to a science.

"Delaney, tell me again when you signed this insurance contract."

Delaney didn't bother looking down at the paper he had pushed under her nose. "I already told you, I've never seen that contract."

"You deny that that is your signature?" Cruz flipped to the back page of the document.

"Anybody could have signed that. Handwriting isn't that hard to duplicate. Once you have an expert examine it, then you'll know it isn't my signature."

Cruz half nodded. "Handwriting analysis, while helpful, isn't a science of certainty. Of course somebody could have forged your signature, but normally that is the case when somebody else stands to benefit. Who would take out a three-million dollar whole life policy with a double indemnity clause and name you as sole beneficiary? I spoke with the insurance company, and it was a pretty hefty premium paid. Somebody might only be willing to pay a premium like that if they *knew* they were going to cash in on the policy."

"Then why don't you check with the insurance company and ask them how that premium was paid? If the buyer wrote a check . . ."

Cruz, two steps ahead of Delaney, presented an image of a cashier's check drawn on Delaney's bank showing her as remitter.

"I didn't buy that cashier's check. Check the bank records."

"It was bought with cash. Whoever paid for the cashier's check used your account number as the reference number. Unfortunately it was purchased just over six months ago, so the bank surveillance film has been destroyed."

"I live paycheck to paycheck. Where would I have gotten that kind of money? You can check my personal accounts. There's never a balance larger than a few hundred dollars each month."

"We've been told by Mr. Paul Daniels, by Misty, and by a few of the staff that Mr. Daniels was known to keep large amounts of cash in a safe in the house. By all accounts, you were one of the few who knew the combinations to some of his safes. You've already told us that you kept a key and the alarm codes."

Delaney's mouth went dry. She had always been a fan of reality crime dramas. Now she was living one. The more Cruz spoke, the better picture she got of the mountain of evidence against her. Hell, if she didn't know she was innocent, even she would think she was guilty.

"There's no way to prove I bought it. The handwriting won't match."

"There's also no way to prove that you didn't buy it. The prosecutor can find a forensic analyst who will argue that you purposely altered your writing to deflect attention."

"Somebody is trying to frame me for my husband's murder," Delaney insisted.

"I demand that you cease and desist this interrogation immediately," Lawrence bellowed as he burst in the room.

Cruz jerked up and cast a guilty look at Delaney before facing Lawrence.

"It's merely an interview," Cruz lied.

"What have you told them, Delaney?"

"Only the truth, for what that's worth," Delaney said. "Nothing incriminating. They have enough without me adding to the mix."

"This interrogation was executed without the benefit of counsel. Any discovery as a result of these questions will be excluded."

"There was nothing to discover." Delaney was instantly irritated that Lawrence assumed there would be. "I didn't kill my husband. I don't know who did."

"Come on, Delaney. We're going home." Lawrence tugged on her arm. "Unless you plan on charging her."

Cruz's eyes shifted to the door and then he shook his head. "I assume that you aren't making any travel plans, Delaney."

"Is that the P.C. way to tell me not to leave town?"

Cruz nodded, then added in a warning tone as if it were necessary, "Don't leave town, Delaney."

"How did things go at the police department?" Lucas's voice warmed Delaney. She hadn't been able to warm up since spending the evening in the meat locker the city liked to call the police department.

"How did you know I was taken in?" Delaney asked.

"I saw you leave with them after the burial."

Delaney got the impression he wasn't telling her everything. "And?"

"And they informed me of their intentions to speak with you."

"You knew I was being taken in for questioning and you didn't warn me?" she asked.

"I didn't exactly know you were being questioned. I knew they wanted to talk to you about the insurance policy."

"You *knew* about the insurance policy?"

Lucas sighed. "It was brought to my attention the day after the murder."

"Why didn't you say something to me?"

Her question was met with silence.

"Well?"

"I was waiting for the opportunity to tell Lawrence, to see how he was going to tackle your defense."

"My defense? You already have me convicted with a needle in my arm."

"That's not true."

"You think I need a defense plan," she protested.

"What I think doesn't matter. . . ."

"I know; it's what they can prove. And they can prove I had three million reasons to kill J.D."

Lucas didn't respond. Delaney tried to interpret the silence by measuring his breaths.

"*You* think I killed J.D., don't you?"

"I didn't say that," Lucas finally said.

"You didn't have to." Delaney hung up the phone and tossed herself on the bed and cried.

The Bar was packed, which was exactly how Lucas liked it. Enough people for him to get lost in the crowd and for him to lose himself in a gin and tonic. Because of its vicinity to the courthouses and the downtown district, it was a favorite hangout for lawyers, judges and other legal types.

"Come here often?" A pretty redhead fanned her hair out of her face. Lucas offered an obligatory but noticeably fake smile.

"Not often," he said. Anymore.

"Me either. I just hate the bar scene."

Lucas wanted to ask her why she was there, so obviously prowling, but he feigned agreeableness and just nodded.

"Can I buy you a drink?" she asked, tossing her hair.

She was pretty. Very pretty. Just the kind of girl he would have gone home with two weeks ago. Full lips. Big eyes trimmed garishly with dark lashes. He should chat her up. Tell her the things he knew she wanted to hear. He could take her home and take her to bed and end this self-imposed celibacy he'd declared since he last spent the night with Delaney.

Delaney. No matter how beautiful the woman sitting next to him was, it was Delaney who haunted his dreams day and night. He finished off his drink and motioned for the bartender.

"I'm sorry, honey, but I'm drinking alone."

She looked at him, blinking in confusion. She was attractive enough that she was obviously not used to being turned down.

"You're kidding me, right?" She glanced down at his left hand just to be sure there was no telltale sign of a happy marriage.

"So you're gay?" she asked incredulously.

"No, sweetheart, just not interested," Lucas grumbled, not bothering to hide his irritation with her.

"Suit yourself." She picked herself up and marched right out the door.

"Martini. Wet and a little dirty."

Lucas recognized the voice over his shoulder. He turned, offering Judah a genuine smile. "I don't know how you can drink that stuff."

"I like my drinks like I like my women," he said, his green eyes flashing. "It's a man's drink. Not like that sissy girl stuff you sip on." He indulged himself in a long swallow from his martini. "You know they say the first sign of alcoholism is a man who drinks alone."

Lucas scanned the crowded bar. "I'm hardly alone. And yes, you can join me."

Judah perched on the stool recently vacated by Red.

"Never thought I'd live to see the day when Lucas Church would send a beautiful woman away . . . unsatisfied. The Lucas Church I used to know would have been all over that girl."

"Yeah, well, maybe I'm not the same guy I used to be."

Judah chuckled. "I've known you for twenty years. You're the same guy all right. It just seems you've got Delaney in your system and you can't get rid of her."

"It might not matter. She might get rid of me."

"She's been nothing but bad news since you met her."

Lucas scowled. "You know, I was enjoying my solitude," he said irritably.

"Fine . . . I'm off my soap box. You want to tell me what happened?"

Lucas shrugged. "Who knows? The cops brought her in for questioning and now she thinks I think she offed her ex."

"Don't you?"

"Huh?"

"Don't you think she did it?"

"No, of course not. She didn't do it." Only Lucas wasn't certain.

"How can you be so sure? After all, she had motive, she had opportunity. They might as well have found her with the smoking gun."

"Well, they didn't. They haven't even found a gun."

"She had plenty of opportunity to discard it."

"Thank you for playing devil's advocate, but I don't really care for you to convict her before she's even charged."

Judah sighed. "So the cops let her go?"

"They didn't have much to hold her. It was all circumstantial, really."

"Lucky break. Damn lucky."

"There's no telling how long her luck will hold out.

They've pegged her as the murderer. It's only a matter of time before they bring her in and charge her. If only I could . . ."

Judah shook his head. "I know what you're thinking and don't think it. Drop it. You're only going to get hurt in all this."

"If she didn't do it she deserves to have a quality defense. Lawrence is as sharp as they come, but it's been years since he's done any criminal work. He'll want somebody who's done criminal work more recently to second chair, somebody who knows a few people in the D.A.'s office. . . ."

"Somebody like you? What if she did it?" Judah finished his martini. "What if she got so sick of the son of a bitch she just waltzed right into that house and up those stairs and shot him square in the forehead?"

"I can't believe she did that. She isn't capable of harming another living thing."

"You don't want to face the facts, man. Aren't you the one always saying it's all about proof? The evidence proves she did it, well then . . . proof is proof."

"Maybe. But just this once, I want to know the truth."

Chapter Thirty-one

The only thing you can count on in pageant life is that it's all downhill the minute you hit thirty.

Delaney was startled awake by knocking at the door. She hadn't meant to fall asleep on the couch, but sleep was so transitory since J.D. had been killed that when she was able to catch an hour or two of rest she took it.

The media circus that had camped out on her lawn around the clock the week before had finally dissipated, chasing a bigger, better story about a local politician and a porn star. J.D.'s murder was still in the papers but only tiny blurbs on page six. They always said the same thing: Delaney was a person of interest, the only person of interest, but she was more than grateful that the media no longer found her interesting.

"Yes?" she called as she stumbled to the door and peeked out the peephole. The bright white star of a Cowboys hat stared back at her. Whoever was there was looking down.

"Can I help you?" she called out.

"I have a delivery for a Miss Mary Mac." The delivery boy chuckled. "Hey, isn't that a rhyme or something?"

Delaney peeked out the window. The delivery guy was balancing an oversize vase of tulips—her favorite. She opened the door.

"Those are beautiful but I don't think they're for me."

"Is this 4025 Silver Birch?"

"Right address, wrong name," Delaney said, her brows knitting.

"Maybe it's a joke or something. I mean, Miss Mary Mac? Come on. Nobody really has a name like that."

"Yeah, of course." She fished out a five and several ones from her wallet.

"Aren't you supposed to be wearing black or something?" he asked.

Delaney dropped the bills. How could such a young kid know who she was and that her husband was just buried? Her face drained of all color.

"Like the rhyme," he said, breaking into a grin. "Miss Mary Mac. All dressed in black . . ." He blushed. "I got a kid sister who jump ropes to that kind of thing . . . I don't really know how the rest goes. Stupid joke. I guess you must get that all the time."

Delaney sighed and smiled. She picked up the fallen bills and traded them for the flowers.

"Gee, thanks!" He crumpled the bills and shoved them in his pocket. "If you ask me," he said as he turned to walk away, "you look much better in pink. Hot."

Delaney smiled as she closed the door. It was the first genuine smile that had creased her face since the news of J.D. The minute the thought of him entered her mind she was sick again. She glanced at the card tucked in the floral arrangement.

Odd.

The card envelope was typed: Miss Mary Mac. An

old-fashioned style typewriter whose "M" was offset, pulling the letter a tad lower than the rest. Who typed an envelope for a floral card? Before she read the words she instantly realized the card was typed also.

She froze after scanning the text. She might have screamed. She might have passed out. She didn't remember. She remembered waking up to low voices murmuring and bleary figures shifting. She blinked several times as she wondered how her home could go from completely empty to full of people in a matter of seconds.

"She's coming to," Macy called out to someone Delaney couldn't see.

Delaney tried to push herself up in bed. Her head was pounding. She felt like she had a hangover.

"You should just lie there." Macy patted her hand.

"What happened?"

"Lucas found you passed out a few hours ago. He called all of us. You came to for a little while, but you were histrionic so Matt gave you something to help you sleep. You don't remember?"

Delaney shook her head. "I can't really remember anything clearly. I remember the detectives telling me J.D. had been found dead. Everything else is just kind of bits and pieces here and there."

Matt was at the foot of her bed nodding. "Classic stress disorder. You might not remember all the events that have happened in the recent past exactly in the order that they happened. But within a few hours you should get most of the information in the right place. Don't be distressed if it's even several weeks before your brain is able to process all information correctly. Right now it's just dealing with the stress of the sudden and tragic loss of J.D. and it can't take on anything else."

Delaney managed a half smile. Matt. Sweet, analytical Dr. Matt. How could the three of them ever even imagine he would do anything as sleazy as routinely bar hop? He was totally dedicated to Phoebe and, obviously, her family, running to help whenever needed. She'd have to remember to tell Phoebe to hang on to this one.

"What do you remember?" Lucas asked.

She turned to focus on his face. His forehead was creased with lines of worry and his normally radiant blue eyes looked red and tired. If she wasn't mistaken, he looked . . . worried.

"What are you doing here?" It was the second time she had asked him that in as many days and this time she intended to get an answer.

"I was worried about you. I thought I should drop in to see how you were doing. Good thing I did. There isn't any telling how long you might have been lying there in need of help."

She didn't thank him. "Where's Lawrence?"

"He had to leave. He had a court appearance." Lucas tried to hide his irritation at her casual dismissal.

"Do you remember anything about this?" Macy passed her a photocopy of the card that had been stuck in the flower arrangement.

She scanned the card and her hands and lips trembled anew.

Miss Mary Mac
All Dressed in Black
One Silver Bullet
Right Through Her Back
The cops let you go. Next time you won't be so lucky.
I don't need evidence to put you away for life.

Delaney shivered. "I remember reading it. Right before I blacked out. It came with the flowers. But I don't understand."

"It's a credible threat," Macy told her.

"The detectives are treating it as such. Given the circumstances," Lucas said.

"No, I mean who would threaten me? Why would anybody want to kill me?"

"We were hoping you could tell us. Do you remember anything about the kid who delivered the flowers?" Lucas asked.

"He just looked like an ordinary kid. He remembered the nursery rhyme, too. He said I looked better in pink."

"Do you think he knew what the card said?"

"No. He genuinely remembered on his own accord. He blushed when he started to repeat it, like it wasn't macho or something. Then mentioned something about his little sister jump-roping to it. I really don't think there's anything to that. He was just a kid."

"Still, the detectives think it's worth checking on. They're questioning the florist to see what info they can gather about the order," Phoebe told her.

"Anybody could have sent those flowers." Delaney scooted herself up in the bed.

Matt, Phoebe, Macy and Lucas exchanged meaningful glances.

"What?" Delaney asked, searching their faces. Lucas, who had evidently been nominated as the spokesman, coughed uncomfortably into his hand.

"This is not being treated as a random act. Whoever sent those flowers sent them as a sign. Not to mention the more serious implications. They know where you live and that you would be back home. But that's not even as big a concern as the fact that they know you. They know your favorite flower is the tulip and they know your favorite color is pink. Whoever sent those flowers wanted to scare you. It is a threat we will have to take seriously."

"This is probably linked to J.D.'s murder," Matt added.

"When we find who sent these flowers, we might find who killed him," Phoebe offered.

Delaney's face blanched and her mouth went dry. "I'll say what nobody wants to say: I'm in real danger."

Lucas finally convinced the others they would better serve Delaney by going on with their normal lives to the extent that was possible. Anybody who might have been watching Delaney might well be watching the others, too. Digressing from their normal activities would be like waving a red flag. After making sure that a police unit watched the house, Lucas ran to the local drive thru, returning with a brown bag special of burgers and fries.

"So you never told me what you were doing here, when you found me."

"I came over after you hung up on me. I came to apologize," he said, avoiding eye contact. "It wasn't fair of me to jump to conclusions without hearing your side of the story."

"Call the five o'clock news, Lucas Church admits he's wrong," she joked, munching on French fries.

Lucas sighed. "And you in no way deserve the things I said to you the other day. When I saw that picture of you and J.D. in the paper, I jumped to conclusions. And I was wrong."

"Is there something more you want to ask me? Something you're not saying?"

"I just . . . I just want you to lay it all on the table for me. I've risked my career, may still be risking my career for you, and I've only known you a couple of weeks. I think I deserve to know the truth. The whole truth."

"What do you want to know?"

"Why did you go to his house the other night?

Alone." His weight was definitely on the word "alone."

"You think I did it, don't you?"

"Let's not jump back into that pool. I'm asking the tough questions. The questions you're going to have to be prepared to answer if the DA decides to take this thing to trial."

"I wasn't sleeping with him. I didn't take out that life insurance policy and I didn't have anything to do with his death. Is that clear enough for you?"

He remained silent.

"I went to his house . . . to our old house that night to collect some of my things. Shannon said he called, wanting me to come get them that night. I didn't think anything of going by myself because I didn't think he was going to be found dead in the hot tub. Hindsight is twenty-twenty."

Lucas rubbed his hands across his face, struggling to find reasons to believe her.

"Maybe . . . maybe we should just . . . I don't know. Things are crazy right now with the cops and now this nursery rhyme lunatic . . . you practically represent J.D.'s estate . . . this thing between us was just . . . really bad timing."

Lucas didn't know how to respond. He had always considered himself pretty good with math, but when it came to J.D. and Delaney Daniels, things just didn't add up. It didn't make sense that Delaney seemed so chummy all of a sudden with J.D. unless she was manipulating him to get close to him. A week ago she despised the man. Then she showed up in a photo spread arm in arm with him. The only reason she had to get close to him was so that she could ensure she got what she needed. But exactly how far was she willing to go to get what she wanted?

He finally made eye contact. His eyes had lost the sparkling blue quality she'd admired. They seemed cold and icy now.

"Fair enough." He smiled, but it was the kind of smile that only barely turned the corners of his lips.

Delaney knew that smile well, the pageant smile. Perfect. And plastic. And false. She had seen that look of distrust a dozen times during her marriage, staring back at her from the mirror. She sighed. As much as it hurt, she had wasted five years in a marriage with a man she couldn't trust. She wasn't going to waste five minutes in a relationship with a man who couldn't trust her. She knew at that moment things had changed between them. What she didn't know was if they could find their way back together.

Stacey Ferris paced J. D. Daniels's spa room at record pace as she finished off the last of a cigarette.

"When did you start smoking?" Lucas asked as he circled the hot tub.

"Oh, about ten minutes after we broke up." Her green eyes flashed at Lucas.

Lucas grinned. He may have broken a few hearts in his day, but Stacey's certainly wasn't one of them. "You know those are bad for your health." He squatted at the rim of the in-ground hot tub.

"*You* were bad for my health," she said.

"You quit me," Lucas remarked without taking his eyes off the white tape that marked where J.D.'s body had been found.

"Oh, if I remember correctly, *you* quit *me*."

Lucas shrugged and circled to the other side of the tub. "You would have eventually gotten around to it. I hear you're hooked up with an assistant DA now."

"Hooked up? Do you have to make it sound so . . . sophomoric? We're engaged."

"So is it true? Is he running for governor?"

"I can neither confirm nor deny."

Lucas looked up at his former lover and smiled. She already had the lingo of a first lady. "Let's hope they don't go digging any skeletons out of your closet." He waggled his eyebrows.

"I'm a forensic scientist. I think that gives me the leisure to have a bone or two," she joked. "Speaking of skeletons . . . what the hell are we doing? You know I could get my ass in a sling if anybody finds out I let you in here."

"You're lead CSI for this shift, right?"

"Right. But I'm not assigned to the case. I shouldn't be here unless there's a reason for me to be here."

"We're not doing anything wrong. We're just two people examining a crime scene."

"You're not working on the defense, are you? You've always been a sucker for a pretty blonde."

"Not officially. Besides, you said yourself they're opening the scene tomorrow. I just want to get a look before the cleaning team comes out."

"What are you looking for? From what I hear around the department, it is pretty much an open-and-shut case. Hostile divorce turns lethal."

"That's what bothers me. It is a little too convenient. Besides, the wife . . . she just isn't the type."

"Cheerleading, pageant-winning sorority bowhead? That's exactly the type. These prima donnas think the world is owed to them. The first time they don't get their way they snap. Might I remind you of a Betty Broderick?"

"She's not like that. She's an ordinary girl from Small Town, U.S.A. She didn't grow up rich or privileged. She didn't even want money out of the divorce.

I happen to know she was offered an enormous alimony settlement that she turned down flat."

Stacey narrowed her eyes and fixed her gaze on Lucas. "Are you hot for her or something?"

"No!" Lucas answered too quickly.

"You horny toad, you! What you won't do for a roll in the hay. But this . . . even this . . . is a record for you."

"This is not about getting her in bed. I'm a lawyer. An officer of the court. I'm seeking the truth."

"Right. I have some cases to freshen up on, I'm going to wait in the car. Don't be too long."

Lucas nodded as he watched her leave and turned his attention back to the spa room. Everything remained as it had the night of the murder. So what was he missing? J.D. had been found in the tub. A black electrical tape "x" marked where there had been two champagne flutes found and another "x" where the champagne chilled in an ice bucket. His eyes canvassed the entire room. There had to be something he was missing.

Then his eyes stopped on it. A tiny little hole. Just to the right of the steam shower. He went over to examine it more closely. Up close it could not be mistaken. A camera. J.D. Daniels had been shot and it was all on camera.

"There aren't any cameras in this house! I lived here for five years; you'd think I would have seen a surveillance room."

"It never struck you as odd, Delaney? That a house this large wouldn't have a more elaborate security system than just door and window alarms?"

"J.D. wasn't hugely paranoid. He was rather trusting, actually. And he was definitely old school. He always said the only protection he needed was a big dog and a bigger gun."

Lucas nodded. "Perhaps. But I've seen clients go an extra step on security since the development of Homeland Security. Maybe he made these additions shortly before you were married."

"Why didn't they find this before? Right after the murder?"

"This system was installed by one of the premier protection firms in the country. J.D. didn't get his money's worth if it was easily detected. Not only that but one can only find the evidence one is looking for. Maybe it wasn't intentional, but you were pegged for this murder the minute Misty dialed 911. They only needed to find the evidence that convicted you. I was looking for evidence that would clear you," he told her.

"Thank you." She inhaled deeply but her eyes were still bright with tears. She switched her attention to the dozens of officers who were scattered like ants throughout the estate, tapping on walls or listening to them with stethoscopes. "What are they doing?"

"Looking for a false wall."

"False wall?"

"False wall, hidden door. Something that might conceal another room . . . a panic room . . . a safe room . . . anything like that where J.D. might have kept—"

"Got it!" a uniform yelled from J.D.'s study.

Delaney and Lucas rushed to the study as the officer revealed a keypad behind a volume of Yeats.

"Do you know his code?"

"Are you kidding? I didn't even know this was here."

"Maybe a pet's name. An old phone number. Anything?"

"He used to have a horse, Blue. He used that as the pin number on his debit card."

The officer tried it. The wall slowly opened, revealing a twelve-by-twelve room filled with television monitors, shelves of canned food and bottled water, even a futon in the corner. Delaney shook her head in disbelief.

"I ate here, slept here. We . . . I . . . he was watching me the whole time and I never knew it. Are there cameras that cover the bedrooms and the bathrooms?" Delaney asked, chewing her bottom lip. She could only imagine an entire precinct of officers getting their jollies watching old recordings of her.

Wayne blushed, understanding her concern. "It appears so, ma'am. We'll have to take all these tapes into evidence but I assure you, the lieutenant will make sure they are viewed with the utmost discretion."

"There's a tape in the recorder. It's stopped recording now, but I'm willing to bet that it is the same one that was in there the night of the murder," Cruz informed Lucas and Delaney. They circled around the monitor as one of the officers pressed rewind, taking them back to the day of the murder, just moments before J.D.'s death. He reclined in the hot tub. Something from the corner of the room, off camera, gained his attention and seconds later he was shot.

"It doesn't show anything." Delaney sighed, dejected.

"On the contrary, Mrs. Daniels. It shows something very important."

"What?"

He pointed to the corner of the screen, the time date stamp. Of course! J.D. was shot and murdered at or around 3:30 in the afternoon. Delaney had thirteen very reliable alibis: her 3:15 ballet class. There was no way she could have been at the ranch at the time J.D. was murdered.

"Once we verify this time stamp, that nobody has tampered with any of the equipment or the video, then I'd say you were free to go," Cruz said.

"It won't be too difficult to authenticate," Wayne added, his voice tinged with sympathy for the first time.

"We'll check out the surveillance from the other cameras. We might be able to get an image of somebody trespassing on the property or entering the house. I just hope he wasn't wearing a disguise at the time," Cruz told them.

She hugged Lucas. "I don't how to thank you. I owe you my life."

Lucas tipped an imaginary hat. "Just doing my job, ma'am."

"No. You did so much more. I owe you."

He grinned his lopsided grin that dimpled his cheek. "And I'll collect. Of that you can be sure."

"The Austin Police Department no longer considers Delaney Daniels a subject of interest. Newfound evidence has taken their investigation in another direction. Daniels, a former Miss Texas, had recently become the sole suspect in the investigation of the murder of her estranged husband, J. D. Daniels, CEO of the Daniels Enterprises conglomerate. Officials will not comment on the evidence they found but said that it promises to yield more information about the death of one of Texas's favorite sons."

"Damn it!" the man screamed as he threw the television remote at the screen.

Newfound evidence? There was no evidence other than what he planted for them to find. She had the motive; she had the opportunity. What the hell more did they want? A snapshot of her with the gun?

He couldn't lose control. That would be detrimental. This was just a glitch in his plan. No matter what evidence the police had found, it didn't point back to him. He'd been careful. He'd driven a rental. He'd worn a mask and a neutral black T-shirt and black pants—no labels. The only things he'd seen after he hopped the fence were a couple of cattle and a horse, and they weren't talking. He retrieved a longneck from the fridge and took a deep swig.

There were other problems right now. The dim-witted accountant, Schuyler, was starting to get nervous. Since J.D.'s death, all he could talk about was needing protection, going to the officials. He wasn't going to let some dumbass bean counter bring him down. Schuyler had to be silenced.

Chapter Thirty-two

Don't be afraid to dream.

She couldn't see his face. The stage lights blinded her. If she shielded her eyes with her hand and squinted she could make out the shadowy figure. No face. But the body. The body was definitely male. He was walking toward her from the back of the auditorium. She tried to smile and wave. Smile and wave. Smile and wave. There were no cheers from the audience. She was just crowned; there were always cheers. There were no cheers. Smile and wave. The roses she carried became burdensome. Crimson concrete. The shadow was moving faster. The flowers were so heavy. The tiara pressed into her head, causing it to throb. Ignore the headache. Smile and wave. The roses were so heavy . . . if she could just drop them. The shadow stopped. He raised his hand. The noise. It was a clap but it wasn't cheering. It was a gun. A bullet. Three drops fell from her head . . . and she was bleeding. And now they were cheering. So she smiled. And waved.

Delaney awoke dripping in sweat. The nightmares.

Nightly. Vividly. But when she woke, she couldn't remember anything from them except the intense feelings of dread and panic. And a gun. Sometimes when she woke it was because she heard herself screaming the word "Help!" But as much as she tried to pull it from the recesses of her memory, she didn't know what she feared or why she needed help. She shook her head and took a long sip from the glass of water she kept near her bed. She had to stop watching *The Sopranos* before bed. She had been cleared of J.D.'s murder. Anybody who might have been targeting her out of revenge had no reason to come after her. She was safe, right?

The funeral had been more than a week ago, and burying J.D. had also buried the press frenzy surrounding his murder. The cloud of suspicion had been lifted, and she was finally comfortable at home. No flashbulbs, no phone calls, no police interviews. Just the more than occasional neighborhood patrol around her, "for the safety and interests of all parties," Cruz and Lawrence had convinced her. She couldn't help worrying if they would imagine that she had paid for somebody to kill J.D., but she couldn't lie awake fretting about that.

Think about the center. Think about the girls. You gotta keep it together, even if it kills you.

She grimaced at her poor choice of words.

Delaney massaged her neck and rolled her head slowly from shoulder to shoulder. She glanced at the clock. Four A.M. No point in trying to go back to sleep. She knew she would stare at the ceiling for several hours before forcing herself to get up and go on her morning jog. So as long as she was awake, she might as well make the best use of her time.

Her thoughts drifted back to Through the Looking Glass. In the last two weeks she hadn't given the center the attention it deserved. But that was going to be remedied this afternoon. She spied the statements she had downloaded from the online banking account and a legal-sized envelope Shannon had left on her porch. She hoped Shannon had been able to do some research and discover the identities of the cash cows J.D. milked for funding. With J.D. gone, she couldn't rely on funding from Daniels Enterprises. Paul had a heart carved from stone; the last thing he was interested in was philanthropic endeavors. Without the financial support of Daniels Enterprises behind her, she was going to need to stick her hands in some deep pockets to keep the center up and running.

Delaney had already made an appointment to visit with a new CPA. If she wanted to be able to speak intelligently regarding the finances of the organization, she was going to need some answers from Schuyler. She had spoken with him twice since the murder, but on the phone the conversations were always cryptic and rushed. He was insistent on speaking to her in person.

Math types.

She rolled her eyes as she got out of bed. Delaney was certain he had gotten wind of the fact that she wanted to seek an independent accounting firm and that he was going to try to woo her into staying with Simon, Simon and Schuyler, but she had already made up her mind. Through the Looking Glass was her baby, and she wanted a fresh start—to sever any ties with J.D. and Daniels Enterprises. Nothing Herman Schuyler said or did could change her mind.

Delaney had paced the kitchen floor long enough. The mug of cinnamon vanilla-flavored coffee had grown tepid while she watched minutes tick off the green digital display of the clock on her microwave. The second the clocked displayed 9:00. She picked up the phone to dial Herman Schuyler, J.D.'s private accountant.

"Simon, Simon and Skiiii-ler. Hold please." The line went immediately to a classical rendition of some pop not-so-favorite. Delaney seethed, wondering how what was probably the first call of the morning could justify a hold.

Three minutes later the receptionist returned. "Simon, Simon and Skiiii-ler. Thank you for holding. How may I direct your call?" the receptionist whined. Delaney thought to ask her if she was enjoying her doughnut, but then pictured a perfectly polished acrylic nail poised and ready over the disconnect button and thought better of it.

"Mr. Schuyler, please."

"I'm sorry, but Mr. Schuyler is out of the office." The receptionist didn't sound sorry at all. She sounded inconvenienced.

"Will he be in today?"

"Nope," she was more than happy to respond.

"Will he be in tomorrow?"

"Nope." She popped the "p" at the end of the word. Delaney hated when people did that.

"*When* will he be in?" Irritation seeped through her words. Delaney decided to avoid the closed-ended questions altogether.

"Mr. Schuyler has taken an indefinite leave of absence," the receptionist recited.

"He has?"

"Yep." More "p" popping.

"Ooooo-kay," Delaney slowly responded. "Is there anyone working with Mr. Schuyler's clients? I had an appointment set up for today. It's very important that I speak to somebody."

"He kind of left all of a sudden. The Simons haven't got that figured out yet..." Her voice lowered.

"What?" she whispered. "I don't know, some chick. Why? . . . What? . . . Well, what the hell am I *supposed* to tell her?. . . . Oh . . ." She returned her attention to Delaney. "I'm supposed to tell you to direct all questions regarding Mr. Schuyler and his clients to our legal firm, Duncan, Kelley and Hilderbrand."

Delaney sighed. *Lucas's firm.*

"Do you know it?"

"Oh yeah, I know it."

Criminology 101: Tie up all loose ends. Schuyler was definitely a loose end. He had been given a perfectly acceptable alternative. He could have taken the money and disappeared somewhere in South America. But he was weak. Whining about leaving his wife and kids. With his cut he could start a whole new family south of the border. Ten million goes a hell of a long way in the third world, for sure. Hell! His wife and kids would have been better off without him. He could have faked his death and left them with a cushy insurance claim on which to soak their salty tears. Schuyler had miraculously sprouted a conscience overnight. He had to be dealt with. He was planning to spill his guts to that beauty queen bimbo and who knows who else? And exactly what did he think that was going to get him? Immunity? Not likely. Bound and gagged in the trunk of his car in the blazing heat of a Texas summer, that's what.

Now he could focus all his attention on the beauty queen. She should have left her Nancy Drew detective card at home. Who the hell did she think she was, stirring up all this commotion? If she would only learn to keep her mouth shut, nothing bad would happen to her. He smiled as he watched her strut into the law firm, hotheaded and hell bent, totally unaware that she was being followed, watched.

Delaney Daniels, another damn loose end.

Chapter Thirty-three

There is no judging conspiracy . . . just really bitter losers.

"I want answers." Delaney dropped a stack of papers on Lucas's desk. He looked up, startled to see her suddenly in front of him. Claire must have taken a lunch; it was the only explanation for why Delaney was here unannounced.

"Do I know the questions?" he said, glancing at what appeared to be bank statements.

"You were J.D.'s lawyer."

Lucas scanned the stack of papers. "You must be under the impression that privilege ceases at death. It doesn't necessarily. Regardless of our relationship . . ."

"I would not use the fact that we slept together to manipulate you into telling me anything you shouldn't tell me." Delaney's eyes darkened with anger. After all they had been through, she couldn't believe he still thought her capable of using him.

"Of course not. Still, I don't have any answers for you. I can't tell you anything about his personal financial—"

"This is not personal. This is about the Looking Glass. I'm still the director of the program, not to mention my name was on the account during the period of time in question, so I have a right to know what is going on with our accounts."

Lucas glanced at the statements again. "I was only his divorce attorney. And only for a very brief period of time. I don't know that much about his business affairs, but maybe if you tell me what we are looking at, *maybe* I can ask Judah a few questions. I'm letting you know—"

"I won't ask you to tell me anything that could compromise your position. I just need a few answers. I don't understand all these transfers in and out of our account to all these foreign companies. We never had any relationship with these banks. I've never even heard of most of them. And all of J.D.'s international ventures were taken care of by firms in those countries. That said, none of those companies ever had a relationship, financial or otherwise, with my center."

Lucas raised a brow and sifted through several of the statements, making note of dozens of transfers that must have added up to millions of dollars over the last year. He handed the statements back to Delaney.

"And that's not all." She produced another stack of papers and dropped them on his desk. "Some of Shannon's friends work in the corporate offices; these are 401k and profit-sharing quarterly statements from more than a dozen employees of Daniels Enterprises ending third quarter last year. These . . ." She produced even more papers. ". . . are the statements ending third quarter this year. Shannon and I have seen similar losses. Where is all the money? It didn't just disappear."

Lucas examined the documents for several minutes while Delaney paced the length of floor in front
of his desk.

"Well?" She fisted a hand on one hip and tapped
her foot while she waited for an answer.

"Yes, at first glance this is . . . curious."

"It's not curious. It's criminal. J.D. Daniels stole our
money."

"I'm sorry. I don't know what to tell you. Honestly,
I don't know anything about J.D.'s business matters.
That was taken care of by a different department in
the law firm. But I can tell you it won't pay to rush in
there and run ramshod over them because they aren't
giving up any information. They'll cite . . ."

"Privilege," she said angrily.

"Privilege," Lucas echoed softly. "Daniels Enterprises, Paul, the board of directors, they are all still
clients of this law firm. It is our job to protect their
interest."

"What a privilege it must be for your law firm to aid
and abet a thief. That is morally reprehensible."

"Perhaps, but it is the law. Even if Judah were to tell
me anything . . . I wouldn't be able to relay the information to you. Paul is still among the living and, right
or wrong, this law firm still represents his company. I
suggest you speak with the investment firm that man-
ages the 401k plan? Maybe it's simply a matter of
careless investing."

"Been there, done that. They refer us to his accounting firm."

"And?"

"And they refer us to you. And you refer us back to
the investment firm." She threw up her arms.

"Look, I know it's frustrating. There is a way to determine what happened to the money. We just have to
find it. You have a working relationship with the ac-

counting firm, right? They audit your books? We'll start there."

"Don't bother. Schuyler stood me up for an appointment to discuss all this. He didn't even bother to have his secretary call and cancel."

A dark expression curtained Lucas's face as he suddenly began to realize the implications of what Delaney was saying to him.

"Schuyler. Herman Schuyler?"

"Yeah, why?"

"I take it you haven't seen or heard the news in the last few hours."

"I stopped watching the news shortly after the three major stations started using my name and photographs as their lead story every night."

Lucas sighed. "Herman Schuyler was found stuffed in the trunk of his car at the bus depot. He was murdered."

Delaney dropped into the buttery soft leather of the office chair as she let Lucas's words sink in.

"Murdered?"

"Unless he managed the feat of binding and gagging himself, climbing into his trunk and closing it, yes. Murdered."

"Who? When? Where? Why?"

"They just found him a few hours ago. He's been MIA a couple of days, so you know, they start their searches at the usual hot spots: airport, train station, bus depot. They found his car at the bus depot and when they popped the trunk . . ."

Delaney held her head in the palms of her hands. "Do you realize what this means? First J.D. and now Schuyler."

"Wait a minute, Delaney. Don't go jumping to conclusions. Yes, it is a coincidence, a mighty big coincidence. But the police have not linked these murders. As far as they're concerned the primary motive in Schuyler's murder appears to be robbery. He was stripped of his wallet, his watch and his wedding band. And the primary motive in J.D.'s murder is—"

"What? Nobody knows why J.D. was killed. Now Schuyler. Somebody wanted them both dead but didn't want the police correlating the murders. And whoever did it put this plan into motion at least three months ago when they bought that life policy on J.D. Somebody who knows me. Somebody who thought I would be the perfect scapegoat."

"You're missing one critical piece—motive. You barely knew Schuyler."

"You want motive?" She pushed the papers she had brought in across the desk, dropping some in Lucas's lap, scattering some across the floor. "What if you tell your shareholders your company is worth thirty billion and in reality the figure is a lot less than thirty million. What if your ex-wife stumbles across this fact when she's fighting tooth and nail to save her silly charity. What if she's not the dumb blonde you thought she was and puts two and two together. We have to go to the Federal Trade Commission or the DA or something."

"You watch too much Court TV."

"They'll want to see what we have."

"What do we have, Delaney? A few bank statements. A dozen 401k quarterly statements. That's not evidence. The best way to be ignored is to make accusations without foundation. They'll say you're under stress, they'll tell you to visit a doctor and ask for sedatives. This," he waved to the papers scattered across his desk, "this doesn't look good but it isn't—"

"Proof," she finished.

"Not to mention two of the key players are . . . dead."

"But there's more!" she insisted. "The day of J.D.'s murder I went to his office to appeal to him regarding the directorship at the center and Paul was there."

"That's hardly out of the ordinary."

"So they were arguing. Fighting. Yelling at the top of their lungs. Now, they've never been the best of friends, but doesn't it seem the least bit odd that they were arguing so viciously right before J.D. was murdered?"

"You think Paul might have had something to do with J.D.'s murder? His own brother?"

Delaney chewed on her bottom lip before answering. She didn't want to accuse him of something so horrible when she had no foundation other than a fight. "I don't know what it means," she finally decided. "I just know that Paul lives, breathes and dies for Daniels Enterprises."

"Which is exactly why he wouldn't be involved in any corporate accounting scheme to ruin the conglomeration."

"It's also why he would do anything to protect the integrity of the company. If J.D. were involved in some wrongdoing and Paul thought it would besmirch the name of the company . . . and the family, I don't think Paul would ever let that happen."

Lucas fixed his eyes on Delaney. "Do you think he's capable of killing in order to protect the company?"

"I don't know. That's why I need your help. If Paul killed them—"

"Delaney, all this is no more than conjecture. I know it feels as though it all fits together like a puzzle and maybe that's how things come together on television, but in real life, real cops and real DAs need real evidence. We don't have any real evidence."

"Let them find the evidence. But they won't start looking if they don't know there's something to look for." Delaney repeated almost verbatim the words Lucas had spoken to her.

"What if you're right? What if J.D. was involved in something sketchy? He lost his life for it. I don't want you getting involved if it means you could be hurt." He knew he should tell her why. He should say that he couldn't live with himself if something or someone harmed her. He should tell her he couldn't live if anything ever happened to her.

"Does it even matter? Because the truth is, J.D. was a big-business billionaire and those murders aren't swept under back-room rugs. Somebody is going to hang for his death and, right now, I'm guessing the APD thinks I'm just as good as the next guy. What kind of life would I have behind bars? Prison would be preferable. It would take a small miracle to keep a needle out of my arm if I'm convicted."

"You aren't going to prison. They don't have any evidence against you. We've already proved that you couldn't have possibly been at the house at the time of the murder."

"Maybe it's just a matter of time before they get the idea that I hired somebody to kill J.D."

She was right. Just because she didn't pull the trigger didn't mean she would be exonerated of any related charges. The thought had even crossed his mind once or twice.

"This isn't even about me anymore, Lucas. So far, I've been lucky. I've had you and Lawerence and Mace and Phebes all looking out for me. Well, it's high time I grew up and started looking out for others. You know I tell my girls at the center all the time how important it is to do the right thing. This is about doing the right thing. There are thousands of people who work for Daniels Enterprises who stand to lose everything because of J.D.'s greed. I'm not saying I can single-handedly make it all right, but somebody has to look out for them the same way you guys were watching my back. I feel like I owe it to them."

On some level Lucas had thought that once her name was cleared, Delaney would go on, business as usual. It would be easier for her to continue to run her organization without J.D. standing in her way. But Lucas should have known better. What he did know of Delaney was that she was a champion of those who didn't have anybody to fight for them. The same energy that drove her to tirelessly practice pirouettes with Penny was the same motivation to get to the bottom of what was shaping up to be one of the biggest accounting scandals in the history of oil.

He sighed. "Let me talk to Judah. See what he knows, if he's heard anything or if he can tunnel out some news before we send the whole Austin Police Department on a wild goose chase."

"Thank you. You don't know what this means to me." She hugged him tightly.

Lucas tensed. It was the first direct contact they had had since their last night together.

"No problem." He rubbed the expanse of her back, reluctant to let her go.

"Really." She pulled away just slightly, enough to make eye contact but not so much to break his comfortable hold of her. "You don't know what it means to have your support, to have you believe me."

Believe in me.

Delaney tilted her chin, inviting a kiss. He pressed her lips to his. At the very moment their lips touched he knew he was in over his head, losing control. He didn't understand it. The insatiable desire, *need*, for her. And he didn't give a damn. He wasn't thinking. Hell, he couldn't think if he wanted to. All he wanted to do, all he could do was feel her. The soft curves of her body as she pressed herself against him. His heart hammered against his chest as he deepened their kiss with his need to possess her.

It had been too long since he'd enjoyed the warmth of release her body offered his. He could have her. Right here. Right now. He thought about the office door, trying to remember when she had barged in.

Was it locked?

Judah cleared his throat from the doorway.

It wasn't.

Lucas pulled away quickly, pushing Delaney back just slightly, and wiped the evidence of her lipstick from his mouth with the back of his hand. He tried to lean against the desk so as to camouflage his raging erection.

Judah's eyes moved from Lucas to Delaney and back again. "Guess I should have knocked," he said.

"Yes, you should have. Mrs. Daniels was just leaving," Lucas responded, hiding his embarrassment behind formality.

"Right. I really need to get going so, if you can check on that thing . . ." she told Lucas.

Lucas nodded. "I'll check on it."

"It was nice seeing you again, Delaney." Judah's voice followed her as she hurried out of the room, as did his eyes. "That's one lady who looks just as good going as she does coming." He whistled. "You know, I don't understand why you're being such an idiot over her but if she is half as good in bed as she looks, I might be getting the picture." He turned to meet Lucas's stony, cold expression. "What?" He feigned innocence. "I was just paying her an innocent compliment."

"I would appreciate it if you didn't treat her like she was just another piece of ass."

Judah shrugged. "Sorry. I didn't mean anything by it."

Lucas nodded. He was much more territorial with Delaney than he had ever been with any other woman. "I'm sorry. I didn't mean to jump down your throat. It's just, I'm worried about her."

"Really?" Judah sat. "What's up?" His eyes fell to the stack of papers scattered across the mahogany desk and floor. "What's all this?"

Lucas shook his head as he retrieved some of the papers and shuffled them into a semblance of order. "Delaney's got it in her head that something fishy was going on at Daniels Enterprises and she thinks that is why J.D. was killed. This . . ." he shook a handful of papers, ". . . is her proof."

Judah reclined in the tufted leather chair. "Proof? A few bank statements? What does she think was going on?"

"Not sure. We thought maybe you could help us out."

Judah's eyes narrowed. "You're 'us' now?" he asked.

Lucas tilted his head in a half nod.

"There was a time when you and I were 'us.' Best friends. You watched my back and I watched yours." Judah shook his head and held up his hands. "Look, if you want to lay your career on the line over a piece of ass, that's fine. But I've got a family to support. I'm not breaking all the rules of privilege when I don't even have the privilege of . . ."

Lucas cut him short. He didn't even want to hear what was about to come out of Judah's mouth. "I'm not asking you to break any rules of privilege. I'm just asking you to let me know if there was anything funny going on with the accounting practices at Daniels Enterprises."

Judah sighed, steepling his fingers in front of his

face. "Exactly what does she know? If she knows of illegal activity, it's her responsibility to go to the authorities. Let them get a subpoena for documents. Do things . . . you know . . . legally."

"She doesn't know anything. She suspects. And I've advised her not to go to the authorities just yet. We don't know that there is anything going on. If she's wrong it will be a headache for the firm and a huge embarrassment for her. I just need to know if you ever noticed any oddities in Daniels's requests."

"As far as I know, everything at Daniels was on the up and up. J.D. was very meticulous with the business of the company. My advice to you, my friend, is to drop it. Let it go. J.D. Daniels might be dead, but our relationship with Daniels Enterprises is not. J.D. was a kitten compared to his brother, and Paul Daniels is not Delaney's biggest fan. If you go stirring up a lot of shit over this, I can assure you that Paul will press for your dismissal. You can kiss your job good-bye."

"I was relying on you to keep any inquiries under the radar, Judah, friend to friend. I'm not entirely sure how much Paul is involved in this whole mess. He might pose a bigger threat to Delaney than we know."

Judah narrowed his eyes. "Threat? Lucas, you can't go accusing one of the most respected citizens of the state of . . . I don't know what. Do you know what you're saying?"

"Nobody's accusing anybody of anything. It's speculation. But if you could do some checking without him finding out, that would be great."

"I can't believe you're risking everything you've worked for. . . . You love your job."

"You're right. I do. But this is more important than a job, Judah. A lot of the employees at Daniels Enterprises have lost a lot of money in the last few quarters.

If this is one of those accounting schemes that J.D. got caught up in, it has already cost him his life, and may mean the livelihood of thousands of others. Not to mention Delaney might be in danger."

"Fraud? Murder? You know what I think? I think you both need to say no to the next episode of 'ripped from the headlines' *Law & Order*. You are beginning to sound like those conspiracy nuts."

"I'm just asking for you to throw me a bone."

Judah stood. "I'm going to give you a piece of advice, *friend to friend*: let her go, Lucas. Better yet, get rid of her altogether. Cold turkey. She's trouble and has been since the day you met her."

Lucas didn't open his mouth to argue because he had the sneaking suspicion that Judah was right. There was something keeping him attached to Delaney, making it impossible for him to walk away for good.

Who the hell did she think she was? Making all kinds of inquiries and accusations. She didn't know she had a shadow. Somebody who watched her every move, listened to her every word. He had tolerated enough out of her. She had to be silenced. For good.

Chapter Thirty-four

Every little girl wants to grow up to be a queen, but I have one question for them: Do you know how many queens have lost their heads?

Delaney stepped out of the Jacuzzi bath onto the cold ceramic floor. She had to remember to get her bath rugs from the cleaners the next time she went by the strip mall. She stared at her reflection. The golden flash normally sparkling in her eyes was absent and had been for several days. Most nights she didn't sleep at all. The nights she did manage to get some sleep, she normally woke up sweating, heart throbbing from the nightmares.

"You look awful, girl," she told her reflection. She had to get some sleep tonight. She had a sleep aid Matt had prescribed that wasn't quite as strong as the ones he had given her previously. *Dirty Dancing* was on TBS, so maybe she would microwave some popcorn, take the pill and let "The Time of My Life" lull her to sleep on the couch.

Or maybe not. Lucas had mentioned that he would call, so maybe she would try to stay awake until she got his call. Or maybe he would decide to come over. Maybe.

She slipped into her Supergirl pajamas, the ones with the bright blue lycra cami and the tiny boxers screen-printed with a repeating red "S," and brushed her honey-gold hair into a loose knot at the crown of her head. A cool summer night's breeze from her dressing room window got her attention. She never opened the window in her dressing room. For that matter, she didn't think she ever locked it, either. The sole purpose of the window was for the aesthetic from the outside view of the house. So unless she was spring cleaning the blinds, she normally ignored that window.

Goose bumps dotted her flesh. She rubbed warmth to her arms and closed the window. She stilled for a moment, listening for any unusual sounds through the house.

Silence.

She shook her head. She could drive herself crazy imagining all the possible scenarios for the window being left open. There was probably a perfectly reasonable explanation. Perhaps the cleaning lady had opened it the last time she had been there. It was the same cleaning lady she had used when she was married to J.D. Even at the ranch, the lady had been notorious for leaving windows open. Every time she cleaned she left random windows open. Something about fumes of cleaning products and fresh air. Perhaps Delaney just hadn't noticed before that it was cracked, and a stiff breeze had pushed it open. Yes, Delaney was certain that was it. That must be it. Delaney would mention it to her the next time she came to clean. Maybe she would purchase a box fan or something to keep the fumes at bay. Or maybe there was still that old box fan in the attic.

Delaney grimaced at the thought of spiders in that dark and musty attic. She shuddered away the crawling sensation that was climbing up and down her spine. That was when she saw him. The tall, dark, looming figure, clad from head to toe in black. He was even wearing a ski mask. Delaney processed incoherent thoughts like a sluggish CPU.

First: *Why is the man in my kitchen wearing a ski mask in the middle of summer in Texas?*

Instead of: *Why is there a man in my kitchen?*

Then: *Where did he find my Henckels meat cleaver?*

Instead of: *Why is coming at me with that knife?*

But the next thoughts were clear and coherent.

Run.

Scream.

Everything she ever learned about standing her ground to face her opponent (you cannot defend yourself from the danger you can't see) and not turning her back to him flew out the window. She turned to run, but within steps his arms were around her. The stupid thoughts returned.

He smells just like J.D.

She kicked and screamed as he tried to tighten his hold on her. She knew any moment she would feel the razor-sharp blade (*Damn that specially formulated high-carbon steel blade!*) split her skull. She would be dead and the newspapers would write stupid headlines about her: *Texas Beauty Queen Loses Her "Crown" in Gruesome Murder. Bye-Bye, Miss Mincemeat Pie.*

She refused to be another stupid headline. The gruesome thought of a gash through her skull and the heyday the press would have with *that* roused her senses and everything she'd learned in her martial arts self-defense classes surfaced. She had taken Tae Kwon Do for self-defense during her pageant circuit days. One year there had been some weirdo who latched on to some random Miss Nobody from Nowhere and sent the pageant sponsors into a protection frenzy. The girls were coached two hours a day on martial arts between the sightseeing photo shoots and dance practice.

The instructor was a very happy and equally tiny woman who informed the contestants that victimization began with a thought; that the first thought when being attacked is, "I'm going to die."

"Just quit that stinkin' thinkin'." She wagged a finger at the dozens of contestants. "If you're being attacked, what do you say?" she asked at the beginning of each session.

"I. Will. *Not*. Die. Today!" Delaney screamed as the words came rushing back to her. She punctuated each word with a brutal stomp on his foot, a half turn, a kick to his chest, a palm to his nose and a knee to his groin.

The man moaned and curled over. His scream was angry. Deep. Gutteral. Again with the thoughts.

He sounds like J.D.

The attacker dropped the meat cleaver, doubled over, then fell to the ground groaning. Delaney snatched up the blade. For some unknown reason, she remembered reading an article once in the paper about how an attacker might cut the Achilles' heel of his victim to prevent her from running away. She didn't know how much reliability that theory held, considering it was in a gossip rag, but weighing her options, she felt it was worth a try. The attacker howled in pain as the blade ripped across his ankle. Delaney dropped the weapon, well within his reach (*Stupid! If the Achilles' heel thing doesn't work*), and ran like hell out the door and down the street.

Lucas slowed his car to a screeching halt and blinked hard to make sure his eyes did not deceive him. No mistake. Supergirl was running down the street headed straight for his car.

"I need you to calm down," Lucas said. "You have to tell me what the hell you're doing running miles from home dressed like a freaking cartoon." He didn't mean to yell at her or to sound so callous, but she was screaming, she was unintelligible and, if he wasn't mistaken, she was covered in blood. And for the first time in his cognizant memory, he was scared.

She heaved in large doses of air, her tear-streaked face glistening beneath the street lights in the dark night sky.

"There's ... there's a man ... in my house ... he tried to ... he was going ... to ..."

Lucas embraced Delaney, holding her tightly in order to suppress her violent shaking. "Delaney, it's okay. You're safe. Did he hurt you? Your legs are covered in blood. Are you bleeding?"

"No. I fought him ... I kicked his ass just liked they taught us in self-defense." She was beginning to calm down.

"Where is he now? Is he still at your place?"

She nodded, still crying but at least not screaming.

"Is this his blood? Did you hurt him? Did you kill him?"

"No. I just cut him. His ankle ... like I read once in the supermarket checkout. They wait under your car . . . I cut his ankle . . . so he couldn't run after me . . . and I ran."

"Did you call the police?

She shook her head.

"We're going to call the police. All right? We're going to call the police and then we are going to wait right here for them, and when the police get to your house and check everything out, then we'll go back there, okay?"

She nodded.

"Delaney, I need to know that you are okay. I need for you to tell me that you are okay."

"I'm okay."

She was still shaking but she wasn't sobbing. Lucas called the police on his cell phone, giving them Delaney's address and the few details he knew about the attack. Delaney paced in front of Lucas while he was on the phone and glanced up at the street sign.

Maple Street?

She had run just over three miles in her red flip-flops and pajamas without even thinking.

"They're on their way. They want us to meet them at the intersection in a few minutes."

The gray wool blanket scratched Delaney's skin, but she welcomed the weight and the warmth it provided. She had never noticed how low she kept her air conditioner until she was forced to sit around in her living room in pajamas and no electric blanket or cashmere throw to snuggle under.

When the police had gotten to her place, the house was empty but for a trail of blood out the back door that was lost in the brush behind her backyard. The intruder had vanished, like a ghost. Neighbors watered their lawns at night, making it impossible for the canine units to pick up a scent past the curb. More than likely the intruder had parked his vehicle close enough to make a speedy escape. The police canvassed the neighborhood and woke her neighbors to ask them what out of the ordinary they might have heard or seen earlier that evening.

"Mrs. Daniels." Detective Wayne, sympathetic this time, approached her.

"Yes?" she asked.

"I know you must be exhausted after your ordeal, but we do have a few more questions if you don't mind."

Delaney shrugged. She had nothing more to tell them, but if they wanted to pick her brain, they were welcome to it.

"You said you engaged in a struggle with the intruder. Did he say anything to you?"

Delaney shook her head. "No. When I entered the kitchen I froze right there at the door, just for a few seconds, when I first saw him. Then I turned to run and he came after me with that meat cleaver."

"Did he make any verbal threats to you at any time?"

"He never said a word. He screamed. But he never said anything."

"He grabbed you?"

"Yes."

"Do you mind demonstrating, with Mr. Church here, how you got away?"

Delaney nodded and stood positioning herself in front of Lucas.

"He had me like this." She wrapped his arms around her waist. "Only a lot tighter. But with only one hand. He had the blade in his other hand. I thought for sure he was going to bring it down on my head if I didn't get away, so I stomped on his foot, the toes, with my heel." She demonstrated in slow motion for the detective. "It surprised him, which allowed me the opportunity to turn. Then I kicked him." She lifted her leg and positioned her foot perpendicular to Lucas's chest. "He stumbled back a little so I took the opening to jab him." Palm to Lucas's nose. "And disable him." Knee in slow motion, very slow motion, to Lucas's groin. "That's when he fell and I cut his ankle. I was going for his Achilles' heel but . . ."

Lucas and Wayne stood open-mouthed after the demonstration. "What?" she asked.

"It's just amazing that you were able to defend yourself against this guy."

Delaney shrugged. "I owe it all to the Supergirl underoos."

Lucas groaned. "Explain how the hell you're suddenly Miss Kickass."

The men nodded.

"You guys have only known me through a pretty rough spell. Despite the recent deluge of tears, I'm not a girl who can't take of myself."

"Evidently," Lucas said.

"You say this man was over six feet?" Wayne asked.

"Precisely six-two," Delaney said.

"You're certain?" Lucas asked.

"I'm absolutely certain."

They exchanged looks. The attack had not been prolonged, by her own account. How could she be so sure?

"Mrs. Daniels, did you know your attacker?" Wayne asked.

"Yes."

Lucas's mouth dropped open. Delaney had not mentioned before that she might have known who attacked her.

"Delaney, if you know who did this to you, you have to tell us."

Delaney looked into Lucas's clear blue eyes. She sighed. "If you must know . . . it was J.D."

Chapter Thirty-five

I once read about a contestant who completely cracked up mid-Miss America. She thought she was competing as the Miss of each of the fifty states and the District of Columbia. Anybody who thinks pageants are all fun and games has obviously never competed.

"Of course she *knows* he's dead. She's just created a separate reality. It happens. When a person endures a number of stressful situations in a relatively short period of time, she may create a more peaceful reality, often going back to a point just before the trigger event. We'll have to keep a close eye on her for a few days. We can all take turns. Besides, until they catch this guy it's probably better that she stay with somebody." Matt stood at Lucas's door along with Phoebe and Macy. He was a horrible whisperer. Delaney heard everything he said.

"We really appreciate you helping out, Lucas." Phoebe absently twirled a lock of hair.

"I wouldn't have it any other way. Since I found her, I kind of feel responsible for looking after her tonight."

And every night.

He wanted to take care of her. He wanted to do whatever he had to do to make sure no harm came to her, now or ever.

"Watch after her, Luke. That's my big sister. The only one I got. I kind of want to hang on to her."

"And my best friend," Macy added.

Lucas said good-bye and shut the door. He turned to his bedroom and ran face to face into Delaney.

"You're supposed to be lying down. Resting."

"I'm not tired. Besides, how can I rest when the people I love most in my life are sitting around discussing how crazy I am?"

Lucas's heart quickened at her words.

"The people I love most in my life."

He searched her eyes for some clue that she had meant to include him among the ranks of those people. He could just ask. But how elementary would that sound? *Do you love me? Check yes.* But he wanted so badly to hear that she loved him. Because he loved her.

That was it. He loved her. He couldn't say how or when it happened. It could have been the first moment he laid eyes on her as she teased the crowded bar from a well-lit stage. Or maybe it was when she turned him down. *That* had been a first for him. Or the time she saw her talking with the girls at the center. The way they looked up at her as if she were the most beautiful woman in the world, and she was. Not because of her face or her body or any of that but because she looked back at them as if *they* were the most beautiful women in the world.

"I mean . . ." she started.

He didn't want to hear her explanations. He

wanted to believe that she felt about him the way he felt about her. So he spoke over her to shut her up. "Nobody thinks you're crazy, Delaney. Matt says it's a classic case of post-traumatic stress disorder. You've had a lot put on your plate over the last couple of weeks. Your brain is just reacting to it."

"Cracking under the pressure?"

Lucas shook his head. "Nobody thinks that. It's just . . . Delaney . . . J.D. is dead." Lucas tried to choose his words carefully.

"You don't understand. I *know* it wasn't J.D., but it was somebody who really wanted me to think it was J.D. He wore the same cologne J.D. wore."

"Maybe it's just a coincidence."

"Oh right, our random burglar always makes sure to splash himself with cologne that cost $130 an ounce before a long arduous night of terrorizing." She spun on a heel and retreated to his bedroom.

He groaned inwardly. He did *not* want her in his bed. Well, better stated, he absolutely wanted her in his bed, which was exactly the reason he did not want her in his bed. She had been through one of the worst hells a person could survive, and watching her walk to his bedroom, all he could think about was taking her in there and making love to her all night long. His groin hardened. It was going to be a hell of a long night.

"Delaney," he called as he followed her.

"You know what? Why don't you just leave me alone? If you think I'm just the idiot who doesn't know which way is up . . ."

"You know I don't feel that way about you."

"No, Lucas, I don't know how you feel about me. I don't even know what I'm doing here."

"I don't want you going back home until they find out who attacked you and have him under lock and

key. As for how I feel about you . . ." Lucas struggled
with the words. He had never even come close to
telling a woman he liked her, much less loved her. He
raked his hand through his hair as he pushed out a
frustrated sigh. Then, taking in the fear and anxiety
held in her chocolate brown eyes, he caved. Melted.
He leaned in, pressing his mouth to hers, greedily
kissing her as she softened against him. Their tongues
danced like two lovers embracing for the last time.
Everywhere he touched, everywhere he stroked, he
found her skin silky smooth and hot. Their hands
were all over each other, exploring each other, consol-
ing each other. Lucas was gone. He wanted her far be-
yond anything he had ever wanted.

In that instant he pulled away. Delaney stared at
him, breathless.

"What . . . what was *that?*" she finally managed to
ask.

"*That* is how I feel about you," he said.

"Oh," she said.

Lucas tried to gauge Delaney's reaction. He had just
poured all his heart and soul into that kiss, but she
didn't say anything further than "oh." He gave himself a figurative kick in the ass for being such a
chump.

He coughed uncomfortably. "If you say somebody
is playing tricks with your head, I believe you. We've
just got to figure out why. I mean, if the attacker came
to your place to kill you tonight, why would he care if
the last thing you smelled was J.D.'s cologne?"

"What if he holds me responsible for J.D.'s death
somehow? Maybe it's one of those Jack Ruby nutsos
who thinks he'll have some divine reward by killing
the killer."

"You didn't kill J.D," Lucas reminded her.

"Right, and there was a second gunman in the

grassy knoll. You know I didn't kill him and I know I didn't kill him but let's face it. I was there. I was taken in for questioning. And to the outside world, I have more motive than anybody else. If somebody wanted attention or a reward for taking out J.D.'s murderer, I would be on the top of their list."

Lucas sighed. "I can't talk about this anymore. I could have lost you tonight, and that scares me." When he said those words he recognized their reality, their gravity. He could have lost her and she wouldn't have known how he truly felt. He thought about their kiss. There was something in that kiss.

"Nothing ventured, nothing gained," he whispered under his breath.

"What?"

His tone turned eerily serious. He tilted her chin so her eyes met his. "I'm going to tell you something I should have told you weeks ago."

She waited, her eyes growing large.

"I'm crazy about you, Delaney. I think I have been from the day I first met you. And, as you well know, I'm not exactly one of those hopeless romantic types who falls in love at first sight. But there is something about you that I can't get over. That I don't want to get over."

Then he said it.

"I love you."

Delaney felt fat tears roll down the apples of her cheeks.

"You're crying? Shit! This is wrong. This is all wrong. With the divorce and then J.D. and then the attack. I'm sorry, I have really crappy timing."

Delaney shook her head. "I'm not crying because I'm upset. I'm crying because I'm happy."

"Happy?"

"I love you, too, Lucas. And I know I have from the day I first met you."

Lucas sighed in relief as he lowered his mouth to hers. "God, tell me you meant that," he whispered against her lips.

"I meant it. I meant every word."

He pressed his mouth to hers and pulled her against the length of his body. Every ounce of blood in his body seemed to surge and collect at a centralized location just beneath his belt. He forgot for a moment the ordeal she had been through earlier.

"Sorry." He loosened his hold on her.

"Don't. I want to."

"Are you sure? I mean, you've been through so much tonight."

Delaney's eyes shifted to his hands. They were balled in fists so tight his knuckles were white, and she realized he was struggling to keep his hands from exploring her body. She wanted him to. To slowly caress every inch, to make her giggle, to make her moan, to make her scream.

She slowly unbuttoned her shirt and watched him as he focused on each button as she slid it through its hole. She felt empowered by the way he could not take his eyes off even the slightest movement. It reminded her of their first time together, the way he had watched her when she stripped for him at the club. Then his eyes had been hooded with lust and desire as they were now, but now there was something more.

She pushed him back on to the bed. "I'm going to dance for you."

The only music she needed was the dull cacophony of crickets from outside and the whir of the ceiling fan overhead. She wasn't just stripping off her clothes, but she was stripping away the shields that she had worn for so many years. She wanted him to see all of her because the way he looked at her made her feel less like a trophy and more like a treasure. She unfastened the last button, then let the shirt drop to the ground.

Her movements were smooth and languid as she worked on the hooks of her bra and slid out of her panties. She traced her index finger from her mouth, between her breasts, down and around her navel, stopping just short of her touching herself where she only wanted him.

He sat without moving, as though he were hypnotized by her dance. Delaney straddled his lap and, still slightly swaying, slowly worked on the buttons of his shirt. She pushed open his shirt and ran her hands down his chest. He was burning, so warm she almost thought he had a fever.

Her fingertips danced down his midriff. Just as she reached the snaps of his jeans his hands caught hers. They were icy.

"Are you sure?" he asked again.

She leaned in and whispered kisses along the column of his neck. "I've never been more certain. Never."

Lucas stopped breathing. He surrendered to his desire and suddenly his hands were everywhere. But this time he went slower, savoring the entire experience of learning every curve of her body. He kissed her and pulled and pressed her more firmly into his lap, not even recognizing when they had discarded the rest of his clothes. Lifting her from his lap, he turned her and positioned himself between her legs and buried himself deeper inside her than either of them ever imagined possible.

He plunged inside her over and over again. Hard,

but not the mindless frenzy of the first time they had sex. Without fully being conscious of it, he was taking note of every move she made, every breath she took and every one she held. Even though it had been longer than Lucas had ever gone without sex, he didn't want to rush to the grand finale. Every thrust wrapped in her silky heat was savored. He wanted her wrapped around him forever.

The more he waited for her, watched her, the more he struggled for control. He felt himself slipping away as she whimpered and moaned and then finally screamed as she tightened around him. Seconds later he relinquished hold on the control that he never truly had in the first place.

It was the first time he could remember watching, seeing while he was having sex. It was the best sex of his life because for once it wasn't just sex. For the first time, Lucas Church made love.

Chapter Thirty-six

I'd trade all my crowns and scepters for one slice of decadent carrot cheesecake consumed without a moment of guilt.

Lucas stood over the stove cursing whatever he was attempting to prepare in the skillet. It smelled like burnt hair and as Delaney walked closer she didn't even want to think about what it looked like.

"I guess it doesn't look too appetizing," he said, noting her crinkled nose.

"So you're not so good in the kitchen. You're brilliant in the courtroom and you're a mastermind in the bedroom." She snaked her arms around his muscular, naked abs. "Besides, I'm not so hungry. Not for food anyway." She kissed his shoulder.

"I bet I could improve my scores in the kitchen," he said, turning and taking her mouth with his. He kissed her and their hands became entangled as they explored each other.

He groaned audibly as he pulled away. "As much as I want to do this all day long, I can't. I haven't been on my A-game over the last few weeks and I'm amazed the partners haven't mentioned it. I have to go in today. I'm seeing two new clients and I think I'm settling another." He didn't unwrap her arms.

"I know." She rested her forehead against his bare chest. "Me, too. Macy's coming over and bringing me an outfit. I have the will thing today. I'm meeting with some guy . . . Dacus?"

"Yeah, Harold Dacus. In estate. Are you reading the will today?"

Delaney nodded. "I really didn't think I would be in it, but he called me a day after the funeral and told me I was. I guess J.D. never got around to changing it or something. I wholly expect Paul to contest anything J.D. might have left to me, which is fine. I don't want his money anyway. I just want this whole thing to be behind me."

"Have you thought of anything? Remembered anything that might explain why somebody killed your husband and is now after you?"

She leaned against the counter and crossed her legs at her ankles. She looked down at the ground. Lucas could tell she was hesitant to share with him. When was she going to understand? He was in this thing for the long haul. If she had any ideas about who wanted to harm her, he would give credit to them, no matter how off the wall they sounded.

"Delaney . . ." He was about to start on a tirade about how they had to trust each other, but something in his tone told her it was time to open up.

"Fine. It's probably nothing but remember when I told you about all those inconsistencies on the bank statements and the losses to the 401ks?"

"Yeah, I'm having Judah check into it."

"What if . . . what if J.D. was in with some bad people? Like organized crime."

"I guess it isn't totally incredible. Do you know of any associations he might have had?"

She shook her head. "No. I'm just going out on a limb actually. I can't think of another explanation of why somebody would want to kill him and attempt to kill me."

Lucas nodded. "I've asked Cruz and Wayne to have somebody watching you at all times so if you notice a tail, don't get nervous."

Delaney rolled her eyes and tried to pretend to be fearless. "Do you really think that's necessary? I mean, nobody is going to attack me in broad daylight."

"I'm not taking any chances with you, beauty queen." He tweaked her nose. "Humor me."

"Fine," she joked. "But part of me believes you just want to make sure there are no guys hitting on me."

Lucas shrugged. "So sue me."

Delaney walked into the large office already occupied by Paul and Harold Dacus.

"Thank you for joining us, Mrs. Daniels." Dacus nodded to a chair next to Paul and across the table from him.

"Delaney," Paul said in greeting.

"Good morning, Paul."

"As you both know, I have called you here regarding the personal last will and testament of James David Daniels the Third."

Paul and Delaney nodded.

"Then shall we get on with the reading?"

More nods this time, accompanied by a brief uncomfortable silence. Dacus covered verbatim most of the formalities of the will, skimmed over some of the technicalities, then hit the high points. J.D. had bequeathed small fortunes to golf associations and his alma mater, smaller fortunes to the Humane Society, the American Heart Association, and Through the Looking Glass. Delaney relaxed, finally understanding why she had been called to the reading. Her heart raced as she heard the sum. Surely Paul wouldn't contest that. After all, it was a philanthropic donation.

Dacus continued to tell Paul that he got, essentially, everything. No surprise there.

"That brings us to you, Mrs. Daniels."

"Me?" Delaney asked.

Dacus peered at her from over his bifocal lenses. "Yes, you."

"But we did my part. Through the Looking Glass."

Dacus checked his papers. "You are one Delaney Davis Daniels?"

"Yes."

"Then it appears you have been bequeathed the following: a 1969 Corvette convertible, red."

She *loved* that car.

"A horse by the name of Domino," he continued.

Her horse? Her horse, which he had sworn she'd never see again? He had given her Domino.

"The deed to a property bought and held mutually by Mr. and Mrs. Daniels in the Pleasant Hills annex of Austin."

Her horse and her house?

"One additional property bought and held mutually by Mr. and Mrs. Daniels on the island of Oahu."

Now this was too much. Her horse. Her house. And now Hawaii. She stole a quick glance at Paul, who stared stone-faced ahead.

"And finally . . ."

"There's *more?*" she asked incredulously. What more could she ask for?

". . . ten million dollars."

"What!" Paul and Delaney exclaimed. Delaney shot Paul an angry look. It was small potatoes for him. A drop in the proverbial bucket. The house and ranch were worth more than ten mil.

"And you're certain that my brother just recently revised this will?"

"This is the *new* version?"

Dacus, of course, ignored her and answered Paul. "Yes, sir. He was much more generous with the widow Daniels in the previous will. I convinced him of the importance of altering the will, considering their estrangement. He was quite adamant about what properties and funds she was to receive. However, if you want to contest the will . . ."

Paul cast a look full of disgust and disdain, then shook his head. "I won't betray a dead man's final wishes. Well, Delaney, it looks like you finally hit the jackpot."

Chapter Thirty-seven

So you've won . . . now what?

.

Dacus finished with the reading before dismissing Delaney so he could cover some other things with Paul. During the elevator ride down to the lobby, Delaney's head swam with how much her life had changed in just a matter of a few weeks. She shook her head in disbelief as she reached for her handbag to retrieve her keys. It wasn't on her shoulder.

"Damn!" she muttered before doing an about-face and marching back to the elevators. She was going to have to get one of those fashion-disaster fanny packs that clipped around her waist. It took the elevator forever and the first car crowded with at least a baker's dozen of people who had been waiting longer than Delaney, so she opted for the second car.

On the ride back up she weighed the pros and the cons of her hefty inheritance. If she invested correctly, she wouldn't have to work. She could devote all of her time to the center until she married and had babies, and then she could stay home for a while. When her thoughts shifted to marriage and babies they automatically shifted to Lucas. The things they had said to each other. He loved her. And she loved him. One day when all this drama and chaos was behind them, he would be the father of her children. She was certain of it. She was just minutes from breaking into a hearty rendition of "The Sound of Music" when her mirth was chased away by a darker, more menacing emotion: terror.

Paul had just exited Dacus's office. He turned and walked in the opposite direction of Delaney. Only he wasn't quite walking. He was limping. Limping! When his stride lifted she saw it . . . a bloody bandage around his ankle.

"It was Paul!" Delaney burst into Lucas's office.

"What?"

"The intruder. Last night. It was Paul." She was breathless from running up the three flights of stairs to his suite.

"Sit down." He offered her a chair and crossed to a stainless steel pitcher on a refreshment valet and poured her a glass of ice water. He handed it to her and she gulped it down in several swallows.

"Tell me what's going on."

"I was here for the reading of the will, you know. With Harold Dacus. And Paul, of course, was there, too. Well, Dacus read the will and I left because he had some things to discuss with Paul. But as soon as I got down to the parking lot I realized I left my handbag in Dacus's office. I'm always leaving that thing behind."

Lucas nodded, beckoning for her to continue.

"Well, I get off the elevator just as Paul is leaving the office and that's when I saw him . . . he was limping."

"Limping?"

Delaney nodded and wet her lips. "And when he walked, his pant leg kind of lifted and his ankle . . . his ankle . . . was wrapped with a bandage and it was spotted with blood."

Lucas reclined against his desk, rubbing his face.

"It's not just a coincidence," Delaney told him. "It explains everything. It explains how he knew my windows would be unlocked. It explains why he seemed so familiar to me . . . so much like J.D. It explains why he would want to hurt me. He probably thinks the cops have let me go and he wants to punish me for the murder of his brother. It makes perfect sense."

"I agree. We should call the police right away. It will just be a matter of a simple DNA test. They will test the blood found at your place with Paul's."

Delaney waited by Lucas's side as he made the call.

"Yes . . . yes . . . of course. What do you mean you don't have it? What about chain of custody? Anytime I've ever looked at a piece of evidence they've all but asked me to sign away the rights of my firstborn. This is crooked. . . . No, I'm not accusing you or the department of anything. Good-bye." Lucas slammed down the phone.

"That didn't sound like they were sending a black and white over to Paul's."

Lucas sighed and took her hands in his. "They've lost the evidence."

"All of it?"

Lucas nodded. "The uniforms from your place signed it in last night, but when the detectives went to retrieve results on the blood type the lab didn't have it. So Cruz and Wayne did some checking and the entire box . . . everything . . . is just gone. Vanished."

"Entire boxes of evidence do not just vanish!" Delaney insisted.

"I agree. Unfortunately, this one has. And without any evidence, without any blood samples . . . well, they can question Paul if they can get to him through his barrage of legal counsel. By that time, who's to say the ankle isn't healed and he denies the whole thing?"

Delaney rested her elbows on her knees and her face in the palms of her hands. "So then he just gets away with it? He tries to kill me and he just gets away with it?"

"They will continue to look for the box of evidence," Lucas said. "We have to concentrate on the positive."

"I'm finding it very difficult to see anything positive about this."

"Now we know your foe. Maybe Paul didn't have any real intentions of killing you last night. Perhaps he just wanted to scare you."

"He had a meat cleaver."

"I meant he's a very rich, very resourceful man. If he truly wanted you dead he could have hired somebody weeks ago. Perhaps last night was a rage of grief. You said he was civil to you this morning, right? Maybe he clicked for a moment and now he came out of it. At least we know who we're fighting. Who we have to look out for, right?"

Delaney nodded. "You're right."

"I want you to go home. To my place. Lie down and get some rest. I only have a couple more clients to see today. I'll take a short day and come home as soon as I'm finished. Okay?"

She nodded.

"There are still a couple of uniforms following you, so you should be fine. If you need them for anything, just dial 911 and give them unit number 3715, all right?" He kissed her on her forehead as he sent her out the door.

* * *

Lucas paced the length of his office for several minutes before picking up the phone.

"Ju-duh!" He answered that way on internal calls.

"Jude, hey, it's Luke. Are you busy?"

"Uh . . . yeah," Judah said. "I'm with a client. But I can spare you a few minutes. He's looking over a contract right now."

"Would that client by any chance be Paul Daniels?"

Judah sounded surprised. "Yeah. What are you? Psychic? Hey, you wouldn't by any chance know if Becca's having boys or girls, would you?"

Lucas tried to chuckle. He wanted to keep this casual. "No, just a lucky guess. But I need you to do me a favor."

"Anything."

"And I don't need Paul to know that you're talking to me."

"Oookay."

"Delaney was attacked last night."

"Is everything okay?" Judah asked.

"She will be. But she has reason to believe that Paul Daniels is the one who attacked her."

Judah chuckled, trying to mask the nervous timbre. "You're shitting me."

"I'm dead serious. And it seems that Paul must have some friends in the police department, because they've conveniently misplaced all the evidence they collected from her house last night."

"You don't say."

"We can't prove anything without that evidence. Unless . . . unless you've found something we can use."

"Like?"

"Like anything that will get this creep behind bars and keep Delaney safe."

"That's priv—"

"Privilege doesn't extend to information or disclosure of future crimes. If you could just get him to say . . . something."

Judah sighed. "I'll do what I can, but I'm not making any promises."

"I owe you one."

"Yeah, you do. And one more thing."

"Yeah?"

"No more favors."

Chapter Thirty-eight

Bill Clinton was elected president, in part, because of his sex appeal. Miss America was crowned because of her political stance on the war on terrorism ... hmmm. ...

It was four o'clock and Lucas hadn't come home early. He'd called and explained to her that he was going to be late. Something about a judge named Codger and a settlement that wasn't settled. But Macy and Phoebe had come over to keep her company, so Delaney wasn't suffering from cabin fever yet.

"I can't believe you're a freaking millionaire," Phoebe said after Delaney disclosed how much money J.D. had left her.

"I know. Now I'll be able to help Momma and Daddy with the girls' college tuition, plus I get to keep my position at the center and concentrate all my efforts there."

"Not to mention all the Giuseppe Zanottis and Luellas you can imagine," Macy said dreamily.

"This is not about shoes and handbags. This is more important than accessories."

Macy shook her head. "Nothing is more important than a great pair of shoes."

Delaney giggled. It felt good to share an unburdened laugh with her friends. It seemed like it had been weeks since she smiled and it had been months since she hadn't had to worry about how to pay her bills. With all the media hype around her divorce, the boutique had requested a quiet dismissal. Delaney understood, but she had been afraid it was going to make it financially impossible for her to live. Now almost as quickly, she wouldn't have to worry about money again.

"And I didn't mention the best part of it all."

"It gets better?" Phoebe asked.

"Any better and I'm throwing up," Macy told her. "Seriously."

"It's about Lucas."

"Yeah?"

"We made love for the first time last night."

Phoebe and Macy returned her smile with blank expressions. "She really has cracked up, just like Matt said," Phoebe whispered loudly to Macy.

"Honey, you know you've had sex with him before, right? Remember earth-shattering. Mind-numbing. You actually screamed. Any of this ringing a bell?"

Delaney rolled her eyes and threw the cowhide toss pillow from her chair at the two of them on the sofa. "That's not what I meant! Of course we've been together before but last night . . . last night it was different. It wasn't just about the orgasm. It was beautiful. It was poetry. It was *love*."

Macy made a gagging sound but then broke into a

smile. "You deserve it, sweetie." Phoebe nodded in agreement but was fighting back tears so she couldn't verbalize it.

"And he said the words. He said them first and I didn't even have to ask him or hint or anything. I'm in love."

She finished sharing the details of her evening with Lucas and went on to tell them about her suspicions regarding Paul.

"Do you think he means to hurt you?"

"I don't know. I don't think so. Paul was always a little on the odd side, you know. He hated J.D. but at the same time he really looked up to him. Maybe it was just like Lucas said and he just clicked."

"So what are you going to do?"

"I'm going to talk to him." She fished out a tiny tape recorder and microphone that she had picked up at an electronics store.

"What do you think you're going to do with that?"

"My own personal wire. I'm going to Paul's to get the information I need."

"You're crazy, Laney; that's not safe," Phoebe protested.

"The cops aren't going to question a man with Paul's power and influence without some evidence. This might not be admissible in court but maybe it will raise some eyebrows. I won't ever feel completely safe and secure unless I know he's behind bars."

Macy shook her head. "If he was in fact the intruder, he's already tried to kill you once; what prevents him from doing it again? And what if this time he succeeds?"

"Lucas has two officers tailing me. I'll have my cell in my hand at all times. If I get there and something goes wrong I'll hit 911 and give them the code. But I really don't think he will try anything with a house full of staff. I just want to get him to say enough to make the DA push for an investigation."

Phoebe shook her head. "I don't like it."

"You have to back me up here, Phebes."

Phoebe cast a doubtful glance at Macy. "If you aren't back in this apartment in two hours, I'm calling the cops myself."

"Fair enough."

When he first started following her, he hadn't expected it to be this easy. Of course, he knew disposing of the officers was going to be difficult, but even that turned out easier than he had expected. He was a familiar face. Hell, he'd even been introduced to them. They might not have expected to see him in front of her house, but it certainly didn't rouse alarm. Getting them to take the laced lemonade was easier than giving candy to a baby. They slept slumped in the leather seats of their "unmarked" car while Delaney drove away, the false comfort that the late model Acura, his late model Acura, was the tail Lucas had arranged for her. Who ever heard of the APD shelling out forty-five thousand dollars on a car for a couple of cops to cruise around the city?

He laughed to himself, satisfied, as she made her final turn. He couldn't ask for better if he guided her there.

But he had to give her credit where credit was due. What she lacked in the brains department, she more than made up in the looks department. Pretty girl like that, it was such a shame she would have to die.

"You have to find Judah and tell him it's time." *Pfff, pfff, whooo. Pfff, pfff, whooo.* Rebecca concentrated on her breathing.

"Rebecca?" Lucas could barely register the voice.

"Yes." *Pfff, pfff, whooo.*

"Where is Judah?"

"I don't know." *Pfff, pfff, whooo.* "I've tried to call his cell." *Pfff, pfff, whooo.* "He said . . . he had. . . . to run an errand out at the ranch." *Pfff, pfff, whooo.* "He never . . . gets . . . reception down there."

"The Daniels ranch?" There was only one reason Judah would have to go out to the ranch and that would be to confront Paul. Lucas tried to keep the sound of alarm out of his voice. He didn't want Rebecca to worry. The only thing she needed to concentrate on was delivering her babies. Judah was his best friend. If Judah were going to confront Paul, Lucas had hoped it would be within the secure walls of their law firm. Judah was potentially in danger because of a favor Lucas had asked him to do. And that simply wasn't something Lucas wanted to consider.

"It just so happens I'm headed to the ranch right now, Rebecca. I'll make sure he gets to the hospital lickety split."

Lickety split?

Okay, so maybe he was trying a little too hard to sound as if everything was okay.

"Tell . . ." *pfff pfff . . .* "him . . ." *whooo . . .* "to hurry. . . ." *pfff pfff. . . .* "Aaaaargh!" Rebecca screamed and the line went dead.

Lucas's head was crowded with thoughts. He had to get to the ranch. And soon.

Delaney's sweaty hands slipped across the leather of her steering wheel. She had almost talked herself out of this idiot escapade a dozen or more times, but now she was at the ranch. Paul's Cadillac was parked under the covered drive. She inhaled deeply and rang the doorbell.

"Marisol. Hello." She smiled brightly.

"Mr. Daniels is busy." Marisol, who had always

been friendly, fisted a hand on her hip and blocked the entrance from Delaney.

"Marisol, I know you must be hearing horrible things about me. About what happened to J.D. I did not kill him, Marisol. You know me better than that."

"Hmmpf." She didn't move.

"I waited at the hospital for thirteen hours with you when your daughter gave birth. Do you remember that? Does that sound like a person who would shoot her husband in cold blood?"

"Money makes people do crazy things," Marisol insisted.

"You're right. It does. And that is why I am here to talk to Paul. I think I might know who killed J.D. I have some important information to give him." Delaney hated misleading Marisol, but she saw it was the only way she was going to get in the door.

Marisol looked at her watch and then back to Delaney. "He will fire me if I let you in."

Delaney chewed her lip. She knew that was a real possibility. "Don't you have somewhere to go? Some shopping to do or something? Because if you left and I just happened to be coming while you were going, he couldn't really hold you responsible for that, could he?"

Marisol looked at Delaney from head to toe again. "You say you know who killed Mr. Daniels?"

"I believe I do, yes."

"I will leave for one hour. And you do not tell him that I let you in."

"Scout's honor." Delaney thought about holding up fingers but she could never remember how many. Delaney had never been a Girl Scout and didn't think she would have been a very good one even if she had tried. To her knowledge, there was no merit badge for speedy false lash application.

"Very well. You wait here. I will get my purse and when you see me drive off, then you go in."

Delaney nodded. She paced around her car until she saw Marisol's electric blue economy car kicking dust down the gravel drive. Delaney fluffed her hair and checked her reflection in the foyer mirror. J.D. had confided in her once that Paul was considerably attracted to her, and though the thought of using her looks to cajole a confession sickened her, she was willing to use everything she had to her advantage. What mattered right now was finding out what had happened to the missing money and who was responsible for the deaths of J.D. and Herman Schulyer.

She just hoped it worked. She knew that desire for beautiful women was a weakness that Paul shared with J.D., but Paul was a shrewd man. He had never been married and he didn't allow himself to get tied down in long-term relationships. This wasn't going to be easy.

The heavy brocade curtains that covered the French doors in the study blocked out any sunlight. Even in the early summer afternoon, with the lights off and the curtains closed, the room was dark. As her eyes adjusted to the dim light, Delaney could barely make out Paul's figure at the desk.

"Paul?"

There was no answer.

"Paul?" she asked again as she groped for a light switch on the wall.

"You can call his name all day, but he's not going to answer." Delaney felt a gun being pressed into her back as the room flooded with the warmth of yellow light.

Paul's body slumped in his oversized leather chair, a single bullet wound through his forehead. Delaney gasped and a scream caught in her throat as the man pushed her farther into the room and kicked the door closed.

"What? No screams? That surprises me."

Where had she heard that voice?

"Lucas said you were a screamer."

Judah!

Chapter Thirty-nine

When the curtain goes up and the orchestra swells it's showtime! Be afraid. Be very afraid.

"Judah?" Her voice was trembling.

"In the flesh. Sit." He pushed her toward a wingback chair. She turned to sit in the chair, finally seeing her foe face to face. She eyed the gun in his hand and obediently sat.

"There are dozens of staff here. Somebody will hear you," she told him.

He shook his head. "No staff. Paul here gave them the evening off with pay. The only straggler was that tightass Marisol and you dispensed of her quite nicely for me. Besides, I don't plan on shooting you. It wouldn't look authentic."

"Authentic?"

"Women, especially attractive women, typically don't shoot themselves when they commit suicide. Even in their most desperate hour they're a bit too vain. Too busy thinking about what they will look like in their pink laminate coffins. No. It would be much more realistic for you to . . . say . . . swallow a bottle of those sedatives you've been taking." He held up a brown medicine bottle and rattled the pills.

"So I shot Paul and then killed myself, is that it?"

"Smart girl."

"Nobody would ever buy it. Nobody would believe that's true."

Judah chuckled as he poured a tall glass of water and handed it to her along with a few pills. "Hasn't your association with Lucas taught you anything? It doesn't matter what the truth is. It only matters what they can prove."

"I won't take them," she said.

"Then I'll be forced to place the gun at your temple and pull the trigger. A lot less glamorous but . . . you're right-handed, correct?"

Delaney thought about the wire she was wearing. If she was going to die, at least maybe the cops would be able to get the truth as they searched her cold stiff corpse.

"Tell me about it."

"Delaney . . ."

"If you're going to kill me you at least owe me an explanation, Judah." She tried not to sound too angry but, under the circumstances, she felt like a little hostility was her right.

"You killed them all, didn't you? J.D. Schuyler. Paul. Why?"

"The four of us were partners in highly profitable, decidedly illegal creative accounting. Paul found out a little while ago that J.D. planned to take the money and run. Fake his own murder and leave us behind like the three stooges, to take the rap for it all. Us and you."

Delaney nodded. It was all beginning to make sense now. "The champagne flute, the brush, the in-

surance contract. They were all props J.D. was going
to use to frame me for his murder when he disappeared. And the will. That's why he left me so much.
He thought it could be used as evidence, too, if he disappeared. He didn't want the authorities sniffing
around, asking too many questions about his disap-
pearance and the lack of a corpse, so he left me a ton
of money. When he disappeared, with all the money
missing from Daniels Enterprises, all the activity
through the organization's, *my organization's*, account.
It all was a bloody bread crumb trail right to my front
door. How positively evil! I can't believe I married
that man!"

Judah inclined his head as he watched Delaney un-
ravel the rest of the story.

"So you conspired to kill him and still frame me.
Paul called Shannon that night because they sound so
similar you knew she wouldn't recognize his voice as
anyone other than J.D."

"I guess the dumb blonde jokes don't have foundation after all."

"Not true. You're blond."

"The famed wit of which Lucas spoke. Cute."

"I just have one question."

"Yeah?"

"What the hell did I ever do to deserve this?"

Judah laughed. "It was never anything personal,
Delaney, as much as it was merely . . . convenient. I've
been watching you from the beginning. And I must
say, for a moment, I almost felt bad for making you
take the fall. But your youth center is a tiny charity,
nobody would ever guess Schuyler was cooking the
books. Not until we had the money we wanted where
we needed it."

"So what then? Why kill Schuyler?"

"You spooked him. You called him asking all those

questions and then, when you were cleared from all suspicion regarding J.D.'s murder, he got nervous. Wanted us to turn state's evidence against Paul."

"But you were too greedy."

Judah shook his head. "My hands were too bloody. Paul had certain evidence that I was the one who pulled the trigger."

"So you had to get rid of Schuyler. And Paul?"

"You already know the answer to that. You discovered that Paul was the one who broke in and attacked you that night. It was only a matter of time before you and Lucas put two and two together. At that point, the bread crumbs lead right to my office at the firm."

"So you dispose of Paul and the only other person who knows the truth. . . ."

"You."

"And how, exactly, do you expect the authorities to buy my death?"

He sighed and dropped a sheet of her pink stationery in her lap. She scanned the words quickly.

Please forgive me . . . I love Paul, have always loved Paul . . . I can't live without him . . . death is preferable to jail . . .

It was her handwriting, only . . . it wasn't. She looked up to Judah, who still had the gun trained on her.

He shrugged. "You know they say, 'the devil's in the details.' All of your personalized holiday cards to the firm gave me an endless sampling of your handwriting. You're right, it's not exact but . . . it's close enough. Any inconsistencies will be reasoned away by the fact that you were so distraught when you wrote the letter. You didn't sign that insurance contract either, but nobody believed you there."

"Truth versus proof."

"Proof will win every single time."

"You're pretty good," Delaney said, looking at the note.

"Forgery. A little trick I learned growing up without parents. You know, nobody even questions your excessive absences or unstable home environment if you only have a note signed by dear old mom or dad."

"So all of this . . . is just . . . about money?"

"Just about money? Easy enough for you to say when you're floating in millions of it. J.D. flashes a million dollars in my face and I'm supposed to turn it down? Do you know how long it would take me to earn that kind of money?"

"With effort and hard work . . ."

"Oh shut up! I'm not one of the little girls you work with. You know what effort and hard work have gotten me, Delaney? Running back when I should have been quarterback. Salutatorian when I should have been valedictorian. Associate when I should have been partner. Second place." He chuckled low and deep. "Second place is just the warm and fuzzy way to say first loser. I was always one step behind your boyfriend, Lucas. And you know how he got first place, Delaney. It sure as hell wasn't hard work . . . it was money."

"You're wrong. He worked for everything he has. So maybe he didn't have as many odds stacked against him but he has earned every iota of respect. . . ."

"Bullshit!"

"Judah, you're a bright lawyer. You can't possibly believe you'll get away with this. If I was able to figure this out, don't you think Lucas will? The cops?"

Judah shrugged. "I'm not an idiot. I don't plan on sticking around. And I have more than enough money to hide for a very long time."

Delaney moistened her lips and quickly tried another tactic. "And what about Rebecca? And the babies? Think about them growing up without you. Think about how awful it was for you growing up without a father."

"My sons are going to grow up in a world that belongs to the rich. I want them to grow up on a level playing field. I owe them that much. There's a few million dollars in an offshore account that I'm leaving them. They'll be fine."

Chapter Forty

Breathe. One Miss America passed out cold when they called her name. Never underestimate the importance of oxygen.

" 'No legacy is so rich as honesty.' " Lucas's voice shocked both Judah and Delaney.

"Lucas!" Judah took several steps backward, widening his range to include both Lucas and Delaney. "How long have you been there?"

"Long enough to know that I don't know who you are, Judah. Why are you doing this?" Lucas's voice was calm and steady.

"You shouldn't have come here."

"I didn't think I would find you pointing a gun at my girlfriend." His eyes shifted to Paul's corpse. "Judah, man . . . help me understand what's going on here."

"I don't expect you to understand."

"Understand what? Understand theft? Murder? All for a little money?"

"Who was it? Shaw? Who said 'the lack of money is the root of all evil,'" Judah quipped.

"If you needed help . . ."

"Shut up! Is it so easy for you to sound so self-righteous? You had it all growing up. Do you know how hard it was watching you open mountains of presents on Christmas and the only wrapped gift I got was what your maid picked up for me? Watching you go to parties every Friday night in college while I went to work? Watching you get all the girls while I couldn't even afford to take one out on a date if I wanted to? That was a shitty life, Lucas."

"That's not true. All those things are superficial. You and I were on a level playing field from day one. Neither one of us had parents for all intents and purposes. And look what an incredible life you have now. You're happily married to a beautiful, intelligent, wonderful wife. Rebecca wouldn't even give me the time of day despite my money."

Lucas saw a warmth creep into Judah's eyes. If he could just keep Judah's thoughts on Rebecca he could end this standoff. Judah laughed. "I remember. Do you remember? We were playing pool and you were all like, 'Man, look at that incredible girl over there.' And you threw every pickup line at her that you ever knew."

Lucas continued, "And after she hustled me at a game of pool, I asked her for her phone number and do you remember what she did then?"

"She marched right over to me and told me to call her and let her know how I put up with an arrogant asshole like you."

"She fell in love with you, Judah. Not your money. Not me. Not my money. You know, she called me just about fifteen minutes ago. She's looking for you. She's in labor."

"You're lying."

"I'm not. She called me asking if I had seen you. She wanted me to find you. She needs you at the hospital by her side. Think about her. Think about Rebecca. Think about the babies. *Your babies.*"

"Shut up!" Sweat poured from Judah's face. "You're lying. She's not due for another four weeks."

"Twins . . . twins come early. Almost always." Delaney's voice was hoarse.

"If you don't believe me, check my caller ID." Then Lucas prayed to the three patron saints of Luck, Fate and Stupidity and tossed the phone at Judah.

The flashing silver object startled Judah and in one instant he lost his guard and fired the gun. The chandelier came crashing down a mere few feet away from Delaney and though she had kept her cool this long, though she had always despised the screeching, histrionic women in thriller films, she screamed.

Loud. Tension-releasing. Blood-curling. Scream.

Judah dropped the gun and it skidded across the varnished floor near the vicinity of Lucas's foot. Just as Lucas realized he could gain control of the gun, Judah had Delaney in an armlock with a shard of glass pressed against her jugular.

"Drop the gun, Lucas."

"Judah, let her go. It's not too late."

"Like hell it's not. Three men are dead, Lucas. I'm not headed up the river to a fancy schmancy federal country club. This is Texas; they'll fry me before the gavel adjourns the court."

"It doesn't have to be this way."

Judah backed up to the French doors. Lucas knew he couldn't let him leave the ranch with Delaney. If he left with her, Lucas would never see her alive again.

"Do you think this is easy? You think I wanted it to come to this? No! It didn't have to come to this. I told you to drop it. But you couldn't. You had to take up with this . . . bitch! It could have all ended with J.D. But you couldn't leave well enough alone, could you? It had to be your personal mission in life to clear her name. I told you to just leave her alone. If you had just dropped her then, her pretty pampered ass would be sitting in a 10-by-10 cell right now and I would be at the hospital with my wife delivering my babies. Why didn't you just let it rest?"

"I couldn't. I love her."

"Congratu-screwing-lations! You hear that, ladies and gentlemen? Lucas Church has fallen in love. You picked a hell of time, buddy. You could have any woman in this whole freaking state and you pick the one . . . the one . . . who holds the only get-out-of-jail-free card for your best friend in the whole wide world."

"I didn't know."

The muted sound of sirens whined in the background.

"You called the cops? Jesus, Luke, who the hell are you? Some kind of choir boy?"

"I thought it was Paul. I didn't know I was coming after you."

"Would it have made a difference? If you knew, would it have made a difference?"

"I would have worked something out."

"What about your little girlfriend?"

"What are you asking?"

"You know damn well what I'm asking. Who'd it be? Her or me?"

Lucas shook his head. Judah was clearly irrational. He had to answer with care. One wrong word and he would drag that knife across Delaney's neck. "Judah, drop the glass."

"Drop the gun," Judah spat back.

"I'll drop the gun when you drop the glass."

"Why don't I give you the chance to choose now?"

"Don't make me choose."

"That's how it is then? You'd sell me out. Me. Your best friend. You've known me twenty years, you've known her for a few weeks, and you'd sell me down the river for a piece of ass?"

Lucas shook his head. How could he answer?

"Then shoot me now, choir boy, because I don't have any reason to live."

"Don't say that."

"What have I got? I've lost it all. My job, my wife, my kids, my best friend in the whole goddamn world. I've got nothing, Lucas. Nothing to live for." He pressed the impromptu knife deeper into Delaney's throat, and a trail of blood drizzled down the column of her neck.

"Rebecca loves you. She would never abandon you." Delaney's voice was calm and measured, her words slow so as not to cause the glass to dig deeper.

"Shut up, bitch. You don't know anything about my wife or my life."

"I know . . . I know the day . . . when I first met you in the park that day . . . I know one of my first thoughts was what incredible love you shared. Don't take that away from her."

"It's already gone. It's too late. Do you think she could bear to stand by me after this?"

"Judah, it's never too late. You can turn this around. You have to let her go," Lucas tried to reason. His voice wasn't his own. It was his father's. Always so damn reasonable. His best friend was holding a knife to the throat of the woman he loved. If there were ever a time to forget reason, this was it. The situation called for action.

"I want you to know, for once, how it feels to have everything important taken away from you."

"I didn't take anything from you," Lucas insisted. "I would've given you my right arm if you asked."

"That's all I am to you . . . your damn charity case. Your project kid."

"That's not true." Lucas's voice grew more intense as he watched the crimson droplets travel down the side of Delaney's neck.

"The gun!" Judah insisted as he pressed the knife deeper.

"Judah . . . I'm putting the gun down." Lucas lowered the gun.

"You don't know how it feels. You never have. You've had the whole world handed to you on a silver platter. For just once I want you to feel what I've felt."

In one second a shot rang out.

Chapter Forty-one

Anybody who can proudly parade around as Miss Pork Princess deserves to be Miss America above anyone else.

He hadn't expected to see her car here of all places. What was she doing here? He hadn't spoken to her since that night. He had picked up the phone a number of times just to place it back on its base. He knew she had called him on several occasions. But every time he went to pick up the phone, he couldn't imagine what he was going to say to her. So he just let it ring.

Then there had been the funeral. The funeral was the first and last time he'd even left his apartment until today. Rebecca had called him and told him she had named the twins. Girls. She wanted him to come over and discuss a time and date that would be good to set the christening. She and Judah had chosen him as godfather and it was to be no other way. Of course he had come straight away but when he got here, there it was. Parked in front of the house. Delaney's pink convertible.

Lucas paced in front of the door, debating whether or not he should knock. Rebecca took his options from him.

"Are you going to stand out here all day or are you going to come in and see your goddaughters?"

"Um . . . well." His gaze shifted over Rebecca's shoulder to Delaney. "I figured you had company."

Rebecca moved to the side to allow Lucas in her home. "Just Delaney. She's brought by lunch and dinner every day since I got out of the hospital. She's driving my mom and aunts crazy because she won't leave anything for them to do."

"Hi." Delaney stood and cleared dishes off the table.

"Hi," Lucas said.

"I'm just going to load the dishwasher, then I'll be on my way," Delaney told Rebecca.

"Really, you don't have to do that. My mom and aunts . . ."

"Are coming over to enjoy the babies. Not to work. I don't mind, really. I want to do this for you," she insisted as she exited the room.

"She's a force to be reckoned with, huh?" Rebecca laughed.

"Yeah, don't I know it."

An uncomfortable quiet stretched between them before Lucas finally broke the silence. "I would have come earlier but . . ."

"But things are awkward. I know."

"Look at these girls." He stood over the bassinets and gazed down at the tiny pink bundles. "They are beautiful."

"Thanks. I've named them . . . finally. Yesterday." Rebecca smoothed the dark silky tresses on one head.

"Really?"

She nodded. "Judy. She's the chubby one. And Lucy. The little one. They had a struggle getting here but now they're here and they're healthy and each one will always have the other to watch her back . . . like you and Judah."

Lucas nodded and swallowed a lump rising in his throat. "I need to know if you blame me for his death."

"I don't blame anyone but maybe Judah." Rebecca peered at Lucas through tear-filled eyes. She brushed away her tears. "He made some really bad choices, didn't he?"

"I just don't know how he could have gotten in so deep . . . if he needed help he could have come to me."

"You know Judah; he had his pride. Part of him felt like he'd been coming to you for handouts his entire life. He just wanted to do something on his own."

"But . . . this."

Rebecca shook her head. "Neither one of us had to grow up like him. I mean, I was poor, but I had two parents who loved and cared for me. Neither one of us had to worry about where our next meal was coming from, or if our mother would come home beaten and bloody. That was deep inside him. For a little while he overcame it. He graduated from college and law school at the top of his class. He was a good lawyer. He was a terrific husband. But his fear of going back to where he came from . . . I guess the stress of the unknown. The twins. The new house. The car payments. He just wanted to know that everything was going to be taken care of. There was a pretty big life insurance policy he took out several years ago, so I guess . . . I guess he figured no matter how things ended, we'd be all right."

"I want to be here for you. And the girls. There are a

lot of things I don't know right now, things I'm not clear on. But I know with certainty that you and the babies were everything to Judah. He wouldn't have wanted you to have to go it alone. As long as I live and breathe you won't have to. They'll know their father as I knew him." He swallowed his sadness. "The way he was . . . before. I'll make sure of it."

Rebecca hugged Lucas. "I appreciate it." She nodded over his shoulder in the direction of Delaney. "You two? She said you haven't spoken since that evening."

Lucas shook his head. "Things are kind of . . . weird right now."

"This is not about Judah, is it? I know he was your best friend and I know you loved him. He was my husband. I loved him, too . . . or I loved who he was before. But Judah was wrong. He hurt her and he killed people and he tried to kill her."

"I know. I know. I just . . . I don't . . . I had to make a choice the other night. And I think I might have made the wrong one. I think I probably could have tried to talk him down. He'd still be here and I wouldn't be responsible for his death."

Rebecca nodded. She wasn't ready to hear about the details of that night. Eventually, she was certain, but not at that moment.

"You can't blame her. She didn't know what she was walking into that night any more than you did. Judah made his choices and you can't punish yourself for the rest of your life because of those choices. And Luke?"

"Yeah?"

"She's a good person. And she has been good for you. . . . I was . . . I was wrong about her."

"What? This is a week of miracles. First you give

birth to the twins and then you admit you were wrong."

Rebecca laughed. It felt good to laugh. "Lucas, whatever decision you made . . . the one that was the wrong decision . . . it's not too late to make it right," Rebecca told him. One of the twins squirmed in her bassinet and Rebecca raised her hand to pat her back to sleep. "That's a lesson I wish Judah would have learned. It's never too late to make it right."

Delaney finished the last of the dishes and turned to leave the kitchen, backing right into Lucas.

"Sorry," she said.

"No problem."

"I've called you. A few times, actually. To see how you were doing."

"I'm good, I guess," he said.

Delaney nodded. "Well, I've got to get to the center. Shannon's on this workout craze and if I'm not there right at twelve she freaks."

Lucas didn't respond. He didn't know what to say to her. How to tell her how he felt about her. How to apologize for ever doubting her. For not protecting her. The scar on her neck was barely visible. It had only been a flesh wound. Looking at it made his stomach churn. What if it had been a deeper cut? And, just as frightening, what if Judah had never intended it to be anything more than a scratch?

She raised her hand to his cheek. "Lucas, he was your best friend. I can't imagine how you must be feeling or dealing with this loss. You aren't responsible for his actions any more than say, Rebecca, or the babies."

"I know that."

But he was still blaming himself for everything that

had happened and for everything that had *almost* happened that night at the ranch.

"I don't think that you do. He was like your brother. For what it's worth, Lucas, if it had been me, I don't know what I would have done, either. I know I love you. I know you are one of the most important people in the world to me. But if the tables had been turned and it had been me and Phoebe, I don't know if I could have pulled the trigger."

"He could have killed you. I should have protected you without hesitation."

"He didn't kill me. Could've, would've . . ." She shrugged. ". . . the choice he asked you to make wasn't fair. But you can't spend the rest of your life tormenting yourself. Or hating him."

One of the twins began to cry.

"They don't have anybody else, Lucas. They're going to need you in their lives. And they need you to be whole."

His jaw clenched. Delaney brought her lips to his, placing a gentle kiss there. "When you've dealt with this . . . call me."

She left. Lucas had never felt so alone in his whole life.

Chapter Forty-two

After the lights go down and the sequins are all swept up, it's comforting to just go back to plain old vanilla real life.

"Hey, Shannon. Is Delaney back there?"

Shannon nodded, her corkscrew curls dancing around her face. "She just started ballet, though; she might be a while."

"Penny's class, right?"

"Right."

"Perfect."

Lucas trotted back to the class where the girls were in various stages of warm-ups, shifting from position to position as Delaney walked down the line adjusting arms, hands and feet.

"Spines straight, arms firm and third position. Legs limber, feet steady and fourth position . . ."

She was interrupted by a tittering behind her back. *Precocious Penny.*

She shook her head and turned to find Penny and Lucas, heads together, whispering.

"This can't be good," she said with her arms crossed in front of her chest. "Penny, do you want to share your secret with the rest of the class?"

Penny's curls bobbed and bounced as she nodded, but Lucas pressed his hand over her mouth.

"I was just keeping a promise to Penny."

"What promise?" Delaney blinked in confusion.

"I told her when I was ready to ask you to marry me, she would be the first one to know."

Penny jumped and attempted a pirouette and cartwheel.

"Miss Delaney's getting married. Miss Delaney's getting married," she sang even as she landed on her butt.

Lucas laughed and shook his head. "She really can't keep a secret, can she?"

But Delaney didn't answer. She was speechless.

"But . . . I thought . . . I mean . . . when you didn't call me back I just thought . . ."

"I wasn't home, Delaney. That's why I didn't call you back. I was . . . out."

"Out?"

"I had a trip to make. To Big Stinking Creek."

Delaney's eyes burned with tears.

"You see, there's this guy down there who's positively loaded down with daughters. His oldest is this incredibly sexy beauty queen. Miss Texas."

"First runner-up, actually."

"And I'm crazy about her. But I didn't want to ask her what I need to ask her without getting her daddy's permission first."

"What did he say?"

"He asked me to take the whole lot of them, actually." Lucas laughed.

"Sounds like a daddy I know."

"So now I've talked to him. I've talked to her." He motioned toward Penny. "There's only one more person I need to talk to. I have to ask her a very important question."

He got down on one knee and the twelve girls gathering around them cried and giggled and cheered and squealed.

"Delaney Davis Daniels, will you marry me?"

Delaney nodded as she tried to examine the ring through her tears. "Yes." She threw her arms around him.

"It's about time!" Macy exclaimed.

Delaney looked up. She hadn't even seen Macy and her family, her *entire* family, enter the room.

"Y'all knew?"

"No," her father piped up. "He only asked me if I would grant permission if he did ask you. He said he couldn't tell us anything further than that or he'd be breaking a promise. Now I understand." He gestured to Penny, who still hadn't managed the perfect pirouette.

Epilogue

No matter how far she roams, the beauty queen always returns home.

Delaney couldn't believe she was standing on stage again beneath the bright stage lights in four-inch heels and a bathing suit. She didn't know how she let herself get talked into this. She wouldn't even be here if all the proceeds from ticket sales weren't going to a variety of children's charities.

"I feel like I have to throw up," she said through a clenched smile without moving her lips.

"Nervous?" the smiling brunette on her left asked.

Delaney shook her head. She had done the pageant thing for too long to ever get nervous. "Nervous? No. I could to this in my sleep," she replied. "Pregnant."

The brunette cast a quick glance. "No!"

Delaney nodded. "Eight weeks."

"Your first?"

"Second. The first is the cotton top in the first row."

Lillian nodded. Earlier she had noticed the dimpled little boy sitting in his proud father's lap.

"The second runner-up is . . . Mrs. Marcia Taylor!" The line of three became a line of two as Marcia cried and waved and retrieved her roses. Lilly squeezed Delaney's hand.

"Good luck," Lilly whispered.

"Oh this? I only do the pageants for the charities," Delaney whispered back.

"Me, too. I was referring to the baby." Lilly smiled.

"In the event that the woman chosen to be Mrs. Texas 2006 is unable to fulfill her duties, the first runner-up will assume the title. The first runner-up is . . ."

Drum roll. Delaney Church.

"Mrs. Lillian Goode."

Delaney froze as the reality sunk in. Lillian hugged her and strode away to collect her roses while the emcee and the previous Mrs. Texas adorned Delaney with a crown and a sash designating her as the new Mrs. Texas.

Thirty minutes later, flashbulbs were still blinding her, but now Lucas was by her side, holding their 10-month-old little boy, as she answered questions about being the first ever to carry the titles of Miss Teen Texas, Miss Texas and now Mrs. Texas.

"So, Mr. Church," a reporter with a wide grin asked, "how does it feel to be married to Mrs. Texas, the most beautiful mom in Texas?"

To which he politely replied, "Wonderful."

SPYING IN HIGH HEELS

Gemma Halliday

L.A. shoe designer Maddie Springer lives her life by three rules: Fashion. Fashion. Fashion. But when she stumbles upon the work of a brutal killer, her life takes an unexpected turn from Manolos to murder. And things only get worse when her boyfriend disappears—along with $20 million in embezzled funds—and her every move is suddenly under scrutiny by LAPD's sexiest cop. With the help of her postmenopausal bridezilla of a mother, a 300-pound psychic and one seriously oversexed best friend, Maddie finds herself stepping out of her stilettos and onto the trail of a murderer. But can she catch a killer before the killer catches up to her?

Rumble on the Bayou

JANA DeLeon

Deputy Dorie Berenger knew it was going to be a rough day when the alligator she found in the town drunk's swimming pool turned out to be stoned. Now she has some big-shot city slicker from the DEA trying to take over her turf. And Agent Richard Starke is way too handsome for his own good. Or hers.

The folks of Gator Bait, Louisiana, may know everything about each other, but they're sure not going to share it with an outsider. Richard won't be able to catch a drug smuggler without Dorie's help. But some secrets—and some desires—are buried so deep that bringing them to the surface will take a major *Rumble on the Bayou*.

GHOULS JUST WANT TO HAVE FUN

KATHLEEN BACUS

This autumn, Tressa Jayne Turner isn't enjoying the frivolity of the season. After being stalked by a psycho dunk-tank clown, all she wants is a slower pace, some candy corn and toffee apples—and a serious story she can sniff out on her own.

She's in luck! Reclusive bestselling writer Elizabeth Courtney Howard is coming to town. So, what's stopping Tressa from getting the dope—besides a blackmailing high school homecoming queen candidate, a rival reporter, and the park ranger who's kept Tressa's knickers in a knot since the fourth grade? Only the fact that the skeletons to uncover are all in a closet in a house only Norman Bates could love.